DREAM WEDDING

She took in a great gulp of air when Jimmy stopped in front of her, but she didn't blink away from his stare. He slid his hands around her waist slowly and easily, as if he had all the time he wanted to do that, and she still didn't even blink, though the warmth from his hands was spreading through her.

He sat her down, and she saw his head move toward her, his mouth move toward her, in slow motion. Missy held her breath and watched as his mouth shortened the distance between them.

He smelled like mint. She always did love the taste of mint. Her tongue flicked out and dabbed her lips. The flecks in Jimmy's eyes darkened like the sky getting ready for a storm to break loose.

BOOK YOUR PLACE ON OUR WEBSITE AND MAKE THE ARABESQUE ROMANCE CONNECTION!

We've created a customized website just for our very special Arabesque readers, where you can get the inside scoop on everything that's going on with Arabesque romance novels.

When you come online, you'll have the exciting opportunity to:

- View covers of upcoming books

- Learn about our future publishing schedule (listed by publication month and author)

- Find out when your favorite authors will be visiting a city near you

- Search for and order backlist books

- Check out author bios and background information

- Send e-mail to your favorite authors

- Join us in weekly chats with authors, readers and other guests

- Get writing guidelines

- AND MUCH MORE!

Visit our website at
http://www.arabesquebooks.com

DREAM WEDDING

ALICE WOOTSON

BET Publications, LLC
www.bet.com
www.arabesquebooks.com

ARABESQUE BOOKS are published by

BET Publications, LLC
c/o BET BOOKS
One BET Plaza
1900 W Place NE
Washington, D.C. 20018-1211

All Kensington Titles, Imprints, and Distributed Lines are available at special quantity discounts for bulk purchases for sales
promotions, premiums, fund-raising, and educational or insti-
tutional use. Special book excerpts or customized printings can
also be created to fit specific needs. For details, write or phone
the office of the Kensington special sales manager: Kensington
Publishing Corp., 850 Third Avenue, New York, NY 10022,
attn: Special Sales Department, Phone: 1-800-221-2647.

First Printing: April 2001
10 9 8 7 6 5 4 3 2 1

Printed in the United States of America

ACKNOWLEDGMENTS

Many thanks to Grace, Pat, Marian and Roz for their critiquing; to Glo and Bill, my mentors; to Bobbie, my sister, for believing in me; to Marilyn, my sister, for leading the way; to Pat, Eileen and Cheryl, my computer tutors; to my family for their encouragements; and most of all to Ike, the hero of my real life romance.

ONE

"Come on, Gertie, not now. Please not now," Missy begged, though she knew it was useless. She looked through the windshield to the empty road. Then she turned and looked out of the back window. The view was the same. Nothing but trees, bushes and weeds, and a long dirt road twisting like a brown ribbon freed from her mama's sewing scrap box.

"Welcome home," she muttered to herself.

The South Carolina summer heat hit Missy when she stepped out of the car. She kicked the door shut, then kicked it again. She stared at the dark green car for a few seconds before she slapped it first with one hand and then the other. None of it did any good, but it felt satisfying. She took a deep breath and glared around her.

It didn't stop the mockingbird hopping in a pine across the road from proving his name. She knew she should have had her old hunk of junk checked before she started the long drive home from Philadelphia. She knew Gertie had been making strange noises for a few weeks, but that didn't make Missy feel any more charitable toward the car now.

"Darn you, Gertie, you couldn't wait fifteen more miles, could you? You couldn't get me home before you decided to quit on me?"

She frowned, lifted her foot and pulled it back, but set

it down in the dark brown South Carolina road dust. She shook her head and sighed. Then she turned her back on the car packed with what her mama would call "all her worldly goods" but what Missy called her "stuff."

Dust devils danced with the heat waves along the road. Missy looked right again, then left as though she expected to see something different this time even though she knew better. It was as if somebody took a stencil and painted the same live oaks and pines with a cypress flaring out every now and then to show where wet parts were. As far as she could see, honeysuckle and kudzu vines wrapped together around the rusting fence wire as if they were fighting over who could cover the most space.

Everything was quieter than she remembered from back when walking was the only way she got around. If it weren't for two crows shouting warnings across the road, she would have thought her hearing had quit on her when Gert died. Missy shook her head.

"I hope *died* is the wrong word. I hope Gert's only passed out." She hit the hood. "Doggone you, Gert. Why couldn't you make it a couple more miles down the road?" She stared toward the left. She knew what was in that direction, but she didn't move.

Jimmy had his place about a mile down the road that way. One-point-two miles to be exact. Missy took in a deep breath and looked the other way. It was about two miles in that direction just to get to the turnoff to Miss Jenkins's place.

Missy looked left once more, hiked her purse further up on her shoulder, patted the clip holding her hair back from her honey-colored face, set her usually full mouth in a tight line and headed to the right.

The early afternoon sun joined with humidity and kept her company as though they thought she'd be lonely on the road by herself. From time to time a breeze waved a breath of honeysuckle under her nose before it moved on, leaving only the pine scent in the air.

She looked to the sky as she used to when she was a kid coming home from the school bus stop, hoping to see a cloud coming to give her shade. It didn't happen often back then. She squinted up at the deep blue sky, looking like a new sheet, and sighed. It wasn't going to happen now.

She trudged through the road dust, leaving footprints that would most likely still be there come evening. Every now and then a bunch of Queen Anne's lace peeped from the deep shadows under heavy shrubs as if they didn't know they were supposed to be long gone by late June.

She shook her head. Some things never learn when their time is over.

Jimmy T's smiling bronze face appeared in her mind, winked at her and faded away. She felt even more alone than before.

She kept walking in the quiet that made her feel as if she were the only person in a peaceful world. So much time had passed since she had felt like this, she had forgotten it was possible. She sure hadn't found a place that gave her this feeling in Philadelphia.

Spanish moss, hanging from the trees lining the road, added its gray to the green leaves and pine needles as they swayed in the slight breeze. From time to time birds warned other birds of her passing, then quiet took over again.

Hot, thirsty and tired, Missy finally arrived at Miss Jenkins's gravel-topped road. A mailbox covered with painted flowers of every color and type imaginable reminded Missy of how much Miss Jenkins loved colors. Missy had discovered that when Miss Jenkins taught art to her fourth-grade class.

"The good Lord put color here on earth for us to use and He expects us to use it," Miss Jenkins had said on the first day of school as she handed out little paint boxes to the class.

Missy smiled at the mailbox standing guard with its little red flag tucked at its side. She brushed her hand over the flowers as she passed by. Some things never change.

She turned off the main road. The live oaks marching along both sides of Miss Jenkins's road gave protection from the sun, but the trade-off was the rough new light-gray gravel covering the road. Gravel and dust. The two flavors of country roads. Missy refused to look at the film of dark brown she knew was covering her new Avia sneakers.

"You just had to go and get white," she muttered. "Your shoes just had to match your new white pantsuit." She brushed the brown film from her white shoulder bag. She wasn't going to think of what condition the soles of her shoes would be in by the time she reached the house. And she refused to look at the bottom of her new pants.

"Walter is worth this, Walter is worth this. I just know he is worth coming home for," she chanted over and over in a voice not as strong as her words. Jimmy's handsome face with its strong nose showed itself in her mind once or twice, but she shoved it away. She wished Walter's friendly but serious face would come to her as easily as Jimmy's, which she swore she didn't want to see ever again.

She kept walking until she saw the forsythias standing guard beside the steps leading up to the wide front porch with its spotless gray floor and white railings. Two wicker chairs faced the road as if set for a parade to march by. She glanced down at her dusty shoes, frowned and followed the brick walkway curving through the side yard and around to the back door.

The azalea and rosebushes in the front yard continued in the side garden. Missy smiled. They appeared fuller, but they were probably the same ones from years ago when she had worked for Miss Jenkins weeding her garden. The green hostas with their white edges, growing in front of the blooming plants, were wider now, but the pansies tucked between them gave dashes of bright color. She'd helped set out these hostas and other pansies. Miss Jenkins hadn't really needed the help that year, but Missy had needed the job.

She swallowed the lump in her throat and blinked away what she was sure couldn't be tears after so much time had passed. A bright plaid dress danced through her mind.

If staring at a dress could wear it out, she would have done just that to the one in the window of Gloria's Dress Shop. Missy hadn't asked for it, but she talked about it so much her mama knew what was in her mind and had to remind her of just how tight money was.

Still, Missy and Annette, her best friend since kindergarten, talked about that dress every day for weeks. Then one day Miss Jenkins asked Missy if she'd like to earn a little spending change. At the time Missy thought she was lucky to get a job just when she needed money so badly. Years later she figured Miss Jenkins had overheard her going on about the dress and decided to help.

Blue and red. The dress was blue and red with a wide red ribbon tied in a big bow at the waist. Up until then her mama had made all her clothes. That store-bought dress was sure to make her the most beautiful girl in the world.

She would put it on, look in the mirror and see a lovely brown princess instead of a skinny girl with pigtails, eyes too large, and a mouth too wide for her face.

The dress had remained in the window for so long that Missy just knew it must have been meant for her all along. Then the next Monday afternoon it had disappeared. She went to visit it and it was gone from the window.

Missy thought she would curl up and blow away the next day when Julie Gaskins sashayed into school wearing the dress. Julie stopped in front of Missy and then twirled slowly down the hall to the classroom.

All day long Julie fussed with the white collar and, when she caught Missy looking at her, she ran her fingers up and down the wide ribbon trailing in her lap.

Missy blinked and the dress that was never hers faded away. Only the garden around her stayed. She walked around back. The smell of the herb garden went with her as she walked up the steps.

The smell of baking bread reached to her through the shed kitchen's screen door and made Missy think of Saturdays in her mama's kitchen.

She knocked on the door and smiled at the thought of seeing Miss Jenkins again.

"I'm coming, I'm coming." A strong voice came from the house. "Just a minute." The voice moved closer to the door. "I don't move so fast nowadays. Leastwise, not as fast as I used to. I guess I got no cause to complain, though. Not many folks who reach my age can race around all over the place. Lots of them have already gone on home to their reward."

A smooth chocolate face topped by a head full of soft white curls appeared at the door. A familiar smile softened the mouth that could be as hard as a live oak trunk when needed.

"Who is it out there in the heat of the day?"

"It's Missy Harrison, Miss Jenkins. I don't know if you remember me. I was in your class in fourth grade."

"Why, Melissa Miranda Harrison, of course I remember you. I remember every one of my students, so you know I remember the good ones. What brings you way out to my place? I was hoping you'd find time to come out for a visit, but I know you're going to be busy with last-minute plans for your wedding and all, so I didn't let myself count on it. It's been a whole lot of months of Sundays since I laid eyes on you. Whenever you came home for Christmas I was off visiting my kinfolk. They always come and get me so's I can spend some time in Hallandale, Florida, with them. They've come to expect me to go. Sometimes I go back in February if the weather here starts to acting up. I can do that now that I'm retired. I'm enjoying my what they call 'golden years,' but every now and again I do miss the classroom. All those children in their 'places with sunshiny faces' as that old song we used to sing goes. Do you remember that song? I expect you do. Do you use it in your class now that you're a teacher, or are they too sophisticated up North for such a thing?" Miss Jenkins nodded slowly. "If I recollect correctly, all of us lower-school teachers used that same song to get our students in the right frame of mind each morning. You can't sing the same words every morning for all those years and not remember them. That repetition is the whole basis of learning the times tables and using flash cards, isn't it? One of the worse changes was doing away with flash cards as a routine drill. Don't know whose bright idea it was to throw out something that worked."

Missy smiled. Miss Jenkins talked as much now as she had when Missy worked for her. Her smile widened. How she missed the nonstop talking. And how she loved this woman.

Missy slapped at the green bottle fly trying to sit down to dinner on her arm. She stamped another one off her leg.

"Come on in here, child, before those flies make a mess of your pretty skin." Miss Jenkins stepped aside to let Missy in, but her words kept moving. "Your mama said you were teaching in some grade school up Philadelphia way. I was proud back when she told me you were fixing to be a teacher. I like to think I can claim at least part of the reason for that. Still, I don't rightly know why you had to go way up North to go to college."

"Yes, ma'am, but I expect to be teaching at the elementary school here next term." She smiled shyly. "You did influence me to go into teaching, Miss Jenkins."

Miss Jenkins went on as if Missy hadn't broken into her words.

"We got some fine colleges down here, you know. I went to the teachers' college right here before it became a university. Course you wouldn't know about that. It was way back before your mama's time even. Closer to your granny's time."

"Yes, ma'am."

The older woman took a breath, but only so she could start again.

"How is your mama anyway? A while ago she told me you were coming home real soon. I saw her again last week, but she was across the street and just waved and hollered her hello. Said she was in a hurry and couldn't stop to talk." Miss Jenkins came up for air and kept on going. "Most folks are in a hurry nowadays. I don't see that life's any better for all the rushing around folks do. Seems they just have more time to make a bigger mess of things. Things were much better back when everybody took their time. Everything still got done and folks didn't have all the stress they complain about nowadays." She looked at Missy and blinked. "Come along, child. Why are you still standing here in the doorway? Anyway, the important thing is that you came to your senses and now you're back where you belong. I reckon your mama talked you into coming on home to stay." She laughed. "Of course, getting married most likely had something to do with you coming on back to Mayland to stay. I know that Walter Wilson will never move far from here. His mama wouldn't hear of it."

"Miss Jenkins." Missy didn't want to talk about Walter.

She wasn't ready to even think of him just yet. "I need to use your phone. Gertie quit on me a few miles down the road."

"You still driving that cantankerous eyesore? Your mama told me how you complain about your car every time she talks to you. Why didn't you say you needed to use the phone sooner?" She nodded. "That explains why I didn't hear you drive up. I know my hearing isn't as good as it used to be, but I still have enough of it left to hear a car pull into my driveway." She frowned. "You know, they don't make cars like they used to, do they? I remember the first car I had way back soon after I started teaching. It was a shiny, black Ford with . . ."

"Miss Jenkins," Missy's voice was gentle. "The phone?"

"Oh, yes, child. Come use the one in the kitchen. I just made a pitcher of iced tea. Now I have somebody to share it with me."

Missy followed her through the shed kitchen at a pace that would make her think there was a treasure on the other side if she didn't know better. *I hope when I reach Miss Jenkins's age I can get around half as well,* she thought. *She has to be closer to ninety than eighty. It doesn't slow her talking, either.*

Car trouble or not, Missy smiled. Now that she was back home, she'd have to come visit Miss Jenkins often. She picked up the phone. First she called Walter and told him where she was.

"Can you come get me?"

"I'm sorry, Melissa. I have a meeting. I expect it to last all day. Don't you have road service?"

"Yes, but you know how slow they can be."

"That's true, but you're practically home. A little while longer won't make any difference. I'm sorry. I have to go. I have people waiting for me. I expect an offer on the Brown place today." Walter hung up and Missy resigned herself to waiting. She made the other call.

She knew the toll-free number as well as she knew her own. Maybe better. After all, she didn't have to call her own number almost every week.

She gave the representative the information. The woman promised her somebody would be there as soon as possible, but however long it took, Missy knew Miss Jenkins would fill the time with news. The woman was a living newspaper, but most of her news was good.

Miss Jenkins sat at the smooth oak table and beckoned Missy to the seat across from her. She slid a glass of iced tea toward her.

"Now tell me. You still fixing to marry that Walter Wilson come next month?"

A long sip of tea came before her answer. "Yes, ma'am."

"Why July? Nothing wrong with it, mind you. It's a perfectly good month, but most girls want to be June brides."

"I-I thought about June, but everything costs more because everybody wants to be married on a Saturday in June. Walter's mother pointed out to me that July is just as good a month as June."

Miss Elberta herself hadn't told her anything. She had sent the message through Walter, who had acted like her carrier pigeon the way he always did.

"Mother says," Walter had told her the day after she had told him she wanted to get married in June, "it's foolish to insist on a June wedding. She said if you settle for July you won't have as much trouble paying for the wedding. A few weeks won't make that much difference. Besides, everybody wants to get married in June. Mother says you should consider being different."

Missy had changed her plans to July, but not because of Miss Elberta. All of the Saturdays had been booked at the Union Hall. July wasn't special to anybody, so she had moved her date to July. If Miss Elberta chose to think she played a part in Missy's decision, what was the harm?

"Walter always was a stuck-up child," Miss Jenkins muttered and stared hard at Missy to see what reaction she might get. There was none so she looked away and went on. "Nothing wrong with a little self-confidence, but Walter carried it a bit too far. He had enough for himself and a dozen other children to boot. Reckon he couldn't help it, though, what with Elberta being his mama and all. That woman acted like the sun only came up each morning so it could shine on her Walter." Her stare found Missy again. "She still acts that way."

Missy didn't nod, but she agreed with Miss Jenkins, who continued.

"He was in my room in fourth grade you know. Right along with you. Any time he didn't get an *A* on a paper, Elberta Wilson insisted something was wrong with my tests." She sniffed. "He might have been a little bright, but he wasn't any genius by any way of figuring intelligence." She sniffed again. "Humph. Bad tests indeed." She refilled the glasses from the pitcher and went to the counter beside the stove. "Where are my manners? Try a slice of this bread, child. I just took it out of the oven. Spread a bit of my homemade jam on it. It's elderberry. If I recall correctly, back when you helped me out with my gardens, you used to love the taste."

"Yes, ma'am. I still do." Missy spread a thick layer of dark jam on a hearty slice of bread.

"Put some of this pound cake on your plate, too. I made it day before yesterday, but a tea towel kept it nice and moist." She put a cake plate on the table and slid it toward Missy. "You got a little peaked-looking since you've been gone. You need to put some meat on your bones to keep you from looking poorly. You've been eating that northern food, is all. Nothing too terribly wrong with it if you're willing to give up taste for good looks."

Missy took the smallest slice and broke off a piece. She thought she looked okay, but nobody dared disagree with Miss Jenkins to her face.

"This is delicious. So is the bread. They always were."

"They came out all right, I reckon." Her hard stare was back. "Speaking of good looks, I seem to recollect that you and Jimmy Tanner Scott were courting each other nigh up to high school graduation, weren't you? The word *handsome* doesn't do him justice. Well? Weren't you two an item?"

"Yes, ma'am." Missy took a sip of tea to push the cake past the lump in her throat that had nothing to do with the food.

"How could you cut him loose and latch hold of somebody like Walter and Elberta?"

Missy shrugged. Miss Jenkins kept staring. She never took a shrug for an answer in her classroom and it looked as though she wasn't going to take one now.

Missy took a deep breath.

"Jimmy T and I . . ." She stopped and started again. "We didn't have the same ideas or the same plans for our lives. We weren't interested in going the same places. Fact is, Jimmy T isn't interested in going anywhere at all. He'll be satisfied stuck right here in Mayland forever." Missy blinked as every word of their last conversation came back.

Missy had told him she was thinking about answering one of those classified ads run by folks who are looking for nannies to go up North.

"I could go right after graduation. I'd only work for a year or maybe two. Then I'd come on back here."

"What would you want to go and do that for? Why would you want to go away from here?" Jimmy had asked.

"I want to get to know other places. Places I've read about and dreamed about. I don't see how you can plan to just stay here when there's so many different places in the world to see and experience. Don't you have any ambition?"

She remembered every word they threw at each other that early evening.

"No, Missy. Not where leaving here is concerned. I don't see any reason to go anyplace else when I'm satisfied right here," Jimmy had said. "Ambition doesn't have anything to do with it."

"But don't you ever get a longing to go somewhere else for a while?"

"Why would I? Everything I want is right here in Mayland. Everything." He had reached for her hand with his strong brown one then, but she had pulled away and put space between them.

"But there are so many other places to experience. Aren't you curious at all?"

"No. I got no reason to go anyplace else. Right here is enough. It's perfect."

"It's not perfect for me. This isn't enough. This will never be enough. I can't stay here forever. When I'm an old woman I don't want to be on my deathbed spending my last minutes on earth wishing I had gone somewhere else. Don't you ever wonder about those places we see in the movies and on TV?" She still remembered the frown she gave him. "Are you really saying you never thought about going anywhere?" She didn't know him at all.

"That's what I'm saying. Right here is just fine for me." Jimmy had inched over to his side of his 1967 Mustang then. "I never knew you were so dissatisfied here. I guess you're not happy with me either. I reckon you want better than me."

"I didn't say that." The car seat wasn't long enough for her to get far enough from this person she didn't know as well as she thought she did. "I just said it'd be nice to go somewhere else."

"There's always someplace else. You planning to see all of them before you settle down?"

"I plan to try."

The chrome door latch dug into her back right through the new blouse she had bought because Jimmy liked salmon pink so much. She should have bought dirt brown.

"I don't know what filled your head with such high-falutin ideas. If you were in heaven, you'd want to go to visit hell just so you could say you saw it."

Jimmy had gunned the motor then as if he forgot he had spent more than two months taking it apart and re-building it.

They shot back to her house as if they were trying to outrun a summer storm.

Her mama hadn't needed to leave the porch light on to keep her and Jimmy out of trouble. Not that night. The light wasn't needed ever again for her and Jimmy Tanner Scott.

Soon after that, Walter started calling her. He looked nothing like Jimmy. Walter was only a few inches taller than Missy and nice, but plain looking. The only sport he was interested in was golf, and that was because his mother said it could help him make contacts when he went into business. Walter was a puppy dog to Jimmy's black panther. Missy liked that about him.

At first he played as though he had forgotten the math assignment or he didn't understand something in science class. Then he didn't pretend he wanted anything except to talk to her. Next thing she knew, they were eating lunch together every day at school.

Walter encouraged her to forget about applying for a job, too, but he wanted Missy to apply for a scholarship instead. He went with her to Mrs. Baker, the counselor, that first time. When one hoped-for scholarship fell through, he encouraged her to keep trying.

He kept asking her out until she said yes. They began

dating on a regular basis, but she was up front with Walter.
She made it clear to him right from the start that she was
only offering friendship; that she was only going out with
him until Jimmy came to his senses. Just until then.

Walter had accepted her terms.

"Missy, I'll have you any way I can get you," he said.
"I'm betting I can get you to change your mind, and that
you'll forget all about Jimmy Tanner."

Before she knew it, it was time for the senior prom. She
went with Walter and had to watch Jimmy, tall and handsome in his tuxedo, and looking like a model on the cover
of a men's fashion magazine, walk in with Julie Gaskins
on his arm.

Graduation came and went and Jimmy's right mind was
further off than ever.

"Melissa? You still with me?" Miss Jenkins touched
Missy's arm and brought her back from her memories.
Missy blinked.

"Yes, ma'am. I was just thinking, is all."

"As I recollect, Jimmy Tanner was a bright boy. Quiet,
well-behaved and right bright. Things came natural to him
like they do to some. He was well past my grade when his
folks moved here, but I heard about him." She smiled at
Missy and shrugged. "You know teachers are no different
from other folks. We do our share of talking, especially
when we come across a child who shows a lot of promise.
Nowadays they say he can take apart any engine, fix it and
put it back together blindfolded. I don't know about the
blindfold part, but I do know firsthand what he can do
to keep a car running. He keeps my Buick going so well
it will outlive me. I see him in town from time to time
even when I don't need car work done. That's no surprise.
You stay twenty minutes in town and you see everybody
who comes in that day." She nodded. "Still, our town's
got everything we need. Jimmy T's doing right well for
himself. He even opened his own . . ." A knock on the

back door stopped her words. Missy stood, glad to get away from the direction the conversation was headed.

"I'll get it." She turned toward the door. "It's probably somebody to see to my car." Then she stopped and looked back. "It is all right if I answer the door, isn't it?"

"Of course it is. You just go right ahead."

Missy rushed through the shed kitchen but stopped short when she looked through the screen door.

There he stood as if a root woman had conjured him up: all six foot three inches of drop-dead, come-back-to-life-and-drop-dead-again gorgeous man. Jimmy Tanner Scott, staring at her with his slow crooked grin, ought to have been declared a hazardous substance by the federal government long ago.

Even after so many years, she was instantly drawn, like a steel plate to a magnet, to the warm brown face that she had traced more times than she could remember. Her fingers itched, ached at the memory. Her gaze stopped at his full lips. Back in the day, when they belonged to each other, after her fingers got done touching his mouth, her lips took over. They always ended up touching his, melting against his, tasting his, longing for more than a kiss from him.

She swallowed and dragged her gaze away from his mouth. There must be some spot on his face where she could look without memories twisting to the surface and closing in on her.

Her gaze stopped at his forehead. He had cut the curl that always hung over his right eyebrow.

Before she and Jimmy got close enough for her to know him, she wondered if he worked to get that curl to drape over his forehead pointing to perfect green eyes. She had commented on the color of his eyes and his hair, and he had just shrugged.

"They're just eyes. They see the same as any others. They show up from time to time in the family and this time I got them. Nobody talks about where they came from. I wish they were brown like everybody else's. Okay?" He had pushed back the curl then. "This probably came from the same place. I wouldn't care if this went away, too." He had frowned at her. "I don't like to talk about it, either. Okay?"

"Okay." She saw the bitterness and sadness in his eyes and never mentioned his eye color again. Nor did she mention the curl.

After they started going together she found out for herself that the curl was just like Jimmy T: doing what it wanted to do and the heck with what anybody thought.

Whenever Jimmy got fed up with trying to tame it back then, he'd threatened to cut it off. Then she would brush it back, move her hand to the back of his head and ease her mouth to his. How she had loved that curl. Now it was gone. Just like their time together.

She shifted her weight and kept looking for a cooler spot even though she knew she wouldn't find one.

"Hey, Missy." His soft words caressed her like always, and she melted like always. The years disappeared.

Heaven help her, his voice was the same and it was doing the same old things to her. She closed her eyes.

Remember Walter, a little voice inside warned her, but it proved too puny to conquer the image her eyes sent to her mind.

"Hi, Jimmy T." She prayed her voice sounded more in control than she felt. Her insides danced and jumped around as if they were at a party going full swing. She was glad the door was between them.

"How've you been?" His voice curled around her and reminded her of what she had been missing.

"Just fine." She blinked. *Until now,* she thought.

"You look more than just fine." His gaze moved slowly over her.

It felt as if his eyes burned a path down her body, so

he could find his way back again later. Part of her was hoping he would. The bigger part of her. What was she going to do?

"Darling, you look better than I remember, but until now I didn't think that was possible."

He looked at her as though he had found the end of the rainbow.

Missy didn't feel like anything as solid as gold. She felt like a bowl of vanilla and chocolate ice cream left out too long and stirred all together. She felt just as mixed up.

"I got a call at my garage about your car," Jimmy said. "I couldn't believe it was really you. I made the insurance woman repeat your name twice so I could be sure."

"Your garage?"

"Yeah. I got my own shop now. Had it for almost two years. I thought you knew."

She might have known if she had let her mama talk to her about Jimmy, but every time his name came from her mama's lips, Missy found something to do somewhere out of earshot. The Jimmy T part of her life was history. She had other plans and he wasn't going to mess with them. Each time her mama mentioned him she told her just that. She didn't mention the pain that filled her whenever she heard his name.

"The lady from the insurance company said you need my help. She told me where to find your car and where to find you."

His voice got husky and Missy remembered other times it sounded like that. How do you erase memories?

"I can't believe it's really you," he repeated. The fire in his eyes almost burned away what little sense Missy had left to cling to.

There wasn't any help Jimmy could give her that wouldn't put her in worse shape than she was now. Why him?

"Was it true about your car or were you just using that

as an excuse to see me?" The glint in his eyes and the twitch at the corners of his mouth that said that he was teasing her, did more to cool her off than getting caught in a sudden rain shower would.

"I didn't even know you had a garage so I couldn't know you'd get the call. Besides, you know the automobile club decides which garage to call." She glared. "I'm tired. I drove a long way today and I'm not in the mood for your foolishness."

Her senses were back where they belonged and were working the way they should. She was glad Jimmy didn't mention the times when she *was* in the mood for his foolishness, and everything else he had in mind.

"My car really quit on me down the road. Besides, why would I use an excuse to see you?"

"Danged if I know, but since I never got a single opportunity to see you when you came home for the holidays . . ." He shrugged. "Well, I just don't know." The twinkle disappeared. "I reckon we don't know each other much anymore." He stared at her and his eyes got wider, as though they needed to see more. "You know you never needed an excuse to see me before, honey. Just because you've been to the big city for a while doesn't mean you need one now." His voice grew low as if sharing a secret meant only for her. "You don't ever need an excuse to see me, Missy. You didn't back then, and you sure don't now. I haven't changed. Don't you know that?"

What was she supposed to say to that? What could she say? She didn't want to remember, but she did. Was it possible to forget something on purpose?

Jimmy waited for her answer.

A sadness filled her. He hadn't changed. He said so. His not wanting to change was the problem in the first place. She'd have to remember that. When she didn't give an answer, he went on talking.

"On the way out here, I saw your car and moved it off

the road. I reckon I'd best go take a look at it," he said, but he stayed firmly in place as if his feet hadn't heard his words. "Want to come with me now?"

"Yes, I-I better go with you. I'll go get my purse." Missy's feet weren't paying any mind, either.

Miss Jenkins came to the door and blinked both of them loose.

"I wondered if you'd get the call." She looked at Jimmy.

"How you feeling today, Miss Jenkins?"

"Just fine, Jimmy, just fine." She looked from one to the other but they didn't even notice. "You want to come in and sit a spell before you get to work? I got a loaf of bread fresh out of the oven just waiting. What do you say?"

"Ma'am?"

"I said how about a slice of my fresh bread with some sweet butter and my homemade elderberry jam? Or maybe you'd rather have a slice of my pound cake?"

"They both sound right tasty, Miss Jenkins. Any other time I'd take you up on your kind offer, but I can't today. I got a heap of work waiting for me back at the shop. Both Benny and Lester called in sick yesterday, so I got to try to catch up on the backwork." He looked back at Missy. "You ready?"

No, she wasn't ready. How could she be? "Yes. Just let me get my purse from the kitchen."

She took in a deep breath and hoped it would cool her off and send strength down to her legs. She was expecting a lot from one breath, no matter how deep it was. She took in another and hoped it would give more help than the first one had provided.

She went for her handbag, glad for a little time to try to compose herself. Maybe if the purse were in the living room she might have enough time. Or better still, if she had to go farther to get it. She sighed and went back to the door.

"You take good care of Missy, now," warned Miss Jenkins. "She was one of my prize students, you know."

"Yes, ma'am, I will." His gaze burned Missy more than the summer sun could. "She's special to me, too."

Jimmy held the door open and Missy managed to walk through without stumbling at the word *special*. She tried not to remember that once she had felt the same way about Jimmy. Once?

A whiff of Jimmy's aftershave teased her nostrils and she had to fight to remember how to walk. She had given him a bottle of Polo for his eighteenth birthday, and obviously it was still his favorite. She blinked and looked back into the house.

"Thank you, Miss Jenkins, for everything."

"It isn't worth mentioning, child. I was glad for the company. I know you're going to be busy what with your wedding plans and all, but you come on back out here to see me again, you hear?"

"Yea, ma'am, I will. I promise."

"You, too, Jimmy. You don't need a broken-down car waiting for you out here for you to come on by for a visit."

"Yes, ma'am, I know."

Jimmy's hand at the small of Missy's back felt like a missing jigsaw puzzle piece placed exactly where it belonged.

"Let's go take a look at your car."

"Remember Walter" played in her mind like a mantra, but with the volume turned down too low. She didn't know how to turn it up.

Jimmy opened the door.

Missy stared at the step almost at her knee level.

"Where's the little stool?"

"Too much bother. We don't need it." He put both hands on her waist and lifted her before she could protest. His hand stayed on her waist way past time to move on.

She looked at him and saw the dark brown flecks in his

eyes deepen to black. Her gaze latched on to his like one of two parts making a whole.

Protest? Protest what?

TWO

Jimmy fumbled with the gearshift twice trying to find first gear. He wasn't this bad the first time he got behind the wheel of a car with a stick shift. That was back when he didn't have enough sense to know he didn't have enough sense.

He wiped his hand on his pants leg and fumbled again, wishing the car designers had made gear shifting easier; wishing for things that didn't have anything to do with cars. Her perfume grabbed at him, and the reverse gear pulled further out of reach. Finally the stick had pity on him and tumbled into the correct slot.

He backed up his tow truck and pulled down Miss Jenkins's road. When he reached the main road, he took a deep breath, gave in and dared to look at Missy.

His heart lurched as though it didn't know whether to slow down or speed up. It was acting worse than a sticky clutch. Heaven help him, she was more beautiful than ever. Would her high cheekbones still crowd her eyes when she laughed? Who did she last have fun with?

He tightened his hand to stop the shaking. Would her honey-colored face taste as sweet as the honey it took its name from? Would her eyes still darken with passion if he held her? Would color fill her cheeks when his words made her blush? Would those sweet, sensual full lips open beneath his like before? Would he ever get the chance to find the answers to his questions?

The last time he had seen her was at her high school graduation and he hadn't gotten this close then. The last time they had been close enough to touch was when they had had that stupid argument about nothing. That was the last time her body had molded its fullness to his in a perfect fit.

He looked away and tightened his hold on the gearshift. He was glad he had decided not to get an automatic truck. Who knew what trouble he'd get into sitting beside Missy and feeling her heat, if he didn't have something for his hand to do instead of wrapping around her arm, her shoulder, her.

He thought his love for her had died from lack of attention, but the sight of her standing at the back door at Miss Jenkins's house proved him wrong. His love had sprung up again as if it had been resting for a few days, instead of having been ignored by her for five years. It was acting as if it last got encouragement from Missy yesterday instead of five years ago.

He shifted in the seat and tried to get comfortable as if such a thing were possible when he was within reaching distance of her. His body was acting as if it were seventeen again instead of twenty-four. Still, he dared another glance at her.

He hadn't seen her in five long years. Five years that melted away five minutes ago. She was perfect. He wanted to pull her close and kiss away the long absence. He wanted to feel if she still felt right in his arms as she had when she belonged there. He wanted to lay her down right here on the truck seat, and remind her of how well their bodies fit together. He wanted her. Right here. Right now. Always.

It was a battle, but he forced his hands to stay on the steering wheel.

A gold clip held her soft curls back. She used to let them fall free for him. If she did now, would they still touch her shoulders like before? He wanted to find out. But that was a small want. He wanted to let those curls wind around his fingers the way they did back when he had a right to touch her; to ease her against him the way she wanted.

He let his glance slip to her mouth. The fullness was bare of color but just as promising, just as soft as when it welcomed his a lifetime ago. He closed his eyes. Many times she had shared its sweet secret with him. Many times. But not enough. Never enough. He moved his left leg to the door searching for yet more cooling space that didn't exist.

His body always tightened when he thought about her. It didn't matter if she was near or not, but it was worse when she was near. With her so close now, he could not have peeled his jeans off if somebody had offered him a bank full of money. Unless it was Missy doing the offering. Then the reward would be worth more than all the money that all the banks in the country could hold. Missy in his arms was always priceless.

He shifted his weight again, tried once more to find a comfortable spot and wished he had put on looser jeans this morning. He shook his head. He wasn't sure that would have helped. He didn't know if anything but having Missy again would help.

A horn blew and he shifted his gaze away from her face and forced his thoughts with it as he looked at the road. He shrugged an apology as an angry driver passed him going in the opposite direction. He tried harder for control of the truck. He didn't want to hurt anybody. That control was the easiest. It was his feelings and reactions that were impossible to restrain. He had to look at her again. How many more chances would he get?

She held her hands together in her lap as if each one

were afraid the other would get away. The sunlight slanted in her window and danced off her barely pink nails. The last time he had touched them they had been cocoa brown and were waiting for him.

When he picked her up that day when they still had a future together, he had kissed each hand as he always did before he pulled her close. Her arms had wrapped as tightly around him as his had around her. Like always. At least like always before.

He blinked. Her body had always fit against his as if it were the other half of him. It still would if she gave them another chance. He let out a hard breath. His head moved from side to side.

Missy and Walter Wilson. His name didn't even belong in the same sentence with hers. Jimmy wasn't going to think of Wilson attached to the end of her name.

His knuckles tightened to keep his hands from checking to see if hers were as soft and smooth as the last time he had caressed them, back when she wanted him to. Back when she welcomed his touch, his body. Him. His jaw tightened and he sighed.

Her hands were probably even softer now. Schoolteachers had soft hands. So did anybody else who worked at a desk. So did folks like real-estate agents. Folks like Walter Wilson.

People like that didn't have hands like a mechanic's: rough and calloused. He looked at his own hands. There was no need for words to tell what he did for a living. His hands and fingernails spoke for him.

His frown still creased his forehead when he pulled in front of Missy's car. He looked over at her. She didn't even know they had stopped. Was she off in a dream? Was Walter with her? Was he holding her the way Jimmy used to? Did he really want to know?

Jimmy's gaze touched her soft cheek, but he kept his hands to himself where they belonged. Was it so terrible for her to be with him nowadays, that she had to escape inside herself just so she could stand it? He took a big breath. He guessed he knew the answer to that one. She was showing him. Showing him good. He cleared his throat.

"Here we are." His words were rougher than he meant for them to be. "You want to stay in here or come watch me give it a quick look?" Back in the day, she always wanted to see what he was doing under the hood of a car.

"I-I guess I should come see." She sounded as if she were preparing for a root canal at Dr. Williams's office.

He went around to her side. This time when he helped her down, he didn't want to, but he pulled his hands away from her as soon as they had done their job.

"Why don't you get on in the car and pop the hood." His hands ached, but she didn't need his help, his touch; not this time. He wasn't sure whether he was glad or sad about that.

"You got to promise me you won't find anything but a little bitty problem, okay?" Her warm brown eyes widened and took him back to the old days when it was okay for him to stand close enough to see the dark lines in them coming from the center like slices in his mama's German chocolate cake. He pulled his feet loose and walked around to the front of the car.

Missy's feet and eyes refused to work at the same time, and right now what her eyes were doing was far more important.

Jimmy's faded jeans rolled with that funny side-to-side walk of his as if they knew his moves before he made them. His backside muscles bunched and stretched beneath jeans molded to fit only him. *Sheriff Andrews should make him wear a warning sign,* she thought. *Beware.* She wondered if Julie Gaskins felt the same way when she watched Jimmy walk. Did Julie appreciate his solidness when she held him close? Missy sighed. She wasn't supposed to care what was between Jimmy and Julie or Jimmy and anybody else. She wasn't supposed to still care about Jimmy, period. She had to work on that. Real hard. She was marrying Walter in four weeks.

Four weeks left. She shook her head. She mustn't think of this as though it were a death sentence. She had to stop letting Jimmy take up space in her mind.

She swallowed hard and made her gaze break free before she got lost in what used to be, and forgot what was going to be.

"You want to take a look at this with me or not?" Jimmy acted as though he found something better for her to look at than him. As if that were possible. Missy shook her head again. At least looking somewhere else would be safer. Looking anyplace else would help keep her mind out of trouble.

She walked around the front of her car and stopped beside him in a fog as if she had no clue as to why she had moved over there. Except to be closer to him. His body heat reached her and made her ache to find out exactly what part of him it was coming from.

Jimmy's top half was under the hood, but the lower part of his body, poured into those jeans that had long ago lost their blue, was in full view. Missy felt herself getting lost, too.

The first time they had kissed they had been standing like this. He had been showing her how to check the oil in her mama's old Chevy. One minute he was looking at the engine, and the next her brown eyes met the green of his in a gaze that made the yard feel like a woodstove in January. That was when she first saw the light-brown flecks scattered in his eyes. She remembered wondering if they were the same shade of brown as her eyes. Then he moved even closer and she stopped wondering about eyes, and thought about his mouth, which was coming toward hers as if it weren't sure of the way.

She had leaned forward to meet him. Then she hadn't wondered or thought about anything anymore. Jimmy's arms had wrapped around her, and she slid hers around him where they belonged. If her mama hadn't picked that time to call her, she might still be lost in that kiss.

She blinked hard. This time there was no kiss, and it was Jimmy's voice that brought her back.

"I know you don't want to hear this." He straightened up and pulled his hands out from under the hood. Missy's gaze followed his hands as he pulled out the cloth he always had tucked in his pocket when he worked on cars. He wiped his hands. They didn't look as strong now as they had felt a while ago when they had wrapped around her waist, and lifted her from the truck and held her close a bit too long. Way too long. But not long enough. Julie would say too long.

When she had come home from college that first Christmas, Missy had heard that Jimmy and Julie were seeing each other regularly. She hadn't let her mama talk about him or Julie after that.

She controlled a sigh. Jimmy belonged to Julie now, and *she* was supposed to belong to Walter. She was marrying him, wasn't she? She swallowed hard.

Jimmy's hands had been gentle but strong the night they had the big fight, too. That was the last time his touch had lit fires inside her. Until today. Today felt almost like old times. Almost. She blinked. It was too late. It was too late for both of them. She had an obligation to Walter and things were probably the same between Jimmy and Julie. She pulled her attention to what was.

Jimmy's voice was easing along now, as if he expected her to understand any of his words that managed to push through the oatmeal that had replaced her brain. She didn't waste time trying to conjure up Walter. She just tried to make sense out of what Jimmy was saying.

"I know one thing wrong is your timing belt," Jimmy said, as if she had been paying attention to his words and knew what he had already said. She made her mind listen to what he was saying now, instead of how he looked. She needed her car working.

"What does time have to do with Gertrude quitting on me in the middle of nowhere? Besides, the clock was working just fine when she cut off so that can't be the problem."

"You named your car Gertrude? No wonder she quit on you."

"There's nothing wrong with the name Gertrude."

"It's all right, I guess. There are probably some nice women named Gertrude. It's just so unusual." He was not going to get into an argument over the name she gave her car. A dumb argument was why they were apart now.

"It is a nice name."

Her chin went up as though she was trying to pick a fight with him. He was too smart to make that mistake again.

"The name isn't the problem, anyway."

He shook his head and a sigh as heavy as Missy's car pushed from him. His look reminded Missy of the one Miss Jenkins had used when somebody in the class missed an easy math problem.

"I knew you weren't paying close attention when I used to show you under the hood, Missy." He shook his head slowly. "Really, Missy. *Something* should have sunk in. I can't believe it didn't."

What could she say? He was right. But he was wrong, too. Something did sink in, but it didn't have anything to do with fixing cars. It was all about Jimmy and the two of them getting together after he was finished playing mechanic. He hadn't had a clue as to how little would get through to her when they were going together and she was within touching distance of him. She tried to make right now the exception.

"From the looks of things under the hood," he went on, "there's probably something else wrong. When was the last time you had this car serviced?"

"You sound just like a mechanic."

"I am a mechanic. I've got a certificate hanging on the wall in my office at the shop that says so. Don't you remember anything from all the times I showed you what's going on under the hood of a car? How many times did I tell you how important it is to take care of a car?"

Jimmy went to technical school after he graduated from high school a year before she did. Back when they were sweet on each other, whenever Jimmy had gotten an itch to teach her about cars and show her what he had learned in school that week, she followed him to the front of the car as he wanted her to do, but she hadn't looked at the grungy motor and stuff. She had been too busy staring at Jimmy up close. She had been fascinated at how his hands took all those big things apart and put them back together. She had been thinking of how his hands were going to feel on her later, after Jimmy got tired of giving her a car lesson. The very last thing she had been thinking about was all those big greasy, dirty things fastened together under the hood of a car.

She hadn't been like her little sister, Beth, who let Jimmy teach her about everything on a car, and in a car, from the front bumper to the back and everything in between. Beth had worked with Jimmy for hours on any piece of car he could get his hands on for practice. Missy was happy to just watch Jimmy work.

Now Beth was in the army doing the same car things by herself and Missy was back here watching Jimmy. Missy blinked. This was far from back then. There was a whole lot heaped between then and now.

"Missy, are you listening to me? I know I told you about everything under the hood including timing belts. You've got to remember hearing about something as important as that. And you've got to remember to take your car in for regular checkups."

She was having trouble remembering her name and he wanted her to remember how a belt keeps time? She had to see Walter and she had to see him real soon. And she had to put some space between her and Jimmy. She took a step away from him.

"That's all over and done with." *Like things between us,* she wanted to add. "Let's forget about the lessons and get going."

He stared at her while a pair of mockingbirds threw a conversation back and forth in the branches of the live oak beside the car. Then he slammed the hood, pushed off and moved away as if he needed space, too.

"Let me hook up the car so I can tow it into my shop."

"Tow" and "into the shop" didn't sound any better here than they did in Philadelphia.

Missy scrambled up into the truck before Jimmy could help her. She kept running Walter's name over and over in her head.

Then Jimmy got in and the truck cab shrank until it was too small to hold the both of them and Walter's name. Walter's name faded away.

Missy had to catch her breath before it left, too. She turned toward Jimmy as he started the truck. She put her purse on the seat between them and wished she had gotten the bigger bag. Then she stared past him as though looking for something among the pines and live oaks standing alongside the road as if they were waiting for something to happen.

"Look, Jimmy, you got to piece my car together, okay? Just so it will run right even if it's just for a little bitty while, okay? I can't afford any major repairs right now."

"I reckon you need all your money for your fancy wedding to Walter." His words came out like a bad taste he wanted to be rid of real quick.

Missy watched his fingers tighten around the steering wheel like he thought it was fixing to run away from him.

"I-I do have a lot of expenses right now."

Jimmy stared into her eyes as if looking for her reasons to pop out at him so he could challenge them. Then he gave up, shifted into gear and eased back onto the road.

A whole lot of pines and live oaks and not a few palmettos rolled past the window before he let any more words loose.

"Why are you doing it, Missy?"

Missy didn't pretend she didn't know what he was talking about. Too much lay between them for her to do that.

"Walter and I understand each other."

"You and I had some pretty good understanding going between us, too, didn't we?"

She could call it a lot of things, but understanding wasn't what she would call what they had back in high school. If she looked at any page of one of her old notebooks in the box under the bed in her old room, somewhere in the margins she would see where she practiced writing *Mrs. Jimmy T. Scott* with curlicues on all the right letters and framed with hearts. Sometimes she practiced *Mrs. James Tanner Scott* for important times when nicknames wouldn't do.

She fought the sadness trying to take root in her. She wasn't going to need any of what she practiced any more than she needed the eleven and twelve times tables she had memorized back in grade school.

"Walter supported my dreams back when you thought they were a silly waste of time." She couldn't remember exactly when Walter had replaced Jimmy in her plans. Looking back, it seemed as though one day it was Jimmy and the next day Walter was coming to see her, but she knew it hadn't happened that fast. Walter had worn her down until she let him nudge into her life. The next thing she knew, he was all the way there. She still wasn't sure exactly when it had happened.

"I never said your dreams were silly or a waste of time. Those are your words. All I said was that I didn't understand them. Then you got to carrying on like you had stumbled into a fire-ant hill and couldn't pull loose."

"I did no such a thing. You said . . ."

"Missy, ain't no use stirring it up again when it's going to come out the same way." Jimmy heaved a big sigh. "Nothing I can say can change your mind when you let your stubborn streak show itself. No matter how hard I tried, I never could back when we . . ." He sighed again. "I don't expect to find the special words to change it now, either."

Heavy silence took the place of words, but Missy didn't say anything. Then Jimmy went on.

"You got your dress like that picture you used to show me, and the flowers and all in place just like you planned years ago?"

His voice got so low Missy could barely hear him, but she didn't lean closer to him. She didn't dare.

"I reckon you won't need your wish book anymore."

Missy heard another sigh come from him like a twin looking for the one that went before.

He was right about her wish book and her plans. She had been keeping that book from the time she was thirteen. The pictures changed until she was seventeen. Then she found a picture of the dress and stuck with it. Everything was going to be exactly like in her scrapbook, and the plans she had made years ago were the same except for one thing: the groom was different.

She stared at her hands and tried to figure out exactly when that had happened and how. And why hadn't she fixed it before it was too late?

"I'll admit," Jimmy stopped as though his next words had gotten lost and he had to wait for them. "I might have been a bit riled. I have to add pigheaded, too. I didn't have a wish book, but I had wishes and dreams for when you graduated. I was waiting for you. I had big dreams that included us together in a house we'd build on the piece of property my grandpa left me. I thought you wanted the same things. I took it for granted that you and me would settle down. I'd open up my own shop. I didn't plan to work for somebody else for the rest of my life." He shifted his head to the side as he did when he was working something out. "I can't fault you for not sharing your dreams about traveling and school before our last day, when I didn't see fit to share mine with you."

He chewed his lip and stared out the windshield, but Missy wasn't sure he was seeing the road.

"I haven't taken anything for granted since then." He looked at her quickly before he looked back to the road. "Before that night, I never reckoned your plans included going off to school and staying afterward. I didn't know your plans included being without me." He shook his head. "I thought we'd get married and settle down right here. I never knew you were even thinking about college."

Several private roads eased past before Missy found the right words.

"I wasn't planning on college at first. I was just going to get a job like I talked about. I didn't dare think about college until after . . ." She swallowed hard. "Until after we broke up. Walter gave me the idea."

Missy stared at her fingers laced together in her lap. Her mama hadn't even known she wanted to go to college. There wasn't any way it could come true and it would just make her mama feel bad that they couldn't afford it, so Missy had kept it hidden. It was talking to Walter after she and Jimmy broke up that gave her the nerve to talk

about what she really wanted. Sharing dreams with Walter
had let her see that hers were possible.

She was as surprised as everybody else when the college
gave her a full scholarship and told her to come on. That
was the end for her and Jimmy.

"I thought maybe, if I tried hard enough," Jimmy continued, "I could change your idea about seeing the world
instead of settling down with me. I figured, if I could get
you to listen, you'd want what I wanted." His voice got
low. "I thought I was at the top of your wish list. I found
out too late I was wrong."

If the steering wheel were alive, it would be having
trouble breathing about now.

"Next thing I knew, Walter Wilson was trailing along
behind you like he was your puppy dog and you were
holding his leash." Jimmy shook his head. "I never did
see that one coming." He glanced at her. "Why, Missy.
Tell me why? How did it happened? Why did it happen?"

She shrugged.

"I knew I could never make you understand. I didn't
wholly understand it myself." She frowned. "You were satisfied being here and spending your whole life within
walking distance of where you were born. I wanted other
places, too. Places where I could get up in the morning,
look out the window and know I wasn't anywhere near
Mayland." She stared at her fingers clutched around the
strap of her purse as if it were the key to some deep secret
and she had to protect it. "One big difference between
you and Walter is that he did understand. He wanted
more, too. He encouraged me to follow my dreams. He
thought college was a good idea. He wanted it, too. You
just wanted to get married."

She had wanted marriage, too. Ever since she and
Jimmy had gotten serious about each other, she had
dreamed of their wedding all peach and white like in one
of those bride magazines she used to read in the library

until Miss Linda, the librarian, decided they were old enough to get rid of.

Missy had cut out pictures of every beautiful gown she saw and put them in her wish book so she could choose the perfect one when the time came.

She had always imagined Jimmy waiting at the end of the aisle in church with Reverend Butler, watching her come to him in her long, lace-covered white gown her mama would make for her. Her bridesmaids and maid of honor dressed in peach would be waiting, too, but she would only see Jimmy, so handsome in his tux, waiting to make her his wife.

She sighed. Her wedding time was here and her gown was prettier in real life than the picture she had finally settled on. It just wasn't Jimmy who would be waiting for her with Reverend Butler. How could she explain how one dream changed into another when she didn't understand it herself.

"Of course Walter would encourage you once he figured he had you. He needs a family and a respectable wife if he's going into politics. Every chance he gets he lets folks know that he intends to be governor one day. It doesn't hurt for the governor's wife to have a college degree, does it?"

"So what if he does plan to be governor? What's wrong with that?"

"Not a blessed thing. Not if that's what he wants and not just something his mama put into his head. Walter's all right. I never heard of him being dishonest or anything like that. That's important for anybody, but especially for a politician. Of course, maybe the reason why he's so honest is because Miss Elberta won't let him be any other way. He doesn't do anything without her say-so."

"That's not true. I'm tired of everybody picking on Walter." Missy wished her words had more power to them, but Jimmy was right about Walter. Every one of her argu-

ments with him had been about something Miss Elberta
had said that Walter agreed with.

"Mother says," Walter had spouted when Missy had
shared her ideas about the food for the reception, "it's
pretentious to serve cornish game hens when chicken
would be just as good. After all, Mother says, that's what
people around here would expect. As for asparagus,
Mother says most of the people you invite won't know the
first thing about how to eat it."

Missy had lists of food she wanted and asparagus and
cornish hens beat out all the other possibilities. They were
staying on her menu even if all folks did was stare at the
food sitting on their plates and the asparagus was still there
when the table was cleared. Miss Elberta was a snob. Other
folks knew as much as she did. Some knew more. When
Missy told Walter that, he had looked hurt the way he always
did when she didn't accept his mama's suggestion.

"Mother was just being helpful. Of course, the decision
is yours since you're paying for it."

"That's another thing," she had said, hating the timid
way her words were coming out. "I was wondering if, since
you have so many more guests on the list than I do, and
since you have more money saved up than I do, I was
wondering if maybe you could at least help pay for the
food?"

Missy blinked as she remembered Walter's answer.

"Mother says it's the bride's responsibility to take care
of all of the wedding expenses." He went on to finish,
dropping Miss Elberta's latest pearl of wisdom. " 'Managing wedding expenses is good practice for managing a
household budget,' Mother says. She said some traditions
are worth keeping. She says she thinks you're clever
enough to work it out so you can handle all of it."

Any other time she would have been pleased at a com-
pliment of any kind from Miss Elberta. That time Missy's

thoughts were stuck on how she would have to cut corners so she could still have the wedding she had always wanted.

It hadn't been easy, but she was doing it. Paying for the wedding wasn't the problem. She was just about finished. Even with the unexpected car repair bill she would be able to meet her expenses. Her problem wasn't the money. She shied away from facing the real problem and latched on to Jimmy's next words.

"Is that what you want, too, Missy? To be the governor's wife? Has living in the governor's mansion replaced your dreams of going everywhere and seeing everything?"

"I never said I wanted to go every place. Those were your words. Your opinion. Besides, Walter and I will be going places. We'll take vacations and he'll have official trips to take and who knows? Maybe he'll move up from governor, and we'll end up in Washington." She glared at him. "None of that has anything to do with why I'm marrying him. Travel is a stupid reason."

"It sure is." He looked at her. "Exactly why are you marrying him? You could have had vacations with me, if that would have been enough for you. And I guarantee they would have been more exciting than any you'll ever have with Walter." His gaze met hers and pinned her in place with its heat. They could have been floating in a spaceship on the way to Venus instead of creeping along service road 26-416. The sun had enough time to go to bed and come up again in the time they sat with their gazes glued together.

A horn blasted behind them and ripped their stares apart. Missy felt more fire in her cheeks in the air-conditioned truck cab than she had felt walking down the road with the sun throwing its full heat on her. She looked away and tried to find a deep breath to cool her off. She was still trying as Jimmy started the truck and continued toward town.

Walter in his three-piece suit, a lace-covered wedding

dress and Jimmy in his faded jeans tumbled through her thoughts as the truck bounced toward town.

Why *was* she marrying Walter?

THREE

"Here we are." Jimmy pulled to a stop in front of the open doors of a garage on Carpenter Street at the edge of Mayland. JIMMY TANNER SCOTT'S GARAGE marched across the top of the building in bold black showing that Jimmy was telling the truth when he said he had his own garage.

Not that Missy hadn't believed him. She remembered years ago, when he first told her of how he was dreaming of owning his own garage business someday.

"I don't intend to work for somebody else for the rest of my life," he had said.

Missy sighed. His dream had come true. As for her own dreams . . . She shook her head. She wasn't going to think about the dreams she had back then. She wasn't going to think about her dreams at all, not now when she was so confused she wasn't sure of anything, least of all dreams coming true. Jimmy always did that to her thinking.

She looked inside the garage. Three men were working under the hoods of three different cars, but none of them looked as good as Jimmy did in his work jeans. None of them could look as good as Jimmy did, no matter what they wore. Missy swallowed hard.

Her gaze followed Jimmy as he walked around the front of the truck to come help her down. Why hadn't he put the dang step in here like he was supposed to?

She held her breath. *Should I keep my eyes open, and watch him close the space between us until I can smell his spicy aftershave that reminds me of what was between us? Should I just sit here and watch him, and wait until I can feel his warm breath caressing my face? Wait like I used to wait when a kiss was at the end of his walk?* She felt her heart rhythm speed up at the memory. *Or should I close my eyes and keep them closed until I can feel his hands remembering their rightful places around my waist.*

Why hadn't he changed so she no longer felt a tug toward him? Why hadn't she stayed in Philadelphia where she had been; far enough away so she didn't have to see him, so she could convince herself that she no longer cared for him? Why hadn't he at least changed what he wanted out of life so the gap between them wasn't too big to close? Why hadn't she seen him when she came home during holidays? Why hadn't she seen him before today? Why didn't her heart know it was too late to care now?

She took in a great gulp of air when Jimmy stopped in front of her, but she didn't blink away from his stare. He slid his hands around her waist slow and easy as if he had all the time he wanted to do that, and she still didn't blink, even though the warmth from his hands was spreading through her.

He set her down, and she saw his head move toward her, his mouth move toward hers, in slow motion. Missy held her breath and watched as his mouth shortened the distance between them.

He smelled like mint. She always did love the taste of mint. Her tongue licked out and dabbed her lips. The flecks in Jimmy's eyes darkened like the sky getting ready for a storm to break loose. Missy's hand used his arm as a stopping place before she found the old path that led around his neck.

"Hey, Jimmy T. I need you to come take a look at this." A voice from the front of the last car snapped the rope holding her and Jimmy together. Missy finally blinked.

She jumped back as if her mama had caught her getting ready to cut a cake made for an ailing neighbor.

Jimmy moved back slowly as if he were still making up his mind about whether he was going to kiss her or not.

"Be right there, Raleigh."

His words were long gone from him, but he was still staring at Missy. And she was staring back. She saw the crease between his eyebrows that showed up whenever he was doing some hard thinking.

She probably had a wrinkle of her own. She stepped to the side so she wouldn't have to look at what she couldn't have anymore.

Jimmy's gaze stayed on her even though his feet were dragging him over to Raleigh. He didn't look away from her until he bumped into the fender of the car that was supposed to get his attention.

Missy moved away from the truck, turned her back on him and stared out to the road. This was crazy. The long walk in the sun this morning must have addled her brain. Things were over between her and Jimmy T. They had been over for more than five years. She frowned. *I haven't laid eyes on him since then.* She tightened her jaw. *He has Julie and I'm engaged to Walter. My wedding plans are in place. My gown is just about finished. The whole town knows about the wedding.*

She struggled to find a picture of Walter in her mind, but it was no use. Jimmy was real, and he was here.

She turned back around. Jimmy's gaze found hers again, and thoughts of poor Walter faded as they'd been doing ever since Gertrude had quit on her.

A lace-covered, off-white satin gown twirled in Missy's mind. *It just needs my final fitting,* she reminded herself as she watched Jimmy look at a machine that beeped and hummed. It looked and sounded as though it belonged in a hospital connected to a person instead of here hooked up to a car.

Jimmy pushed back his cap, and Missy remembered the thick curl that used to caress his forehead. Missy thought of the time she first let that curl wrap around her finger. She shoved that old picture away and thought of pure-white roses and orchids the color of sunlight behind morning clouds. She had ordered as many of them as she could afford in spite of Walter's mama's opinion expressed, as usual, through Walter.

"It doesn't make sense to waste that kind of money on roses and orchids when you'll only use them for a few hours," Walter reported Miss Elberta had said. "Carnations would make better sense. They come in all sorts of colors."

Walter didn't know a thing about flowers. He had told her that when she started making arrangements. He was just delivering the message as if his mama were playing ventriloquist behind a curtain nearby and Walter were the dummy.

Right then and there Missy had thought about changing from roses to gardenias, but common sense came through when Lureen told her how much more they would cost.

Walter's mama faded along with the roses and the orchids. Missy watched Jimmy press a lever. Her car slowly lowered to the ground. She hoped it would take long enough for her to find her common sense.

All too soon he unhooked her car from the truck, and came toward her. She stiffened to get ready for the next battle with herself.

"I'll run you on over to your mama's house." Jimmy smiled at her and the battle was lost. He didn't know about her struggle. He kept on talking. "Or do you want to go to her dressmaking shop?"

"I don't want to put you to any trouble. Dropping me at the shop will be all right." Why did the shop have to be clear across town? "I'll use Mama's car to go on out to the house later."

"You can't." Jimmy shook his head and his lopsided grin appeared. She used to like that grin. "I got her car here in the shop. I still have some more work to do on it."

Was this some kind of conspiracy? Was there some car virus going around and the Harrison cars were both infected?

"Sorry about that." He didn't sound sorry at all. He didn't look sorry, either.

Missy knew he made his money fixing cars, but did he have to be so happy about it? She sighed. She suspected it wasn't just money that had Jimmy sounding so cheerful, but that didn't make sense. She frowned. He couldn't want her. He had Julie. They must be close to planning a wedding of their own by now. She tried to ignore the lump filling her throat.

"I can run you by your mama's shop so you can see her before I take you out to the house. It's practically on the way."

Missy wished she weren't worn out from hours of driving. Then she could just wait for her mama to close up the shop. She wished their cars hadn't decided to go out of commission at the same time. She wished a different mechanic had been called. She wished Walter wasn't sitting in one of his important meetings. Then she packed her useless wishes away.

"I've got to go out to the house. I've been on the road since daybreak, but I would like to stop by the shop first, if you're sure it won't take too much time or be too much trouble. I know you're shorthanded, but I haven't seen Mama since Christmas." She swallowed hard. "Never mind about the shop. I reckon I can wait a bit longer to see her. She might be planning to go on home early today.

Maybe I'll call her and tell her I'm here when I get to the house."

"It's not too much trouble to take you by there, Missy. I'll take you wherever you want to go." His hard look bored into her. "Anytime you want. Just say the word and you got it. Okay?"

Right now what she should want shouldn't have anything to do with Jimmy Tanner Scott. She should be calling for help to get as far away from him as fast as she could, but her voice had run off somewhere, as the rest of her should do. She nodded and hoped that was the right answer to break her loose from his spell.

"I'll be just a minute." His smile softened. "I'll bring the things from your car over to the house later this evening, but do you need to get anything to take with you now?"

"Yes." Missy was glad her voice had seen fit to come back. That was a start.

She walked to her car wishing it were farther away. What was she going to do when she was trapped inside his car with him?

She pulled a few things out of her backseat, and put them into Jimmy's open trunk. A small kit was already tucked against one side of it. Another kit with EMERGENCY in big red letters was in the back. Could she call her situation an emergency? She sighed. There wasn't anything in the kit to help her.

The rest of the space was clean and waiting for whatever was put into it.

Jimmy had once told her you can tell what kind of lives people have by looking at how they keep the trunks of their cars.

Missy thought of her jumbled trunk when it wasn't packed with the things she was moving. She thought of the way things were going in her life. Jimmy was right.

"Remember this car, Missy?" His words came from just

behind her. Her memories came from further away than that. They flew all the way from a Saturday near the end of the last term of school in her junior year.

Jimmy had bought an old clunker from Mr. Ray and had rebuilt just about everything under the hood. The seats were the last thing to fix. She had handed Jimmy the tools when he was putting them back in place after he had reupholstered them. It had taken him a long while to redo them since he had insisted on taking off the old fabric. He had said he wouldn't be satisfied with seat covers when he knew what a mess was underneath.

"That's like trying to hide the truth," he had said, "and the truth will always come out."

They had gone for a long ride to try out the seats that were looking like new again. Jimmy's arm had been around her shoulders and she was glad he didn't have bucket seats. They hadn't talked. They didn't have to. They knew what was going to happen between them. It had been coming for months and, without discussing it, she knew today was the day.

Jimmy had stopped the car at the creek on the piece of land his grandfather had left him. He had pulled her close when they got out of the car. Missy couldn't get close enough to him. Even though it was May, she felt cold when he left her and went to the trunk. She wrapped her arms around herself, but it wasn't the same. Nothing felt as good as Jimmy's arms around her.

He took out the blanket he kept folded and tucked into a plastic bag in his trunk. Missy helped him spread it under the branches of the weeping willow on the bank. She imagined they were in their house making the bed together before they . . .

Excitement and anticipation tumbled through her at

what was going to happen. Apprehension joined in. They shouldn't do this.

He had reached to her, and she had walked into his arms as if she were home. All of the shouldn'ts were forgotten.

His mouth covered hers, making her complete. He trailed a line of fire down the side of her neck. Her mouth was blazing a trail of its own across his chest. When his hands brushed against the side of her breast, she thought her bones had melted. Her fingers found the belt loop on the back of Jimmy's jeans and she used it to hold on.

"I want you so much." Jimmy's words at the side of her face said what she was thinking.

"I want you, too." Missy heard her own words push out before her lips brushed the hard nipple on Jimmy's chest. Her fingers did the same to the twin. His body tightened against hers. She did some tightening of her own. She felt as if a stove were blazing inside and sending lines of fire to all parts of her body.

His hand brushed the front of her blouse and circled one breast. Suddenly her blouse was too tight against her sensitive breasts. Her denim skirt was too hot. Somebody had stolen the air from this spot.

If she could open her eyes, she knew she'd see steam coming from her body. If she could open her eyes.

The air tried to cool her as Jimmy fumbled to open first one button and then another. His mouth welcomed each new bit of skin that was revealed as his trembling fingers worked their way down her too-heavy blouse.

Missy wished there had been a button shortage when her blouse was made. It was taking him too long. She wished Jimmy had put on a regular shirt this morning instead of the pullover he was wearing. Then her fingers would have buttons of their own to work at. She had pushed her hands beneath his shirt and smoothed over his chest, stroking the thick curls waiting there.

Jimmy had groaned against her neck, and her groan had met his. She had tightened her hands against him, searching for an anchor. She felt as if a riptide were pulling at her, threatening to drag her out to sea.

Jimmy had eased her blouse off her shoulders and it slid down her arms. She guessed it fell to the ground, but she was too busy to wonder. Jimmy's mouth had found her breast and his tongue was like a match to the now hard tips. Flames shot down to the private space between her legs. Jimmy's hands found the clasp of her bra and it went wherever her blouse had gone. His mouth found her other breast and she found herself being consumed by more heat than she imagined was in the world.

"Are you sure about this?" Jimmy sounded more out of breath than when he finished running miles around the school track. He pulled back his head and looked down into her eyes. She felt him take in a deep breath before he asked again. "I mean, are you really sure?"

Jimmy asked as if there could be any answer besides yes. She was planning to do something she had never done before. She was about to give him something she could only give once, but she refused to think about what she was about to do. After he asked his questions, she loved him even more than she had imagined was possible.

"I'm sure." She flicked her tongue over his nipples and his hands tightened at her waist. Then his hands slid her skirt down.

Jimmy's belt buckle acted as though it were satisfied being closed. Missy's hands weren't having much luck changing its mind. Jimmy had eased her to the blanket, pulled a little packet from his pocket and enclosed it in his hands. He had known this would happen today, too.

The blanket seemed as wide as the ocean while she

waited for him to pull off his shoes and let his jeans drop on top of them.

Missy remembered how strong he looked coming to her. She remembered how lucky she felt. She remembered how she closed her eyes and heard the foil packet whisper open. She still remembered the shiver that went through her. Then all she had felt was Jimmy beside her, above her, inside her. She remembered it all.

"I remember," she whispered. Too much, her mind added. This car had been the magic chariot that took them to their love haven in their world that was too perfect to last. "I see you still got it."

"I couldn't get rid of it. It holds too many memories." His words sounded as though they were having as hard a time getting through his memories as her words had had getting through her own. "Sometimes memories, the right ones, are better than real life."

When he set down two of the bags from her car as though they were full of eggs, his hands were as shaky as hers felt. Then he eased the bags against the ones Missy had already put in the trunk, and she was glad for a safe distraction.

"There's nothing in those bags but clothes, Jimmy." Her words were weak, but they found their way out. "No cause to be so careful."

"I figured as much, but things aren't always as they appear to be." He slammed the trunk lid closed. "I reckon we can leave if you're ready."

Missy slid into the seat, glad it wasn't high enough to need his help. She was going to have to do some serious sorting out when she could get far enough away from Jimmy for her brain to work the way it was supposed to. She blinked. Was there such a place as far enough away from Jimmy?

He slid behind the wheel. Missy shifted toward her door. She knew this wasn't the faraway place she was looking for.

The car carried only two people, but Missy learned that things you can't see can do a good job of weighing down air and cramming up space. How had she gotten into this mess? Better still, how was she going to get out of it without hurting anybody?

Walter came to her mind and made himself at home there.

He had first proposed to her on graduation day. They were off to the side of the gym drinking punch and eating cookies. It was one of the hot days June was known for, but the only admission to the temperature the kids made was to open their graduation robes. They looked like a flock of crows mixed with doves flitting around the room. Nobody was ready to let go of the last day of their childhood.

Walter had just brought her a cup of punch she hadn't wanted. She was leaning against the wall watching Jimmy standing across the room talking with Julie and her folks. He had looked so fine in his dark gray suit. Better than anybody else in the whole gym.

Some schools only allowed family members at graduations. Right now that seemed like a good idea.

"We can get engaged now." Walter's words had snatched her back to him as effectively as if he had touched her.

The word *engaged* hit her the way the basketball had one time when she wasn't paying attention in gym class.

She watched as Julie tipped her head closer to Jimmy and put her hand on his arm. Jimmy had smiled at her the way he used to smile at Missy. Missy had trouble looking at Walter.

"What did you say?"

"We should get engaged before you go off to school. We won't get married until after our next graduations, though. First things first." His laughter was all alone between them.

"I can't get engaged to you, Walter," she had told him. "I like you well enough. You're a good friend to talk to, but I don't love you. I told you that from the get-go."

"I know. I'm satisfied with being friends and having you just like me. My feelings for you are strong enough for the both of us. We get along so well. And who knows what might happen later? You could grow to love me."

His puppy-dog eyes wouldn't let her break things off between them then. Maybe he was right. Who knew what would happen later after she got over Jimmy?

When she went away to college, Walter wrote to her every week. Sometimes twice a week. She didn't write to him as often, but that didn't slow his letters. He kept her caught up on the news and what was going on with their classmates. If they ever had a reunion, she wouldn't have to wonder what everybody was doing. She'd know from Walter's letters.

Each letter ended with a proposal. Once he had asked her how many it took to make a complete set.

"I hope," he had written, "it takes one more proposal than your supply of no's."

It had. That and news of Jimmy's engagement to Julie Gaskins. She sent her "yes" by return mail and told Walter she wasn't interested in hearing anything more about Jimmy and Julie. She knew they weren't married yet, though. If they were, her mama would have broken her promise not to talk about them.

She thought about her present situation. She had fooled herself into believing she was over Jimmy; into thinking she could ever get over him. What a mess she was in. What was she going to do?

* * *

Jimmy wished Missy's mama, Miss Sally, had her shop way over in Georgetown. If he had to go that far, if he had enough time, he could find the right words to get things out in the open between him and Missy. All he needed was enough time, the right words and a giant-size miracle.

He wondered if Missy still had the little scar on her arm where she had banged it against the motor hanging in the garage over Mr. Grady's car. She had been so mad that day when he told her he couldn't go to the movies with her because he had to finish the job, that she whirled around fixing to run off. Jimmy sighed. Seemed like she was always getting mad and fixing to run off from him. He closed his eyes.

You made it this time, sugar. After July fifteenth you'll be running off, back to Walter.

He swallowed hard. He didn't want to imagine Missy with Walter at all. Not the way he had seen them at the prom or their graduation. He still carried those pictures in his head. He certainly didn't want to imagine them together after she tacked Walter's name to the end of hers. Walter and Missy Wilson. If it weren't so serious he would laugh about the two of them together.

He glanced over at her sitting as still as a store window mannequin. *What picture did you pick from your wish book for your gown, I wonder?*

They had been going together for a good while before she showed him her wish book.

"Every time I find a picture of a fancy dress I like, I put it in here." She set a scrapbook on her lap and rubbed her hand over it as most folks would a pet. Her fingers stopped at the peach ribbon winding through the wide white lace running around the outside edge. Narrow ribbon hemmed in the inside edge of the lace. "I keep articles about flowers, bouquets and reception menus along with the pictures." She smiled. "I found something on writing your own wedding vows. That's in here, too." She had patted the book.

"It's right pretty." He didn't know anything about lace and ribbon, but if Missy made it, it was pretty.

"Mama gave me some scraps left over from Debbie Hanover's wedding dress. That's where this fabric came from." Missy's hand had moved over the puffy cover again. Her fingers had stroked the curly edges of the lace. "I've been keeping this for a few years, now." Then she had let loose a little giggle the way she did when she wasn't sure she was doing the smartest thing. "I guess you think this is silly." She had opened her eyes wide enough to take all of him in. Her voice had gotten all soft and gentle. "When I get married I want everything to be perfect. I only expect to do it once, so it has to be perfect; my dream wedding."

He had struggled to keep from getting lost in her eyes that were loving him as if they had made their promises to each other and the wedding were over.

"I don't think it's silly," he had managed. "One wedding should be enough for anybody." He shook his head slightly.

He wouldn't have agreed if he had known her one wedding wouldn't be to him.

He turned onto the street leading to Miss Sally's shop without finding any magic words to make a difference in the way things were going to turn out, but he wasn't ready to give up. Many a car would be sitting around in pieces, and rusting into the ground if he were a quitter.

"Here we are, Missy." Jimmy came around and held her door open.

All she had to do was make it past him standing within

hugging distance of her, and resist stopping for the hug. That's all she had to do. She could manage that, couldn't she?

She stepped out of the car carrying a load inside herself much heavier than the full purse she pushed up on her shoulder.

FOUR

Missy was wrong again. She had one more time to move close to Jimmy and pretend it didn't have an effect on her. Just one more time to ignore the way her body still ached for his touch after all these years. Just once more and then never again. She should feel relieved that this was the last time. Why didn't she?

She watched Jimmy duck his head to keep from banging it against the shiny bells hanging from the shop door.

The first time he knocked into the bells it was because he hadn't realized they were so low. The time after that it was because they had been kissing in the car and bells were the last thing on his mind. If she had been tall enough, she would have set them off, too.

Jimmy stood in the doorway holding the door and letting the day's heat in. His stare was so strong that Missy felt her own temperature rise a few notches. The shop's air-conditioning wasn't in danger from the outside air; it was Missy that would make it work harder. She looked at Jimmy's intense stare. His heat would be added to hers.

She took a deep breath, looked at her feet where it was safe, and stepped through the doorway and past Jimmy. Once inside, she took a normal breath.

Her mama's shop had always fascinated her. Wide shelves lined three walls all the way to the ceiling of the tiny storefront. Huge windows flanked the door. Today they were empty. Her mama must be planning to put up a new display before she left for the day. Missy turned her attention back to the shelves. She hadn't been in the shop since last Christmas, but she knew where things were stored.

Fabric samples took up one whole side of shelf units, but one section always drew her attention. Her mama made all kinds of garments, from casual outfits to business suits for men and women to prom dresses and other formal wear, but the fabric for those clothes never interested Missy. From the time she was a toddler, she always headed for the swatches for wedding dresses. She still did. She liked to run her hands over the large squares of creamy silks and satins, plain or embossed with intricate patterns, that took up the whole middle three shelves of the unit closest to the cutting table.

Before Missy was school age, her mama had made rag dolls and dressed them in clothes she made from fabric scraps. After Missy learned how to use a needle and thread, her mama gave her the sample swatches she no longer needed. Missy promptly turned them into gowns for her grown-up dolls. She had given away all of her other toys when she outgrew them, but she kept her collection of bride dolls. The shelf in her bedroom and special boxes under her bed held her treasures wrapped in the same paper brides used to preserve their gowns after their weddings. Missy smiled as she looked around.

On other shelves, boxes and bins tried to contain a variety of contents, but here and there bits of ribbon uncurled into the air and lace strips peeked from open tops. Spools of thread of more colors than the rainbow stood on spindles in a covered rack that was fastened to the wall, glinting in the light slanting through the wide windows.

Missy took in a deep breath. The smell of new fabrics and hopes and dreams drifted to her. She blinked. Somewhere on the rack tucked in the alcove and filled with hanging garments was her dress and those of her bridal party. She sighed. Would she be in a lighter mood if Jimmy weren't standing too close beside her? Would she be filled with happiness like the other brides-to-be who came into this shop?

She shook her head. Her mama had worked so hard, and for so many hours on the dress Missy had dreamed of wearing since she first saw a picture of it in a wedding magazine so many years ago. She sighed again.

"Mama?" Her voice stumbled out. She smoothed her slacks as if she could keep all those hours of sitting behind the wheel from showing in her clothes. As if she could smooth out her thoughts into some kind of order. Wedding jitters. That's all it was she was feeling. Wedding jitters. "Where are you, Mama?"

"Missy? Is that you, baby?" Sally Harrison rushed from a back room. She brushed her hair back from a face that showed what Missy would look like in twenty-two years.

"Now, how many other folks you got around here calling you Mama?" Missy met her halfway and wrapped her arms around her. She squeezed tight. She was home. Everything would be all right.

"Still smart-mouthed as ever, I see." Her mama's arms met around Missy's back. "Child, where have you been? Another few minutes and I was fixing to send out a search party for you."

Missy smiled and eased away. Her smile deepened when it was matched by one from her mama. Then they both giggled. Whenever Missy was five minutes late coming in from anywhere, that was the line her mama used. When she got older, Missy realized it was to cover up real concern.

"My car broke down. I didn't call you because I didn't tell you what time I'd be here in the first place." She put her hands on her hips. "It's not my fault you got some specific time frame in your head." She pulled her mother close again for a quick hug.

"You had to rescue my baby, huh?" Sally looked at Jimmy still close behind Missy. "Just like those knights in shining armor in the storybooks."

"Hey, Miss Sally. Something like that, only I used my truck. It'd be hard towing a car with a horse. How you been keeping yourself since I saw you last?"

Missy noticed that Jimmy's voice didn't have the same huskiness it had shown to her.

"Hey back to you, Jimmy T. I've been just fine. How about yourself?"

"Can't complain. Won't do any good."

"And nobody wants to hear it anyway, right?"

"You got that right."

He chuckled and Missy realized that sound was another thing that she missed over these past years.

Her gaze caught the edge of her own wedding dress poking out from the others hanging on the rack. His laugh was one of the last things she'd have to get used to doing without.

The seed pearls looping along the bottom of her dress caught the light from the window and threw it at her. Her mama had put a lot of work into that dress.

"Come have a glass of iced tea with us." Sally led the way to the workroom in the back. "I was just fixing to take a little break. I'm all bleary-eyed from sewing those tiny seed pearls on Stella Carter's dress. I swear, oysters are going to have to work overtime to avoid a shortfall after the way I had to dip into their supply." She looked at Jimmy. "Of course, Missy's gown put a hurt on them, too." She and Jimmy stared at each other, leaving Missy out. "I have a bit more to do, but Stella's dress will be ready for the final fitting tomorrow afternoon. It's cutting it close for her wedding this Saturday, but she didn't give me much notice. If I weren't friendly with her Aunt Louise,

I probably wouldn't have agreed to do the dress. Doesn't matter, now, though. I'll keep my promise. I just have to make my eyes and fingers cooperate for a few more hours." She flexed her fingers and rubbed one hand over the other, circling each knuckle on the way. She patted the dress as she passed by. "That dress will be ready in time," she repeated.

"I just wanted to stop by and see you before I go on out to the house," Missy said before her mama went on. Missy didn't want to hear anymore about wedding dresses. "Jimmy offered to run me out there. He said your car's in his shop." She stared at her mother hoping Jimmy was joking, but knowing he wasn't.

"That's right." Sally nodded. "Been there since yesterday morning when it decided to act the fool."

"I don't think she believed me, Miss Sally."

"I didn't say that." Missy didn't miss the twinkle in his eyes. She turned to her mother. "I guess we best be going. I'll pass on the iced tea. I don't want to take up too much of Jimmy's time."

"I've got time for a glass of iced tea." Jimmy's gaze set on Missy and stayed there.

"You said you're shorthanded. You didn't have time for tea at Miss Jenkins's house."

"I worked up a thirst doing all that talking on the way into town and over here." He smiled at Missy's glare before he went on. "I always did enjoy Miss Sally's iced tea."

"There's nothing special about Mama's iced tea." Missy's glare grew stronger. "Everybody in town uses the same tea and the water comes from the same supply."

"Maybe it's the company that makes the difference." It felt as if Jimmy's stare was looking through her eyes and right into her soul. Missy blinked so he couldn't see the questions bouncing around inside her.

"Stop arguing and y'all come on to the back."

After staring from one to the other, Sally led them to

the small table in the room in the back of the shop. She pulled out a chair. "I swear, all a body has to do is put you two together in the same room and wait for fireworks." She laughed. "Y'all behave yourselves while I get the pitcher."

The smell of new fabric was stronger in this back room. A picture of a wedding dress was tacked on the shelf beside the long table taking up most of the room.

Missy looked at the bolt of the palest pink satin spread out along the length of the table and wondered if the bride who would wear the dress was happy. She blinked. Of course she was. All brides were happy, weren't they?

She took a sip from the glass her mama handed her, and forced the sweet tea down.

"I-I don't want to stay too long."

The room was closing in, crowding her with the promises of happiness the dresses held. "I'm kind of tired and I need to get some rest."

"You did say that before, didn't you?" Jimmy drained his glass. The ice cubes slid around when he put the glass down. "I'm ready to go if you are."

Missy put her nearly full glass beside the pitcher and stood.

Sally stood beside her.

"I reckon I best get back to work, anyway." She hugged Missy and walked to the door with her arm around her shoulders. "I'll see you this evening for supper." She kissed her cheek.

"Jimmy T, you drive careful, you hear? You're carrying precious cargo."

"Yes, ma'am, I will." He looked at Missy. "And I know." He turned away but turned back. "I'll be by to carry you home. Just give me a call when you're ready."

"I can get Quinton to run me home. He heads on out my way not too long after I normally do. I don't want to put you out."

"No problem. You don't want to have to hang around here waiting for a ride when Missy will be waiting at home. Just give me a call. Consider it part of the service until I fix your car." He held the door open for Missy.

She stiffened as she passed by close enough to catch a whiff of his aftershave that tried to pull out memories. It was going to be another long ride.

"Missy, are you sure about this?"

They had barely pulled onto Main Street when he spoke.

"Yes. I have to go to Mama's."

"I'm not talking about you going out to your house, and you know it."

Missy sighed. She'd been doing too much of that since she got home.

"I don't want to talk about it."

"That's not the right answer from somebody fixing to get married in a month. You should be talking up a streak of every color in the rainbow. Happiness should be bubbling from you like the water in the stream flowing through my piece of land."

"It's none of your business."

"I'm not so sure about that. Your business and mine used to be wrapped up tight in each other. Just like we used to be."

"Jimmy, I'm tired." Missy closed her eyes and leaned her head back.

"Making mistakes will do that to you."

Missy swallowed hard, but kept her eyes closed.

"Missy, don't do this to us."

"There is no us, Jimmy. Not anymore."

Things could never work out between them. Just like the attraction between them, the differences were still there, too. She pictured being stuck in the same place for the rest of her life. She imagined never seeing anything more of the world than what she had already seen. It would strangle her.

"There could be an us again. It's not too late. It can't be."

Missy thought of all the wheels she had set in motion. The Union Hall was rented. The food and flowers were ordered and paid for. Beautiful embossed invitations were waiting for her to address and send to folks who had already marked the date on their calendars. Her dress was almost finished, for crying out loud. She imagined the hours her mama had spent working her love into it along with the yards of lace and pearls. The contract with the band was signed, and they were ready to play "Forever with You" for the first dance taken by the bride and groom—for her and Walter, not her and Jimmy T.

"It's too late. Way too late." Missy felt tears gather behind her eyelids. She tightened her lids so the tears couldn't escape. She couldn't let Jimmy see them. He'd never leave the subject alone if he did. He'd be like a dog with a new bone. It was too late for her and Jimmy. She had to make herself accept that. He had to accept it, too.

She was pretending to be asleep when the car stopped.

"You can quit your make-believe now, and open your eyes. We're here." Jimmy got out and opened her door.

Missy stood in the quiet of the small front yard and breathed in the smell of June at home.

When she was little, she used to tell her mama she could smell the difference between their home and any other one. Her mama had smiled.

"Love has a sweet smell," she had said. "You must be picking up the love wrapped around our house." Then she'd hug Missy.

It was true about the scent, though. Maybe part of it was the love, but a goodly part was the jasmine and roses mixed with azaleas and honeysuckle that her mama had planted thick around the yard. They mixed their scents together like perfume in the fancy store where Missy used to browse. She couldn't afford to buy anything, but they didn't charge for looking.

She always walked past the perfume counter on her way out. Someone would offer her a spritz of the perfume they were selling that day, and she'd go home sniffing her wrist every few minutes.

She breathed in deeply again. None of those perfumes smelled this wonderful. It was good to be back home again.

The newly painted front door welcomed her home. Her mama had put a new coat of blue paint on it as she did every year.

"A blue front door means good luck," she had said years ago when Missy had asked her about the color.

Missy sighed. Would the good luck share itself with somebody who needed it? Would it share itself with her?

"If you open the door, I'll take these in." Jimmy stood close behind her with a suitcase in each hand.

How had she forgotten he was there? How had she ever forgotten Jimmy? She blinked. *I must be a lot more tired than I thought.*

She fumbled with her keys, unlocked the door and stepped inside the cool house.

The room looked the same as it had ever since she could remember. The couch and chairs changed from time to time, but the new furniture was always set in the same place as the old. Her mama had hung new flowered drapes over the lace curtains since Missy had been home last, but they didn't keep out the heat of the day any better than the old ones did. She smiled. It felt great to stand in this room again.

"Where do you want these?"

Again she had forgotten Jimmy. If she could figure how she did it, maybe she could remember the trick.

"You can just set them over there beside the end table."

She pointed to the mahogany table that had belonged to her grandmother. It was covered with one of the lace scarves her grandmother crocheted. Missy ran her finger along the top of the smooth metal frame holding her mother's high school graduation picture right next to her own, and managed a smile.

The little ceramic dog Missy had given her mama for Christmas many years ago was still beside the picture. Some things were still where they should be.

"I can't leave the bags out here in the living room. They're too heavy for you to carry."

And some things weren't. She frowned.

"Who do you think had to put them in the car?"

"Only because I wasn't there to carry them for you. See there? That's another reason for you to come home. Northern hospitality can't compare with ours." He gave her a smile like in the days when a kiss followed it. He wasn't talking about just carrying luggage anymore.

Missy swallowed hard. His smile added ten degrees of heat to the house that had felt cool when she first stepped inside. Her stare met his. If she were looking at it, she could have seen the red line spreading upward in the thermometer on the wall in the living room. She took a step backward and thought about Julie Gaskins. That helped a little.

"Okay, bring them on back here." If she didn't get him out of the house soon, when her mama got home she would find a pile of ashes where her house used to be.

She took a deep breath and tried to ignore Jimmy's footsteps close behind her in the hall. She sighed and never glanced at the family photos lining the walls. Her mama had told her so many stories about her grandparents, great-grandparents and aunts and uncles, until Missy felt she knew them. Today they could be gone for all the notice she gave them. Jimmy had all of her attention again.

From the day she met Jimmy, she'd never had any success ignoring him for long. Why should now be any different?

She walked into the last room on the left. The deep pink drapes and matching bedspread she had made during her last year in high school were still in place. Her white dresser was still against the palest pink walls, although her things were missing from the scarf on the top. They were packed away in one of the boxes in her car. They'd never go back on this dresser. The bedroom she'd share with Walter would be the next home for her treasured things.

Missy swallowed hard and almost managed to get rid of the lump trying to choke her. She swallowed again and turned away from the dresser with its top bare except for the lace scarf.

"So, this is your bedroom. The drapes look just like you described them to me that time over the phone. Remember?"

She remembered the conversation. She had told him about the new drapes she had just hung. Then they talked about how they would decorate their home after they got married.

"I don't know about pink," he had said. "I'm not sure I can sleep in a pink room." Then his voice had gotten low, but it sounded as though he were right there with her. "I don't expect us to do much sleeping, though. I reckon we'll find better things to do at night. During the day, too, whenever we get the chance. You got to hurry and set our wedding date."

The next Monday, outside the chemistry lab, Walter showed her a booklet his mama had sent for. It told about all kinds of scholarships. Walter had underlined a few and talked Missy into going to see Mrs. Baker, the counselor. Missy hadn't known seeing the counselor and filling out papers would come between her and Jimmy. She hadn't really expected anything to come of it at all.

That Friday Mrs. Baker had sent for her from English class. Because it was so late, the counselor had called some of the places in the booklet for Missy. She had the widest smile Missy had ever seen. She had found a scholarship offer.

"All that hard work you've been doing in your classes has paid off." She had hugged Missy. "It's as if the scholarship I found was waiting for you. I know your mother is going to be so proud of you."

Missy had walked out of the office in a fog. She could go to college. Missy Harrison, college student. College graduate. She had been thinking about going up North to work for a year. She never even dreamed she could go to college.

When she met Walter in the hall outside the office, he was as pleased as Missy was. It was Jimmy who didn't like the idea of her going away.

"What if you go up there and find somebody else?" he had said when she told him later that evening.

Neither of them knew he'd be the one to find somebody first. He'd found Julie Gaskins. And the somebody she'd found was right here all along. Walter Wilson.

She set the small bag and her purse on the bed. All of that was a long time ago.

"I reckon a pink room isn't so bad after all." Jimmy's words brought her all the way back to the present and her small bedroom. "The color doesn't matter. What's important is who you share the room and the bed with."

Again Missy's stare locked with his. Hours may have crept by before she could break free.

"You-you can just set the bags down anywhere."

"I reckon this is the same bed you had back then."

Missy nodded since words refused to show themselves.

"The one where you used to stretch out while we talked

on the phone for hours on end?" He set the bags to the side and took a step closer to her, pushing aside the air she needed. "All those times when we used to make plans for the future we were going to share together, this is where you were?"

She managed another nod, which was almost impossible since her body had gotten as tight as a piece of new lumber.

"Do you remember those conversations?"

"Don't. Please don't dredge up all that. It won't do any good." She blinked away tears that were trying to escape.

It was Jimmy's turn to sigh.

"I know you remember. I sure do. I've been thinking about it every day since you went away." He stepped away from her. "I'll see myself out." His last words were soft, but his footsteps in the hall were softer.

Missy watched him leave. She was still standing in the same spot when she heard the front door click shut.

She walked over to the window and fingered the drapes without really feeling them.

When she and Jimmy broke up, she thought about getting rid of them. *New drapes for a new life,* she had thought. Her mama had told her it was too expensive, not to mention foolish, since she was leaving so soon for college.

In spite of the cost, she wished she had replaced them. The very last thing she needed now was a reminder of Jimmy, especially in her bedroom.

She went to fix a cup of tea, but on the way her attention was grabbed by a large white box next to the silk roses in the centerpiece on the dining room table. Her mother had picked up the invitations.

Missy had thought about having them sent to her in Philadelphia so she could get them out earlier than the four weeks left, but her mama had pointed out that everybody already knew the date. The invitations were just a formality.

She lifted the top and stared. Then she got a pen and her mailing list and began addressing the envelopes without reading the message inside that would set her future forever.

Jimmy slapped the steering wheel. Why was she so stubborn? She still had feelings for him. He could see it whenever she looked at him. It was there in the way she kind of swayed toward him whenever he was near. He knew she was fighting it. Why? Why wouldn't she admit she still felt the attraction to him? Why did she have to start crying so he had to back off?

He let out a hard breath. She was so stubborn. She wouldn't even admit to herself how she still felt about him. So what if her plans had been made? You don't go through with a marriage to the wrong man because food has been ordered, and a dress has been made. You don't go through with it even if you're standing at the altar and the preacher is waiting for an answer by the time you realize you made a mistake. What did she mean, "It's too late"? It's not too late until the preacher introduces the new husband and wife. And not always then. Why didn't she know that?

Jimmy thought of how she looked standing in her bedroom. His body tightened as it always did whenever he thought about her. He imagined himself and Missy in a bedroom wrapped in each other's arms loving so deeply it wouldn't matter if the room was pink with green and yellow spots and purple stripes thrown all over the walls and ceiling. He wouldn't notice and his loving would be so strong, she wouldn't notice, either.

Her lips had been waiting for his kiss. He hadn't imagined that. She had licked them to get ready for him. He had expected to burst into flames right there in her room. But he didn't touch her. If he had kissed her he wouldn't have been able to stop at a kiss and he was sure she wasn't ready for that yet.

Did she remember how much pleasure they had found in each other? He remembered every part of her body and how hers was a perfect fit to his. He remembered how she moaned his name when they rode to paradise together. She couldn't have forgotten how she had clung to him and how they lay together after they returned to reality. Their spot under the willow tree on the bank had to be as strong in her mind as it was in his.

He shifted his weight trying to get comfortable. If he spent much more time around Missy, he'd have to get some jeans a couple of sizes bigger. That way the whole world wouldn't know the effect she still had on him.

He pulled off the road and rested his head on the back of the seat. There had to be a way to make her see that she was making a mistake. He just had to figure out what it was.

He pulled back onto the road and headed for town. Walter's wedding ring wasn't on her finger yet. With any luck, it never would be.

Part of Jimmy's mind was working well enough to get him back to the garage, but not well enough to make him stop. He drove right past the lot and had to turn around and come back. His mind was working on something more important. It was searching for a way to get Missy back with him where she belonged.

By late afternoon Missy had finished addressing the creamy envelopes, and was back in her room. She put a suitcase on the bed, but she didn't even open it. She just sat beside it, forgot about it and got lost in her thoughts.

Jimmy had been in her bedroom. There had been times, back when she was younger and things were different, when she would have been glad to have him here.

She breathed in deeply. Did she still smell his aftershave hanging around like her memories or was it just her imagination? It hadn't seemed that strong when he was here standing next to her bed, talking about their old plans, but maybe it had been, and something else had held her attention and blocked out everything, including his aftershave. Maybe her long-ago wishes had joined with his and refused to let anything else through.

For a few minutes she got lost in her memories. Then she came to her senses. She shook her head. No. She was marrying Walter. In one month she'd be Mrs. Walter Wilson and Jimmy Tanner Scott wouldn't bother her anymore.

Julie would make Walter happy just as he would her. She sighed.

Why didn't she believe that?

FIVE

Missy thought about the thick bundle of invitations that would seal her future forever. They were stacked neatly in the mailbox down at the road to be picked up in the morning by the mail carrier. Folks would have them the day after tomorrow. The bundle was nice and orderly. How could she get her life that way?

Why was it so hard to stay out of Jimmy's arms? They had had that dumb argument about a pink bedroom as if it mattered back then. It did now, though. She didn't know what color she'd use in her home with Walter, but it wouldn't be pink.

She had to talk to somebody. She called Annette, her best friend since kindergarten.

"Hey, Missy, how you doing?" Nettie's voice held a smile that Missy really needed. "You got home all right, I guess."

"Yeah." She'd tell her about Jimmy and her car later, after she had sorted things out. *When would that be?* She swallowed hard. "I just finished addressing the invitations and putting them in the mail box."

"Oh? I thought you wanted me to help you. We could have done it this evening while you told me all about big-city life."

"I decided to get it over with."

"Missy Harrison, doing your wedding invitations is not something you want to 'get over with.' It's something to savor as you dream about the future with your soon-to-be husband. Girl, we have to do some serious talking. Face-to-face. Lunch tomorrow. Our schedule here is light, and Bessie can handle any walk-ins who come into the shop. Meet me somewhere. Lil's Soul Food is a great place if you don't mind setting your diet back a month. It's on Main Street not far from your mama's shop."

"I can't meet you. My car broke down on my way here, and had to be towed. Mama's car is in the shop, too."

"Jimmy Tanner Scott didn't happen to be the one who towed your car, did he?"

"Yes."

It was a good thing it wasn't a toll call. Missy would be paying good money for dead air space.

"Uh-huh. I see." Nettie had run out of words, too. Then she found some while Missy was still trying. "We have to talk. I wish I could make it tonight, but I have something scheduled. I'll come to your house for lunch tomorrow. Twelve on the dot. Fix something delicious. And don't do anything else stupid."

"Nettie, I don't want to . . ."

"Got to go. See you tomorrow. 'High noon' as they say."

Missy stared at the phone. Then she called Walter's office and left a message for him to call her as soon as he could. She hoped it would be real soon. Like now. She needed him to chase away these doubts that were growing and trying to take over. She needed to see him so he could convince her that she needed him, that all she was feeling was the jitters every bride-to-be feels. Something had to shove Jimmy T back where he belonged. She hoped Walter was the one to do it.

"Come on." She frowned at the phone. "Ring."

She jumped as the phone answered her plea. She didn't let it ring a second time.

"Hello, Missy." Walter's words marched sharply into her ear. "I see you got home safely."

"Yes." It depended upon what he meant by safely. Later when she saw him, she'd tell him all the details. Maybe by then she'd even be able to tell him that Jimmy was the one to come get her, and maybe she could sound casual while she was telling it. By then she should be back to normal.

She shook her head. And maybe the rocker on the front porch will grow wings, fly up into the magnolia in the front yard and settle there, too.

"I told you many times before that you should get rid of that car." Walter continued. "It's not suitable for you to drive it anymore. It was barely all right for a college student, but you're past that now. You're a professional woman. You have to think of your image. Mother says image is important."

"Yes, Walter." This certainly wasn't the way to make Jimmy disappear. If anything, his image was stronger. Maybe she should have fought this battle without Walter.

"I have another meeting in a little while, but Connie said you asked me to call you as soon as possible. She said it sounded important." Walter's crisp voice went on. "Is something the matter?"

"No. I just wanted you to know I got here safely."

"Oh. Okay. I'm glad you did." Walter sounded as if she were telling him the newspaper had been delivered and he were saying he'd read it when he got around to it. "I won't be finished until real late tonight," he continued. "I've got a lot of paperwork to do. I'll see you tomorrow. Why don't we plan on dinner at Debbie's Kitchen? I'll pick you up at six-fifteen sharp."

"All right."

Missy still held the phone after it clicked and the dial tone hummed in her ear. Would Jimmy have waited until tomorrow to see her if she were marrying him?

You're not marrying Jimmy, she reminded herself. She kept reminding herself as she opened a suitcase. Unpacking wouldn't last nearly long enough. She'd have to find something else to do to keep busy after the suitcases and boxes were empty. Something, anything to keep her busy until her mama came home to help take her mind off her problems.

"It sure smells good in here," Sally said as she came in that evening. Jimmy was right behind her. He looked every bit as good as he had this afternoon.

"Hey, Missy. I brought some more of your stuff over."

"My car's not ready yet?"

"No, I don't know when I'll be finished." Jimmy sounded too happy about her car problem to suit Missy. She frowned, but he went on as if he didn't see it. "I'm still checking on some things."

"Just fix what made it stop on me and give it back."

"Can't do that. Might be something else seriously wrong. What kind of a mechanic would I be if I missed a problem? You'd lose faith in me." He grinned at her. "In my work I mean, of course. You don't want to get stranded again, do you?"

"No, but I don't see why . . ."

"You don't want to have an accident, do you?"

"Of course not, but . . ."

"That's what I thought." He nodded. "That's why I intend to give it a thorough going-over." He held up two bags. "I'll just take these things on back to your bedroom. I remember where it is." He ignored Missy's glare, and strolled slowly out of the living room.

"Oh? He knows where your bedroom is, does he?" Sally turned to Missy after Jimmy went down the hall. "How long ago did that happen? When did I miss that?" Sally's hard stare waited for an answer from Missy.

"He carried my suitcases into my room earlier today, Mama."

"Oh. I reckon they were too heavy for you?"

"I told him I could carry them myself, but he insisted."

"And you can't resist Jimmy when he insists."

"Mama, don't read something into it that's not there."

"I set them beside the bed." Jimmy's look told Missy he was thinking more about the bed than about the things.

She felt the blood rise up her face. The words *Jimmy* and *bed* didn't belong together in the same thought. Missy had to swallow hard before her answer whispered out.

"Thank you." She swallowed again. "I guess you're anxious to get back, so I won't hold you. Thank you again."

"I don't have any place more important to be than here."

"I invited Jimmy to join us for dinner."

Missy's lips parted, but no words came out as she stared at her mama.

"It's the least I could do since Jimmy went out of his way to bring me home, and to bring more of your things out here. We have to show our gratitude. It's the neighborly thing to do."

Missy's stare met its match in Sally's. Sally's chin tilted up. Missy had learned years ago that when her mama did that, it meant end of discussion.

"I'll go finish dinner." She had to get out of the room. Then she'd be able to get a grip. Maybe this evening wouldn't be so bad after all.

"I'll come help." Jimmy took a step toward her.

"Oh, no, you won't." Missy took a step back from him. "You're Mama's guest. You can go on into the front room and visit with her."

"I'd rather come keep you company in the kitchen while you finish fixing dinner."

"No. You go visit with Mama. Talk about her car. Talk about her car that should be fixed by now." Missy glared.

Jimmy grinned.

Sally cleared her throat.

"Actually, he can't visit with me. I've got to go change. I'm tired of looking at these clothes." She touched her skirt. "I been in them all this long day and they're too hot. Way too hot. I don't know what made me put these things on this morning." She looked down at her sleeveless blouse and lightweight skirt.

"Mama . . ."

"I don't know how long I'll be. I'm too tired to move too fast. And you know you can't leave company sitting alone in the front room. I taught you better than that. It isn't neighborly."

"Mama . . ."

"I'll be out when I'm finished."

Missy's glare hardened but it was wasted. Her mama was already moving slowly toward the back of the house.

"Good old southern hospitality. I love it."

"You stay out of my way, Jimmy Tanner Scott."

"Yes, ma'am, Missy Miranda Harrison." His grin widened and Missy swore there was a twinkle in his eyes as they crinkled at the corner. "Lead the way and I'll follow." His voice got low and his next words rumbled out. "I'll follow you anywhere, anytime, sugar. Just say the word."

Missy almost stumbled over the doorsill that had been in place since they had moved into the house fifteen years ago.

"Careful." Jimmy steadied her. His chuckle skipped to her. "You don't want it to be said that you fell for me. Again."

His last word whispered out and wrapped itself around her. She didn't dare turn to face him. His hand on her arm was more than enough for her to handle. His touch was dragging out feelings best left hidden, and those feelings were spreading through her, and pushing away the past five years as if they were no more solid than spiderwebs.

She was able to pull away from him only because he let her go. She managed to make it into the kitchen.

Six chairs were around the dark oak table, and Jimmy had to sit in the one that was facing her. He just had to look at her, didn't he. His stare was touching her. Reminding her.

The heat she felt wasn't all coming from the stove. She wished the kitchen were ten times bigger.

"Sure you don't want my help?"

"The only way you can help is to get out of here."

"Can't do that. You heard Miss Sally. Besides, you love Walter Wilson, and you're fixing to marry him. Me being here shouldn't make no never mind to you."

She had to look at him then. He was right, but it didn't feel like it.

"You do love Walter, don't you?" His stare wouldn't let her stretch the truth.

"Walter and I are very fond of each other."

"Marriages built on love have a tough enough time of it. How do you expect one built on 'fond of' to have any chance at all?"

"I-it's none of your business."

"It could be." His words got husky. "It should be, Missy, and you know it. Don't do this."

The only answer she could find was to take the chicken out of the oven. Glad to have something to do, she put the green peas on to cook. As hot as Jimmy's stare was, she should have him stare at the vegetable instead of her using her mama's electricity.

She mashed the potatoes, and was still beating them long after they were ready.

"I like the way you put a meal together. I like watching you. No matter what you do. I always did. Whether you're cooking or . . ." Jimmy turned up the heat in his eyes a few more notches. ". . . or anything."

Missy dropped the spoon she was reaching for and got

another from the drawer. She dropped it, too, but she still didn't look at Jimmy.

"You've been practicing your cooking. Remember that time you insisted on fixing dinner for me?" The smile in his voice was wasted on her. She was busy remembering. Her spoon stopped stirring the peas. She swallowed hard, and wished she had used the microwave instead. It would have been a lot quicker, and the food would have been done sooner, and she wouldn't be trapped alone with Jimmy. She looked at the pan. It was true. A watched pot didn't boil.

"You wouldn't let your mama help you that evening. You wanted to do it all by yourself. The pork chops were extra crispy, you burned the bread, the potatoes were lumpy and the string beans were half cooked." His voice got soft. "Everything was delicious because you cared enough to take the trouble to fix it for me. Just for me. You cried when you took your first taste." His chair scraped against the floor.

"Don't." She shook her head slowly.

"I kissed away your tears." His gaze pinned her in place as he took a slow step closer to her. "Like this."

She knew she should move away. She should leave the room. She should leave the house. But she couldn't move from her spot. All she could do was wait for Jimmy.

His hands were on her shoulders as he eased her toward him inch by inch. She had enough time to get away. If she wanted to.

Step back, something inside told her. *Think of Walter. Think of anything but being here with Jimmy.*

Then Jimmy's arms were around her just like the last time, and all the other times before today.

Her hands slid up his chest to push him away, but she forgot what they were supposed to do. She held on fast and pushed her body closer to his.

Jimmy's stare grabbed hers and fused the two stares together, the way her body was trying to do with his.

She thought she had found her voice and opened her mouth to tell him to stop, but he covered her mouth with his. Her moan got out, but was swallowed by his kiss that rocked her world.

The fires she had told herself were dead sprang to life, and threatened to destroy her. One of her hands found the old path leading to his neck and her fingers tightened in the curls waiting for her. Just like old times.

Walter who?

Jimmy eased her away just as slowly as he had pulled her in. They stood facing each other, both lost in the same place.

She tried to find just one reason for her reactions. He looked as if he was waiting for her to admit the truth about her feelings to herself and to him. Then he closed the space between them, and their bodies were touching again, melting into each other, lost in each other.

His hardness pushed at her softness. His hand found her breast through her blouse. His fingers stroked across the tip that had already tightened. She gasped and he swallowed her gasp with his kiss. His fingers kept up their too-slow movement.

She was back with him under that old willow tree ready for him to love her.

"You need any help out here?" Sally stopped in the doorway.

Missy jumped away from Jimmy too late. Way too late.

"Oh. I guess not." Sally stared. Then she turned away. "I'm sure I forgot to get something in my room. I'll be back. Sooner or later. Most likely later. It will probably take me a while to find whatever it is."

Missy blinked. She moved over to the stove and refused to look at Jimmy, who was still standing too close. Any place in the house would be too close.

A spoonful of potatoes landed on the top of the stove instead of in the white ironstone bowl that had been her grandmother's. Peas tumbled on top of the mound of spilled potatoes as though that was where Missy had meant to put them. A serving of salad ended up on the table. Missy was glad she had already moved the chicken to the safety of the platter. It was the only chicken she had cooked, and somebody might want meat with their meal.

Finally—too late, but finally—everything was ready.

"I'll go get Mama." She didn't look at Jimmy still standing there. She didn't dare.

There was a time when her mama solved everything for her. Not this time. Nobody else could take care of this. She had to do it herself. She had never felt more confused or more alone.

A mother would be proud of a child who had the appetite that Jimmy was showing during the meal. Missy stared and wondered how Jimmy could be so unaffected by what had happened between them. She pushed the food around on her plate trying to find the best spot for each thing to make the food look smaller. Her mama wasn't doing much in the eating department, either, and their talking was about like their eating.

"This is delicious, Missy," Jimmy said. "It's just as good as it smelled when I came in the door." He took another bite of chicken. "You got to give me the recipe."

"You plan to do some cooking?"

"I can cook real good. Been doing it for years."

"How many years?"

"Since I was a teenager." He put more mashed potatoes on his plate and poured gravy over the mound.

"Back when I cooked supper for you, you could cook then?"

"You mean back when we were sweet on each other?" He looked as though he had forgotten he had food on his plate. "When we were making plans to spend our lives together? Is that when you mean?"

"Jimmy." Missy shook her head. "Don't." She would not look at him.

"My mama taught me to cook before we moved to Mayland. She said anybody who knew how to eat should know how to cook." He leaned back. "I didn't agree with her, then. Cooking was girl's work. I had the nerve to say as much to her. She told me the work was for whoever had time to do it." He smiled and Missy felt her heart flutter. "I got right good at cooking, too. Still, I didn't tell my friends. And I kept learning." His smile widened. "My smothered pork chops will make you hurt yourself." His smile disappeared and desire flared in his eyes. "I got right good at a lot of things." He blinked. "When I finish my house I'm gonna have you over and let you taste my cooking for yourself."

Missy blinked and stared at her plate. *Not in this lifetime would that happen. Had he forgotten that Walter would have to come with her?*

"Pork chops aren't all I can fix. Isn't that right, Miss Sally?"

Missy stared at her mama, who stared back.

"That's right, Jimmy. Your chicken potpie puts mine to shame. You have to fix that soon for us, too."

"Oh, go on. It could never compare to yours. I'd rather have a smidgen of yours than a whole plateful of mine any day."

Missy looked from one to the other.

"He's cooked for you?"

"More times than I can count." Sally took a forkful of chicken and chewed vigorously. She looked as though she had found her appetite.

"Don't feel left out, Missy. You and I can play catch-up."

He didn't sound as if he were talking about food anymore. It was her fault. She had encouraged him.

Missy swallowed hard. *How could I act like I did when he kissed me? How could I feel like I do now, when I'm marrying Walter?* She didn't have an answer. Her body didn't need an answer. Just thinking about that kiss had her body reacting by spreading heat from it as if the house were cold and it were doing a favor by sharing.

"Did Jimmy tell you he's just about done building his house?"

"No."

Jimmy hadn't told her much of anything with words. He had let his body do the talking and there was no mistaking the message it gave, nor the response hers made.

Sally began asking Jimmy about the house and he answered. Missy didn't hear any of it. She had her own conversation going on in her head.

"Missy, what are you going to do?"

Jimmy had gone more than an hour ago. While they were cleaning the kitchen her mama hadn't said anything about what she had seen when she walked in on Missy and Jimmy, and Missy had begun to think she could get through the rest of the night without her mentioning it. She needed time to work things out. She had almost convinced herself that her mama would go to bed without calling Missy's attention to the problem, and let Missy figure things out on her own. She should have known that wouldn't go her way, either.

"Mama, I don't know."

"You can't be still planning to marry Walter."

"I don't know what I'm going to do."

"You got to sort things out, and you don't have much time."

"I know, Mama, but so much has already been done."

"Life can be too long if you love one man and are tied to another." She touched Missy's shoulder. "You got to follow your heart. Just do what your heart tells you to do, and things will turn out all right." She kissed Missy on the cheek. "I'll see you in the morning, baby. Try to get some rest."

Missy went into the living room and sat down in her grandma's oak rocking chair. Usually she took comfort in this connection with her grandma. She had survived hard times. Missy could take strength in her grandma's triumphs over adversity. Maybe, if she tried long enough, she could find some strength now.

She was still trying when the stillness in the back of the house told her her mama was in bed.

SIX

Missy got up with the sunrise, something she hadn't done since before she started first grade. She should have slept until afternoon, since she had spent most of the night trying to get far enough away from her problems to find peace of mind. She had failed. She was no closer to a solution than she had been when her mama left her for the night.

She pulled on a pair of jeans and a T-shirt and made her way to the live oak that had been spreading its branches at the end of the yard since before she and her mama had moved into this house.

She sat on the few leaves that covered the moss growing thick like a piece of scrap dark-green velvet. She brushed her hands back and forth over it the way she used to do when she was young and was trying to figure something out. Her problems back then were nothing like the one she had now. *What am I going to do?*

She leaned her head back against the twisted trunk and closed her eyes, not expecting a solution—an easy one— to come to her. She was still there when the sun rose high enough to poke through the branches and into her eyes. A mess. Things were a mess no matter what she did. And she knew she had to do something.

Hours later she headed back to the house knowing what

she had to do, admitting she had known, before she left the house, the only thing she could do.

She read the note about her mama hitching a ride into town with Sam, their neighbor. She dropped the paper into the waste basket, glad Jimmy hadn't come to pick her mama up. She had had too much of Jimmy yesterday.

She listened to a message on the machine from Nettie canceling their lunch. It was just as well. She wasn't up to talking to Annette about her situation. Not yet.

She was eating a bowl of cereal that tasted like the morning newspaper when the phone rang.

"Missy, I find I have to be out in that area in about an hour on an errand for Mother. I trust you'll be home?"

"Yes, Walter, I'll be here."

"Good. I'll see you then."

Missy held the dead phone. No "I can't wait to hold you." Not even an "I want to see you." No "I love you." Nothing that he wouldn't have said to anybody else.

She didn't know how much time he could spare her, but they had some serious talking to do.

Missy found her mama's rubber gloves, and started the task that always took her through hard problems.

When Walter knocked on the back screen door Missy was giving a final wipe to the inside of the oven door. She looked at the sparkling oven and thought about asking her mother not to bake for a week. Then she shrugged. She hadn't cleaned the stove just so they would have a sparkling oven.

Walter knocked again and she went to unhook the screen door.

"Hey, Missy." Walter smiled, but he didn't touch her.

She wouldn't have been surprised if he had offered her his hand as he did to his clients. Jimmy would have touched her. He could do that without using his hands. His look would have . . .

She shook her head. No. Last evening Jimmy *did*. She shook her head again. Walter wasn't Jimmy.

"Come in, Walter. Want a cup of coffee?"

"No, thank you. You know I don't like instant. If you're going to drink coffee, Mother always says, you may as well take the time and make the real thing."

"Does she say anything about tea? Like maybe I should grow it, pick it and cure it myself?"

"Missy, what's come over you? You never talked like that before. And about Mother. What other bad habits did you pick up while you were up North?"

"North has nothing to do with it." She took a deep breath. "Come on in and sit down. We have to talk."

"I can't stay long, Missy. I only came out to give Miss Sutton the clothes Mother got together. You know Mother took the family under her wing year before last when Mr. Sutton ran off and left Mrs. Sutton and their four children to fend for themselves."

"I know, Walter." The whole town knew about Miss Elberta's charity project. Some of the teachers at school in Philadelphia adopted families, too, but they only let others know to get them involved with the project, not to impress anybody with their charity.

Missy shook her head. Miss Elberta and her project didn't have anything to do with what Missy had to say.

"What I have to say is important."

Walter sat at the table. Missy put a plate of cookies close to Walter, but he didn't take any.

She looked at Walter. He was a good-looking man. And he was kind. Walter wouldn't know how to be mean. And he was ambitious. Everybody said so. He had planned his future back when he was in high school. Actually, when they were in fourth grade, he told Missy that he knew what he wanted to do with his life: work with his mother in their real-estate office, and, when the time was right, move into politics. A report he gave in fifth-grade social studies class was about the duties of the governor. At the end Walter told how he intended to be governor himself one day, and what changes he would make. There was no doubt in Missy's mind that he would make it. A woman could do a lot worse than Walter. He was steady. Dependable.

"Walter, I've been thinking about the . . ." She swallowed hard and started again. "I've been thinking about our wedding." There, it was out.

"What about it? Everything's going according to schedule, isn't it?"

"I guess so. I mailed the invitations yesterday." Before Jimmy T, who wasn't on the schedule, pushed his way back into her life.

"There isn't a problem, is there?"

"Yes. There's a big problem. I don't think I can go through with the wedding."

"What do you mean, you can't go through with it?" Walter jumped up as if somebody had yanked him. "Everything's set. All my kinfolk from out of town have made plans to come. Mother has made reservations at the Seasons Hotel for them. I already have the tickets for the honeymoon. I've had them for four months. You can't do this, Missy. Mother invited our congressmen. She even has a commitment from the governor to attend. He doesn't attend many functions outside of his relatives and fellow politicians, but he agreed to come to our wedding. You can't change your mind at this late date. It just isn't done."

"Jimmy T was the one who came to get me when my car broke down. I'm not sure anymore that I'm doing the right thing."

"You take one look at Jimmy and throw our plans away?"

"It was more than a look." *One look was all it took to start things, though.*

"You've been away for a long time and your memory has faded. When you two were going together, you had a major argument once a week. You need at least two calendars to count the number of times you broke up." He frowned at her. "You're back home one day, and you decide to throw away the rest of your life?"

"I'm talking about us, Walter. You and me. Not Jimmy. I think we're making a mistake."

"Did Jimmy tell you that Julie works at the little shop next door to his garage?" Nobody ever said Walter was stupid. "They see each other all the time. Most days they have lunch together either in his office or at a restaurant."

"Walter, this doesn't have anything to do with them." She didn't want to think about Jimmy with Julie. Her mind was still holding the picture of them together at the prom.

"You just have wedding jitters," Walter continued. "That's all. I read about it in an article a while ago. It's a natural feeling. Every bride goes through this, so don't feel you're the only one." He reached over and patted her hand. It was the first time he had touched her since he had gotten there. "Nothing has changed between us to make you change your mind, has it?"

He was right. Nothing had changed. Maybe that was what was wrong. Nothing had changed since she first saw him in grade school. Her feelings were still the same. They were friends.

"Walter, I like you. You know that. And I'm grateful for how you encouraged me to go to college, but I . . ."

"Missy, think about it. Think about all the plans you've made. You just mailed the invitations yesterday, so you didn't want to change your mind then. What happened since then?"

How could she tell him that what had happened was a kiss? Just a kiss. She blinked. "Just a kiss" wasn't the right

way to describe what had happened between her and
Jimmy. Did any other engaged woman react to a man as
she had with Jimmy? She doubted it.

"Give it time," Walter said. "Think about it some
more." He stood. "Mother told me to invite you to dinner tomorrow evening. She told me to be sure and tell
you. She said she's sorry for such short notice, but Lois
wasn't sure until this morning that she could fix dinner
tomorrow. I'll pick you up at five-thirty. I know it's only
a fifteen-minute drive from here to home, but Mother
is used to eating at six o'clock sharp, and I don't want
to take a chance on something coming up on the drive
here or back home to throw off her schedule."

Walter acted as if Missy hadn't said anything about
changing her mind about marrying him. She sighed.
Maybe it *was* just wedding jitters. She hoped so.

"We're still on for dinner tonight, I trust? You aren't
going to back out of that, are you?"

"No. I'll still go." Maybe dinner with Walter would help
her sort things out and get herself together.

"I'd best be going. I'm expecting somebody in the office in an hour and I have to make sure the paperwork
is in order. I'll see you this evening."

"Yes. I'll be ready. I'll be here for the rest of the day."

He placed his hands on her shoulders, but he didn't
pull her close, as Jimmy had. He didn't press her body to
his as if he couldn't get close enough. He leaned his head
in, brushed his lips across hers and stepped away.

Nothing. She felt nothing. She could tell he didn't
either. If his lips hadn't been warm, she might as well have
kissed the door frame.

She walked him to the door on steady legs and leaned
against the screen after he went outside. Her gaze followed him as he backed his black Ford slowly out of the
yard. She looked at her ring catching bits of sunshine.
Then she closed her eyes.

She liked Walter. His mother wasn't her favorite person, but he was okay. She liked him. That would be enough. So what if bells didn't ring, and she didn't go all soft in the knees when he kissed her? What if she didn't have trouble breathing and forget everything when he touched her? They would have a nice quiet marriage. Nice and quiet would be good. Peaceful. No turmoil. And Walter wouldn't interfere with her dreams. He'd be supportive of what she wanted.

Her mama had married for love and look what had happened. There was always a storm brewing when her mama and her daddy were in the house together. There was always a warm making up after they had a heated disagreement, too. They had just made up from their latest argument the day he died in a car accident.

Missy didn't need storms in her life anymore. She had had enough of them when she and Jimmy were going together. Seemed like every day they had some disagreement over some dumb stuff. She blinked hard. She never saw one of their disagreements coming until it was there, and it was too late to head it off. Then neither one of them would back off until days later.

She needed peace and predictability in her life. She was comfortable with Walter. She'd be all right with him. They both had ambition, they both planned to do something with their lives. They weren't like Jimmy. He was contented to spend the rest of his life within ten miles of where he was born.

Missy took down the loping shears and went out to prune deadwood from the shrubs out back.

She was still there when her mama came home.

"Child, what have you done to my poor boxwood bushes and trees?" Her mama's loud words broke Missy from her thoughts.

She looked at the tall piles of twigs marking her trail from the front of the house to the end of the backyard.

"All I did was cut off the deadwood and neaten things up. They needed it. It's been a long time since it was done."

"I've been calling you since I got home. You should have heard Quinton's car when he dropped me off. You must have been doing some heavy thinking not to hear us." She shook her head and looked around. "I was wondering where you had gotten to. Now I see. I didn't know you left a trail a whole lot more visible than bread crumbs." She put her hands on her hips. "You know I always let Mother Nature take care of those trees and bushes back here." She stared at Missy. "I guess, if I look, I'll find a spotless oven in the kitchen waiting for fresh spills."

"I'm sorry. I didn't mean to mess the bushes up. Do you think I did permanent damage to them?" She had already messed up enough since she got back.

"They'll grow back. You know. Like your hair." She smoothed her hand over Missy's hair and gave it a final pat. She stepped back and gave her a hard look, but her words were soft. "Things aren't permanently damaged as easily as we think they are." She smiled and took Missy's arm. "How long you been out here?"

Missy shrugged.

"Come on in and keep me company while I fix a salad for dinner." She led her back into the house.

"I'm not eating here, Mama. Walter's taking me out."

"I know." They went into the house. "He must have called while you were trying to kill everything in the yard. He said he tried three times to reach you. I guess you didn't hear the phone. The way you've been going at things out there, I suspect you wouldn't hear anything. At least not anything not in your mind."

Missy's answer was to wash her hands. She was still wiping them long after she had rubbed all of the water onto the towel.

"He called at the shop trying to track you down. He said you told him you'd be home all day. He was quite put out that I didn't know where you were. I reckon he thought I was lying to him. I can understand that. I'll bet he don't go nowhere unless he gets his mama's okay first."

"Oh, Mama."

"Don't 'Oh, Mama' me. You know I'm right." She shook her head. "Honestly, why you want him to be *your* Walter is beyond me. I thought you had better sense. You go off to the big city to go to school and then you ruin it all by coming back here and getting caught by the likes of Walter."

Missy heard the sigh her mother always tacked on the end of Walter's name as if it were a part of it.

"Mama, please don't start on that again. There's nothing wrong with Walter."

"He's a nice enough man." Sally nodded. "Except for the way he lets Elberta run his life, I can't find no fault with him. I just can't picture you married to him."

"I don't want to hear that again. I got enough problems as it is."

"What kind of problems? Does Walter's mother object to you taking Walter on a honeymoon and leaving her behind?"

"Mama . . ." Missy glared, but her mama ignored it.

"A honeymoon with Walter." Her mother shuddered. "It's enough to turn your stomach. At least my stomach. Yours must be made of the same iron as my heavy skillet." She pulled a head of lettuce from the refrigerator. "Can you help me, or won't Miss Elberta let you?"

"Mama, you're in a mean mood this afternoon. You know I don't have to get permission from Walter's mother for anything."

"You will if she has her way. She'll have you jumping through hoops right alongside of Walter. She'll be able to charge admission for folks to see you perform like those dolphins in the water show in Orlando."

"Mama."

"Missy, reach me a cucumber out of the refrigerator."

Missy found a sigh of her own and released it. Her mama ignored it and went on.

"Now you take Jimmy Tanner Scott." Sally sliced the end off the cucumber. "Ain't no way Diane would try to interfere in his life." She scraped a fork down the sides of the cucumber, and admired the dark and light squiggly stripes running to the ends. "Not that Jimmy T would let her. He's got better sense than that."

"Don't go starting singing that tune today, Mama. I ain't in no mood to hear it."

"You just watch your tone of voice with me, Melissa Miranda Harrison. I'm still your mama, and don't you forget it."

"Yes, ma'am." It wasn't often she heard her full name.

"I'm just expressing my opinion. I want you to know how I feel." She sliced the cucumber into the bowl.

Missy didn't comment. She already knew how her mama felt about Walter. She had told Missy every chance she got.

Missy made sure her mama's back was turned before she swiped a slice of tomato from the salad bowl. She dipped it into the sugar bowl before she bit into it.

"You stop that." Sally slapped Missy's hand lightly just as the last of the tomato slice disappeared. "Come on, sugar baby. Sit down and talk to me. I know you been thinking all day about what went on with you and Jimmy T last evening. I been thinking about it, too." She put two glasses on the table and filled them from a pitcher of iced tea.

"Walter stopped by this morning."

Sally stopped pouring and set the pitcher on the table.

"He finally decided a man should see the fiancée he hasn't seen since Christmas, huh?"

"He had to come out this way on an errand."

"Oh, so it wasn't just to see you? What was he gonna do, wait until the wedding to give you a welcome-home kiss? In all fairness to him, though, you haven't been so anxious to see him, either. Maybe you decided the altar was the best place for your next meeting, too. Oh, I forgot you're going to dinner with him tonight. Y'all could have waited until then to say hello. What happened?"

"You're just gonna say 'I told you so.' "

"Did I?"

"That ain't got . . ." Missy shook her head. "I mean doesn't have anything to do with nothing. I mean anything."

"You pour your troubles out at me and I'll do my level best to keep my 'I told you so' words to myself."

"I don't know what to do about my hair."

"Your hair? After what I saw last night, all you're worried about is your hair?"

"Right this minute, yes." She figured she'd start with a problem small enough for her to handle and work up to the big one. "For the past month or so, I've been planning to get it trimmed. Just a teeny bit. You know how I'm always fooling with my hair."

"Ever since you were little. You used to say you wanted to be a hairdresser when you grew up. You and Annette were gonna open up a shop. That was okay by me. Then you put your hands to a computer and hairdressing flew out the window. That was okay, too. When you set your heart on going up north to Philadelphia to learn to be a teacher, I scuffled to help you get what you needed, though I didn't understand why you had to go way up there. I just want my baby to be happy." She shook her head. "That's why I don't understand about Walter."

"Mama, please don't."

"Okay, baby." Her mama shrugged. "We'll get back to that another time." She brushed her hand over Missy's hair. "What's wrong with a little trim?" She patted her own short curly cut. "You got such a pretty face you can wear just about any style. Any style except that shaved-side look you wore your first year in high school."

"That was a long time ago. Soon after that, Mr. Tucker put Walter and me on a social studies project, remember? We decided to do the work on Walter's computer. Miss Elberta took one look at my hair and I thought she was going to have a conniption fit. My hair was still growing out then. Miss Elberta said if it was growing out, she was glad she hadn't seen it at its worse. She cut her eyes at me the whole time I was there. I told you about it. Remember?"

"Yes, I remember. I was afraid to guess at the next style you had in mind. I was glad you had moved on to a hair-coloring phase, even though you changed it every week." Sally frowned. "I think her opinion about your haircut was the first time I agreed with Elberta Wilson about anything." She smiled. "As a matter of fact, it was the only time."

Missy glared and went on with her story.

"I knew she wasn't happy when Walter invited me to stay for dinner. I only accepted to make her mad. Then I was sorry I did. Miss Elberta spent most of dinner that evening explaining how a woman's hair is her crowning glory. She said the good Lord means for a woman to wear her hair as long as He lets it grow."

"Humph. I see she don't feel she should wear her hair all frizzy around her head like a pot-scrubbing pad when that's the way the good Lord made *hers.*" Sally glared. "You didn't pay no never mind to me, your mama, when I told you not to shave your hair off that long time ago. You give her the same listening now that you gave me then."

"I reckon I will." Missy's chin went up the way it did when she decided she'd listen to herself and not let anybody mess in her business. "I'm going to make an appointment with Nettie at her shop."

"I'm glad that's out of the way. You didn't have Walter come out here to talk about your hair?"

"No, ma'am."

"Then why did you have him come over? I know you weren't just itching to see him, though you should have been if you're still fixing to marry him. Are you?"

Missy glanced at her mama, but let her glance slide away.

"I told him I'm not sure I can go through with the wedding." She took a deep breath and let her next words rush out. "I told him I'm not sure it's right for either of us."

Sally set her glass down carefully over the water ring it had made. She watched a drop slide down the side.

"What did Walter have to say to that?"

"He said I just have bride-to-be jitters."

"And what did you say?"

Missy shrugged. "Maybe he's right."

"Oh, Missy." Sally shook her head slowly from side to side. "You don't believe that."

"Mama, I don't know what to believe anymore. I feel like I'm going down a hill with no brakes on my car."

"Jitters can feel like that. I still remember my own. But you know that's not all of it." She stood. "I said my piece last night. The rest is up to you, but if I were you, I'd yank real hard on the emergency brake. Think on it." She put her hand on Missy's shoulder. "Think real careful like, and don't be so stubborn. It's not a sin to admit you made a mistake. It *is* wrong not to correct a mistake when you realize you made it." She gave her a quick hug. "Now I got to go rest my eyes for a bit. Those seed pearls and rhinestones worked my eyes something terrible today, but

I did a lot of work on Clarissa's gown. First Stella and now Clarissa. Someday maybe it will be popular for weddings to be held in September and October, too. Sort of spread the work out." She smiled. "But for now, I'm thankful for the work at any time. I'll see you in a little while."

Missy didn't need her mama to tell her to think on it. This situation was all that had been on her mind since she saw Jimmy through the screen door at Miss Jenkins's house. Now the problem had gotten so big she knew she had to do something.

Missy was ready when Walter came for her that evening. The clock in the hall chimed six-thirty at the same time the doorbell rang. Missy brushed her hands down the sides of her blue flowered skirt and wondered again why she had agreed to think things over some more when she already knew what she had to do.

She still hadn't found a reason to wait, when they followed the hostess to their table.

"Eva opened this place after the last time you were home, didn't she?" Walter slid Missy's chair in to the table before he sat across from her.

"Yes, but Mama told me about it."

"Try the herb chicken. I don't know what she uses, but it's the best I've ever tasted. It's better than Lois's but don't tell her I said that." Walter smiled. He had a nice friendly smile. Missy tried to smile back.

"When are you planning to go see your new classroom?" They had ordered and were waiting for their food.

"I'm glad you brought that up. I wrote and told Mrs. Parsons, the principal at Jackson Elementary School, that I'd be there next Tuesday morning, but now I don't have my car. Do you think you can take me out there?"

"My schedule is heavy all next week. I won't be able to get away. When will your car be ready?"

"I don't know. Jimmy said he's not done checking it over."

"Why can't he fix what's wrong and be done with it?"

"That's what I told him, but he said he wanted to make sure it was safe and wouldn't quit on me again. He said I wouldn't want to be stranded again." She shrugged. "I couldn't argue with that. I hope . . ."

Missy's hopes had nothing to do with what happened next. She watched a familiar couple come toward her. The restaurant was crowded, but the table across from theirs wasn't the only one empty.

"Is this one all right?" She heard the hostess ask. Missy knew the answer wouldn't be no.

"Hey, Missy. I heard you were back in town." Julie Garrison tightened her hold on her date's arm as though she wanted to make sure everybody saw it, especially Missy.

"Hi, Julie." Her words were for Julie, but her gaze was aimed at Julie's date.

"Hey, Missy. How are things going?" Jimmy's question would be general if it weren't aimed at Missy.

"Okay." So Walter had been right. Jimmy *was* still seeing Julie. What game was he playing with her, then? Why had he kissed her? Because he knew she'd let him, that was why. Because he wanted to prove he could do it, that was why. That was the only reason. She looked away. She had always been a fool for Jimmy T. Up until now. She glared at him.

"I just love this place. It's so cozy." Julie's giggle sounded like chalk being dragged across a chalkboard. She wrapped her arm tighter around Jimmy's. "No matter how often Jimmy brings me here, I never tire of it." She sat, but kept on talking as Jimmy pushed her chair in. "I'm going to have the pork medallions. It's Jimmy's favorite so I like it, too. What are you having, Missy?"

"Walter recommended the herb chicken."

"That's good, too. You should at least try something

when your fiancé recommends it." She shifted back in her chair. "How are you this lovely evening, Walter?"

"Just fine, Julie. Just fine."

"I reckon you're more than 'just fine' now that Missy came back home to you. I reckon you're just counting the days until the fifteenth of July."

"Do you want something to drink, Julie?"

Jimmy's question pulled attention to him as if Missy needed to hear him for that to happen. She was glad Julie answered yes. At least she couldn't run her mouth and drink iced tea at the same time.

The waiter put Missy's dinner in front of her, and looked as if he expected her to be able to eat it. Missy glanced at Jimmy.

He was giving the waiter his order, but he was looking at her. She should have ordered something smaller. Something that wouldn't take much time to eat.

She tasted her chicken and took Walter's word that it was delicious. She could have been eating the menu instead, and it would have tasted the same. She closed her eyes. *Please let Walter eat faster than he usually does,* she prayed.

By the time Walter had finished eating at his normal pace, Missy had learned to tune Julie out. She couldn't tune out Jimmy, though, even though he didn't say much. She hadn't expected to be able to.

"Are you finished? Didn't you like the chicken?" Walter finally laid his napkin on the table.

Missy looked at her almost-full plate.

"It was as good as you said," she lied. "I guess I wasn't very hungry." That part was true. "I'm ready to go if you are."

Walter pulled out her chair for her and took her arm.

"See you, Missy." Jimmy's words were a promise she hoped he wouldn't keep.

She spent the ride home wondering how serious things

were between Jimmy and Julie. If they were so tight, why had he kissed Missy the way he had? Had he been trying to show her what she was missing? Had he meant to make her sorry for their last argument; sorry she hadn't made the first move to make up?

She didn't know. She wasn't sure about anything anymore. She couldn't remember what their last falling-out had been about. Although it had felt like it at the time, it probably wasn't important. It certainly couldn't have been serious enough to end things between them.

Of course, Jimmy didn't care about that anymore. No matter what he said, he couldn't. He had Julie now, and he looked like he was satisfied. Julie wasn't like Missy. She liked what Jimmy liked. What else did he share with her besides pork medallions? And why should Missy care about any of it? She had Walter, didn't she? She was going to marry him, wasn't she? Wasn't she?

SEVEN

"Missy? Missy? Aren't you up yet?"

Missy thought about pulling the sheet over her head and hoping her mama would go away. She'd try it if she thought it would work. She turned over and waited.

The door opened after two quick taps.

"Do you know what time it is? It's after ten." Her mama stood in the doorway with her hand on the knob. "I've done a full day's housework already this morning, and here you are still in bed. I declare, you went up North and picked up all kinds of bad habits."

"North doesn't have anything to do with me sleeping in this morning." She sat up. "Folks up North must have burning ears all the time for all the talking about them and the blame put on them down here." She sat up. "I had trouble falling asleep last night. It was after four before I dozed off."

"Maybe that little voice everybody carries around inside them was trying to tell you something. If so, I hope you didn't cut it off like you did me."

"Mama, the only way I can cut you off is if you let me." She stretched. "Did you wake me up to talk about the time?"

"You always did have a smart mouth when you didn't get your sleep. I see going North hasn't changed you."

"Sorry."

"That's a sorry apology, but I guess it will have to do until something better comes along. Annette is asking for you." She handed Missy the phone. "That cordless you gave me for Christmas does come in handy. A body can take a call and still lay up in bed like it's the middle of the night."

Missy sighed. "Thank you, Mama."

"You're welcome. I'm hitching a ride into town with Sam. It's a good thing that I open the shop late today. Otherwise, you'd still be in bed when I come home this evening. I'm going to wait on the porch. I have to put the finishing touches on Clarissa's gown and her attendants' outfits today. See you this evening." She stared at her. "I hope you'll be out of bed by the time I get back." She left before Missy could say anything else. Missy plumped a pillow and put it behind her back. She had to agree with her mama about cordless phones.

"Hi, Nettie. What's up?"

"I guess you are, now. I heard Miss Sally getting on your case." She laughed and Missy laughed with her. "She sure sounded like old times." She laughed again.

"Not really. Back when we were in high school she made me get up before nine. She must have felt charitable this morning." Missy shifted the pillow behind her. "Are you in the shop?"

"Yep. Some of us have to be at work early."

"Don't even try it. My day will begin earlier than yours when school starts."

"That's true. Anyway, I called to apologize for canceling our lunch yesterday. Folks booked appointments after you and I set things up. I didn't even stop for lunch, so you know I was busy. Those ladies acted like something special was going on last night and today that I don't know about." She laughed. "We both know that's impossible. I pride myself on knowing just about everything that goes on around here. Speaking of which, I tried to call you last

night, but you weren't home. Miss Sally told me you went
to dinner with Walter. Did Miss Elberta go with you?"

"Don't be mean."

"I'm not. I'm being realistic."

"No, she didn't."

"Why didn't you call me when you got in last night? I
know Walter didn't keep you out late. Now if you had
been out with Jimmy T, you might not be home yet."

"Nettie, don't you start. It's too early for it. I didn't call
you because I didn't feel like talking."

"Call the doctor. Missy must have a serious illness. She
didn't feel like talking last night."

"I see you had a dose of sarcasm with your breakfast
this morning."

"I know you haven't had breakfast yet, since you're still
in bed, so your sarcasm must be left over from yesterday.
Tell me about dinner."

"Dinner was dinner."

"I reckon it wasn't anything like dinner the night before last. I heard that Jimmy had dinner at your house
then. I want to hear all about that, down to how many
peas he put on his plate. Wish I was there. I always did
enjoy the show you and Jimmy T put on when you get
together. Better than the fireworks display staged by the
Chamber of Commerce every Fourth of July."

"Has Mama been talking to you or was it Jimmy?"

"You know I never reveal my sources. Now to get back
to my brilliant comparison. As for you and Walter, that's
another story. Watching you two is like watching the grass
grow, only the grass is more exciting."

"I'm engaged to Walter. I wish everybody would quit
talking about him."

"As the umpire said, 'I calls 'em like I sees 'em.' Walter
is all right, if you want boring. I just don't think you will
be satisfied with boring."

"Walter is settled."

"The foundation of my mama's house is settled. Walter is boring. But enough about him. What you got planned for today? Our schedule's not too heavy in the shop. I guess everybody got their hair done yesterday. It sure felt like it. Kim and Lottie can handle the clients we have scheduled and whatever walk-ins we get."

"Sure, come on over. The only thing I have today is dinner with Walter and Miss Elberta tonight."

"Girl, I'm coming over to help you get ready. You can't start too early to meet Miss Elberta's standards. She'll be putting you under the microscope and any other scope she can find to make sure you pass her test."

"Come on. She won't be that bad."

"You've been away so long that your memory has dimmed, though I don't know how you managed that. Probably a survival technique. I don't think Miss Elberta is sure yet that you're worthy of her Walter. She's probably working hard to find a way to stop the wedding. It has to be in good taste, though, and worked out so it won't reflect on her baby."

That makes two of us trying, Missy thought. She took in a sharp breath. *That's not true,* she argued with herself.

"I'm going to marry Walter. Miss Elberta wouldn't stop the wedding. It would be a breach of etiquette after all the plans have been made, and you know how she is about doing things right."

"Get dressed. I'll be there in an hour. We can talk about your future mother-in-law then."

Missy tried to breathe normally at the thought of Miss Elberta as her mother-in-law. She was still trying when Nettie rang the bell and called out.

"Okay, open up. I know you're in there. Let me in and nobody gets hurt."

Missy opened the door.

"Girl, it is so good to see you." Nettie pulled her close and rocked her in a hug. "I've missed you."

Missy stood back.

"I've missed you, too. And I love your hair." She touched the long, thin braids hanging just below Nettie's shoulders. "They're perfect on you."

"They better be, as long as it took to get them in." Nettie gave her another quick hug. "I'm glad you're back to stay even though it took your upcoming marriage to Walter to make you come home."

"Come out to the kitchen. I think I would have come back anyway. I was ready. Don't get me wrong. I love Philadelphia. You turn a corner in Center City and there's another little theater. The talent is fantastic. As if that isn't enough, it's so close to New York City and the Broadway shows that I went as often as I could afford to. Philly is rich in history, too. You should have seen me with my class when we went to Independence Hall. I was more in awe than they were."

"Then what was the problem?"

"I couldn't take the winters. No matter how hard I tried, I could never put on enough clothes to get warm in the winter. It may only have twenty-eight days, but February is the longest month of the year. Getting laid off only gave me the final push."

"You would still be there if not for the layoff. You don't know how to give up on anything." She pinned her with a stare. "Usually not giving up is a good thing, but not always. Sometimes you got to know when to admit you made a mistake, and cut your losses. It doesn't matter how many plans have been made."

"How did the conversation get to that so fast? Did you come over here to pick on me?"

"I'm not picking on you. I'm just giving you an opening to discuss things."

"You should have been a psychologist."

"I'm a hairdresser. We do the same thing, only I don't get paid as much for it, and I have to make the clients look good, too." She shook her head. "Some of the things my clients tell me . . ." She shook her head again. "Ooh, child. You wouldn't believe it if I told you—which I won't. I consider it all privileged information." She filled her glass from the pitcher of iced tea on the tray on the kitchen table. "Now tell me about you and Jimmy T."

"There is no 'me and Jimmy T.' I'm marrying Walter. Besides, you live right here. You should know Jimmy and Julie are going together."

"I don't know any such thing. Who told you that?"

"My own eyes. They came into Debbie's Kitchen for dinner last night when I was with Walter. Julie was latched onto Jimmy's arm like she used a whole tube of super-glue. They sat at the next table and every word out of her mouth was to let me know Jimmy belongs to her now."

"She has been hounding him. He probably got tired and gave in. Especially after you and Walter hooked up." She pinned Missy with another stare. "I know you can understand how getting tired and giving in can happen." Nettie took a sip of tea. "Why are you marrying Walter? I still don't understand it. I know I'm your maid of honor and all that, but I just don't get it."

"Walter and I get along well." She was tired of defending her actions to everybody. "We care a lot about each other."

"I care a lot about old Mr. Vaughn, too, but you don't see me marrying him. How can you settle for lukewarm with Walter, when you can have sizzling with . . ."

"Don't even say it. If you are my friend as you have claimed to be for the past eighteen years, you'll drop the subject right now."

"I just want you to be happy, girlfriend." Nettie squeezed her hand. Missy had to lean close to hear these last words.

"I know you do and I will be." Missy stood. She wished she was as sure as her words sounded. "Let's go out to the porch swing. I sure have missed its soothing rhythm."

When they got outside, she set the tray on the white wicker side table.

"Tell me what's been going on in your life." Missy brushed her hand over the familiar blue flowered cushion her mother had made for the swing. She pushed the swing back and forth with one foot. "How are things at Right Hair for You? What's going on? And who are you seeing?"

"The shop is doing great. I have a new hairdresser starting Tuesday, but I will do the honors for you on Wednesday." She sifted a strand of Missy's hair through her fingers. "Any idea what kind of style you want?"

"Nothing drastic. Not too short."

"I know what you like. I'll give you a do even Miss Elberta will approve of." She patted Missy's hair back in place. "Enough about that. I got something much more exciting to tell you about. Or I should say *somebody* more exciting. Wait until I tell you."

"You met somebody and didn't tell me?"

"I knew you were busy making plans and I didn't want to bother you."

"Uh-huh. You met somebody and didn't tell me?"

"Okay. Truth. Every time I told you about somebody special, things didn't work out."

"Are you saying that I jinx you?"

"No." She hugged Missy. "I should have called you, but I wasn't sure. I was afraid that I would jinx things. Besides, I knew you were coming home. I figured that, if it was for real, I could tell you when you got here. Which I'm doing now. Besides, you owe me forgiveness. I had to hear about you and Walter from Walter."

"Okay, okay. I'm too curious to stay mad at you."

"Good, because it's a fantastic story."

* * *

For the next hour Nettie filled Missy in on everything that had happened since she had last seen her, including how she met her latest boyfriend.

"I fell for him. Literally. I tripped on something just as he was passing by. He caught me before I hit the ground. I looked up into his warm velvet brown eyes and got lost. I was afraid Michelangelo was hovering nearby to swoop the man away so he could do a better version of David, only in bronze this time. Mr. Young was afraid I was going to sue him, because I was in front of his laundromat when I tripped. I told him I was about ready to give him a reward for finding Kyle." A faraway look glowed in her eyes. "That's his name. Kyle. Isn't that a beautiful name?" She looked as if she had forgotten where she was and whom she was with.

A streak of envy fluttered through Missy. She'd never felt that way about Walter, and she was marrying him.

"Anyway, that's how I met Mr. Right and I hope Mr. Last for me. I expect to hear that important question any day now." She laughed. "If he doesn't hurry, I'm going to ask it myself and let him do the answering."

They went back inside and talked while Missy fixed lunch. By the time they had finished eating, Missy knew everything that had happened with everybody in town since she had been home last Christmas.

"The chicken salad was delicious, and the company was fantastic, as usual, but I have to go back to the shop so I can leave early this evening. I have a hot date with Mr. Love of My Life tonight, and I haven't decided yet what to wear. Who knows. Tonight might be question-and-answer night, and I don't want to wish I'd worn a different dress to keep in my memory."

Missy smiled as they walked to the car. Nettie opened the door, but didn't get in.

"We never did go through your wardrobe to decide what would meet Miss Elberta's approval." She shook her head. "I'm afraid you're on your own. Just pick the most conservative dress you have and dress it down. Nothing fancier than a strand of pearls; a single strand, of course." She got behind the wheel. "I'll call you sometime tomorrow. We'll exchange dinner stories. Too bad there's no prize for the best one. I know I'd win." She laughed. "I'd win if I was staying home all by myself."

She was still laughing as she pulled out of the yard.

Missy stood there long after the dust had settled, and a couple of crows called back and forth from the magnolias in the side yard.

Then she went back inside and wondered what she would do with her time until she had Miss Elberta's test. Too bad there wasn't another oven to clean or more bushes to prune. Maybe she could straighten out the linen closet. Maybe if she didn't have time to look at the clock, time would go faster.

She didn't believe that even as she thought it.

Although the door was open that evening, Walter rang the bell. Missy glanced at her watch. Exactly on time. Had he ever been late for anything?

"How are you, Missy? Are you ready?" He brushed his lips across her cheek. His aftershave didn't have a hint of spice to it. She was glad.

"Of course I am. Have I ever made you late?"

"No." Walter had a what-did-I-do-wrong? look on his face.

Missy picked up her purse and followed him out. How could she be mad because he was on time? She was still wondering when they walked into his house fifteen minutes later.

"Good evening, Melissa." Miss Elberta's gaze moved from Missy's hair, down her dress, and back to her hair.

Missy wondered what Miss Elberta would say if she knew about Missy's Wednesday appointment with Nettie. She shook her head slightly. No, she didn't wonder. She knew. But it was her hair and what she did with it was her own business.

She fought the urge to tug on her skirt to make sure it was as smooth as Miss Elberta's blue dress with its crisp white lace collar.

"Come on in, dear. Hello, Melissa. Lois is waiting to serve dinner." She sounded as if Missy were late.

By the time the meal was over, Missy had given a full report of her life since she had been home last. She included more details than in any term report she had made in college. Then she had to go over the wedding plans for Miss Elberta.

When Walter suggested at 8:30 that it was time for him to take her home, Missy thought it was about two hours too late.

Before his good-night peck on her cheek, Walter reminded Missy of her promise to take the rest of the week to think about the wedding. Maybe a miracle would happen and her doubts would disappear. She crawled into bed. *Yeah, right.* She turned over. Then she turned over again.

The next morning the phone jarred her awake early. She was glad she had hooked up the extension in her room. Her mama had gotten in late and this was her only chance to sleep in.

"This is Missy."

"Missy, Lureen here. I'm sorry to call you so early on a Sunday morning, but I just got some bad news. Actually, it don't have to be bad news for you. You might decide it's just a second chance to save big money."

"What are you talking about?"

"I just found out my orchid and rose supplier had a bit of bad luck. Actually, luck ain't had nothing to do with nothing. Cliff's fiancée caught him with his old girlfriend and they wasn't talking about flowers. Fact is, they wasn't doing much talking at all. Anyhow, she burned his green-house clean down to the ground. Don't worry, though. I got an idea that will save you money."

"No roses? No orchids? Can't you get them somewhere else?"

"Maybe roses, but I don't know about all white. Most folks want red or pink or peach. And I know I ain't gonna find those orchids no place else. Not with less than three weeks before we need them. But don't have a fit, now. Just calm down." Lureen's voice sounded as if she were trying to convince herself. "I know where I can get my hands on more carnations than you could use. They can do carnations in any colors you want. They have this thing they do with dye that is amazing. They can even put two colors in one flower. That's the nice thing about carnations. That would still let you keep the color scheme you got your heart set on. Carnations would look right nice in that peachy pink. You couldn't hardly tell them from orchids from far away, and you'd have over half the money coming back to you. Why don't you let me go ahead and put the order in?"

Missy could have taught the summer sun to glare. Was Lureen in a conspiracy with Walter's mother? Why was everybody concerned about her expenses? No. Missy corrected her thoughts. Miss Elberta wasn't so much concerned about Missy's expenses as she was about Walter's money. She was afraid that he was going to have to pay part of the expenses. She had almost said as much last night when she brought up the flowers again, even though she knew they had already been ordered.

"Do I have your go-ahead to place the order?" Lureen's voice pulled her back.

"No. Hold off. Let me think about it." All she wanted was white roses and peach orchids. Was that too much to ask for?

"You ain't gonna find nobody else who can find them roses and orchids for you at this late date."

"I didn't say I'm going to look for flowers anyplace else."

"Well, you want to make sure you got them suckers locked down. You don't want to be disappointed again."

"If you can get them so easily, why do I have to hurry?"

"I just mean to say . . ."

"I can't deal with this right now, Lureen. I'll get back to you when I decide what I'm going to do."

Walter's voice in her head was as plain as if he were standing in front of her.

"Mother says it's wasteful to spend that kind of money for roses and orchids," he had said when she first mentioned them. "Carnations would be a lot cheaper and just as pretty."

"Shut up, Walter," she told his image. "I don't . . ."

The phone jangled him away.

"Morning, Missy. Haroldine, here. Sorry to call on a Sunday, but I just found out something that might upset you a teensy bit. Just a teensy bit. Hear me out before you say anything, okay? It's not the end of the world even if it feels like it after you hear what I have to say. Remember, it's not my fault. I did the best I could. I always do my best. What I'm about to tell you is practically an act of God."

Missy tapped her fingers on the bed. She counted to ten. Three times.

"What is it?" Haroldine was still the same as she had been back in grade school when it took her an hour to answer a simple problem. "Are you still there, Harold-ine?"

"Yes, I'm still here. I'm trying to figure out the best way to tell you. I thought I had it all worked out in my head, but it doesn't seem so right, now. I should have written it down, but I thought I'd remember the words." She sighed. Then she cleared her throat. "I guess I'll just have to tell you straight out."

"Good idea." Missy waited.

"Well, anyway, here goes. I have a problem, but I have a solution too, so hear me out completely before you say anything, okay? Promise me that?"

"Haroldine, just say what you have to say. Get on with it."

"Okay. Here it goes. My cornish hen supplier said he's got a work stoppage on his hands. He expected it to be over in time so he didn't say anything to me before now, but he says the girls in the plant are being ridiculous about benefits and all and refusing to come back to work. Ain't no way he can fix that many cornish hens for us by him-self. I checked around and can't nobody else get their hands on that many hens on three weeks' notice. I can get you some plain chickens and fix them up right fancy, and I can fill in with salisbury steaks if I can't get enough chickens. Maybe this is a blessing instead of a problem. Chickens will save you a pretty penny and they'll taste just as good as those hens. They got more meat on them, too."

Missy rolled her eyes even though Haroldine couldn't see her. Chicken and glorified hamburgers for her recep-tion instead of cornish hens.

"The problem with asparagus is a godsend, now."

"What problem with asparagus?"

"Joel's fields flooded and ruined every one of those little spears. I been calling every supplier from here to East Jablip trying to find more. I was fixing to call you about the hens when Joel called me. I can fix you a mess of string beans with fancy slivered almonds that will make you forget all about asparagus. With them green beans sitting alongside my fancy chicken you'll see this as a god-send the way I do. Folks around these parts wouldn't appreciate cornish hens and asparagus, anyway."

Had Miss Elberta dropped her pearls of wisdom, and Haroldine picked them up?

"Are you still there, Missy?"

"I'm still here."

"What do you think about my idea? What do you want me to do?"

"I think I don't want you to do a thing."

"What did you say?"

"If I change my mind, I'll get back to you."

"But what are we going to serve?"

"Nothing. Cancel the contract."

"But-but you can't do that."

"Sure I can. You can't supply, you broke the contract."

"But what about your reception? What are you going to do?"

"Good-bye, Haroldine. I'll call you if I change my mind." The phone rang right away as if there were a line waiting outside a phone booth somewhere.

"Yeah, what is it?"

"Is this Missy Harrison?"

"Last time I looked."

"This is Neil Carson. You know, of Neil's Nailers? I got some bad news for you."

"Join the club. There seems to be a special on it today."

"Huh?"

"Never mind. What's your bad news?"

"I was painting my mama's house yesterday and fell off a ladder. I broke my arm. I won't be able to play at your wedding reception and the guitar and bass won't sound any good without my keyboard. I can get you a good deal on my cousin, Ralphie. He's got his own group, the Heavy

Mentals, but as a favor to me he'll play keyboard for your gig by himself. I was going to go ahead and tell him to save the date, but my mama said I'd better check with you first."

"Your mama is a wise woman." Missy knew she was considered mental by her mama and Nettie, but she didn't need a rock group to confirm it. She wasn't going to need a group anyway.

"He ain't played much oldies," Neil went on, "but he's willing to give her a try."

"Oldies? I asked for music from seven years ago."

"To a kid who's seventeen, that's oldies. Only thing is, I got to let him know now so he won't take the job at the Electric Socket over on The Grand Strand that night. What do you say?"

"I say never mind."

"But what are you gonna do for music? You can't have a reception without music. Your guests will be sitting around with nothing to do. How're you gonna have the first dance with your groom without that number I been practicing? It's tradition."

"Don't worry about it. It's my problem." He was right, but if she didn't have a reception, she didn't need music.

Missy hung up and propped a pillow behind her back. No flowers, no food and no music. What next?

As if to answer her question, the phone rang again. She shook her head. *Let me guess. Reverend Butler can't perform the ceremony because he expects to preach a funeral that day.* She sighed and answered on the sixth ring.

"Yeah, what is it?"

"I was about to hang up."

"Hello, Patty. I'm going to take a guess. You have some bad news, right?"

"How did you know? Did that Laurie Belle Pace call you and try to plead her case?"

"I haven't talked to Laurie Belle since last December when I signed the contract for the hall."

"That's the problem. I'm at the office now trying to get caught up on some paperwork before I go to church. I came across your papers. That dizzy Laurie Belle put your contract in the folder for the wrong date and didn't see that Sue Ann Drake had already signed a contract for her family reunion for the whole weekend of the fourteenth. I just this minute caught the mistake, and only now because something told me to check up on her after she messed up on the Reynolds' anniversary party yesterday."

Missy listened. It was fitting. What good was a hall when she didn't have any food or music? Or flowers?

"That child needs to learn," Patty went on, "that two things can't occupy the same space at the same time. I don't know what you're gonna do. I'm so sorry. I wish I'd thought to check sooner. I'd be glad to help you get out a notice to the folks you invited. I'm sure we can find another date for you. Of course, we'll also refund your money, and we'll compensate you for the aggravation we caused."

Missy heard Patty take a deep breath. She sounded more upset than Missy was.

"Maybe you can use Miss Elberta's backyard? If you decorate it real nice with your flowers and all, it will look as good as it does when she has that fancy shindig for her flower guild. It's a beautiful sight to behold, and I'm not just saying it because my cousin does the decorations. Let me know as soon as you decide so I can help you get out the notices. I'd make Laurie Belle do it, but I'm afraid she'd mess that up, too. If she weren't my sister, I'd fire her. I might fire her anyway."

"Okay, Patty. Thanks for calling."

"You don't sound as mad as I was afraid you'd be. I'm not complaining about that, mind you, just commenting."

"I kind of expected something like this."

"You did?"

"I'll get back to you. Probably tomorrow."

Missy hung up and turned the ringer off. "I don't know why I did that," she said. "There's nobody else who can call, except the reverend, and I don't want to know who's going to die in three weeks." She got up.

Somebody was sending her a message. Not only was it loud and clear, it was beating her over the head.

"Who was on the phone?" Sally stood by Missy's door.

"Which time?"

"I heard it ringing like this was an office or something. And on a Sunday morning. Even the Lord took a day off to rest."

"I'm sorry it woke you."

"It was time I got up anyway. What's going on?"

"Let's go get a cup of coffee. It's a long story. We'll probably finish your special Sunday breakfast before I'm done telling you."

"Say whatever you want," Sally said when Missy finished telling her about the phone calls. "Somebody is sending you a message." She wiped her mouth. "Maybe you'll listen to them more than you do to me."

"I'm about ready to agree."

"Listen, baby, it's good to marry somebody that can give you a good life, but it's better to marry somebody you can't live without. Your daddy and I struggled from one paycheck to the next, but I wouldn't have traded one second with him for a lifetime of mansion living. We had our differences, too, as you witnessed, but we had our love to see us through mean times and mad times. When you have to choose, choose love. Like I told you before, life is too long to spend it with somebody you don't love."

Missy had heard some of this before, but she hadn't been ready to listen then.

"You're right, Mama."

"You have to call Walter."

"You spent so much time on my dress." Missy felt tears fill her eyes. "More time than on anybody else's. It's a shame to let all your work go to waste."

"A dress isn't a reason to get married, sugar baby. You can save it until you find the right man. Or you can hang it on the wall like a piece of art. If you don't want to do that, we can hold a cookout and you can wear it, and parade around in the backyard right here at the house. We can pull out your old baton and you can march around the backyard in a one-woman parade."

Missy's face was still wet with tears, but a smile found the way through. Then a giggle.

Sally squeezed her hand.

"You can do anything you want with it, but please don't marry the wrong man because I made you a dress."

Missy's smile widened. Sometimes Mama was good for what ailed her.

"Why don't you go call Walter now?"

"I want to make sure there are no more messages."

"Who else is there to call?"

"Good point." She sighed. "I reckon I'll invite Walter over. I can't do this over the phone." She took a deep breath. "I may as well get it over with."

Missy was sitting on the porch swing when Walter pulled up and rushed up the steps.

"What is it? What's wrong? I was getting dressed to go to church with Mother. We had to call around to find her a ride back home. Then I dropped her off—much too early, I might add. We barely caught Deacon Clayborn before he left. He graciously agreed to take her home after services. I hope this is worth all the trouble."

"Have a seat, Walter."

Walter sat on the edge of the chair beside the swing.

Missy twisted her hands in her lap. "I can't go through with the wedding."

"What happened? You promised you'd think about it for the rest of the week."

"I don't need any more time to think about it. It's all I've been thinking about the past few days. I got a lot of phone calls today that should have upset me, but they didn't. I knew for sure then that I had to do this." She told him about the calls. Then, she didn't want to, but she looked at him. She owed him that much. He looked lost. "If I waited until I saw you standing at the altar waiting for me with Reverend Butler, I'd still come to the same conclusion, only then it would be worse."

"It's Jimmy T, isn't it? Why? You saw for yourself that he's involved with Julie."

"I told you before, Jimmy doesn't have anything to do with you and me. It's over between him and me. It has been for years." She closed her eyes. Then why had it hurt so much to see him with Julie? She swallowed hard. "I would have called things off anyway."

"It's Mother, isn't it? I know she can be . . ." Walter frowned. "She can be a bit overbearing at times, but she only wants what's best for me."

Missy thought *interfering* was a better word, but it didn't matter.

"That's true. She is." She nodded. *Might as well be truthful all the way.*

"I'm all she has since Father passed."

"Your daddy's been gone for eight years." She didn't remind him that his mother was running his life before then. "How long are you going to let her interfere with your life?"

"You don't understand." He looked more hurt by the words about his mother than by the words ending the engagement.

"You're right. I don't. But she doesn't have anything to do with this, either." Missy took off her engagement ring and laid it in his hand. "I can't wear this anymore."

Walter sat staring at the ring as though he was waiting for her to take it back and put it on again.

"You deserve somebody who will appreciate you. You deserve somebody who will love you."

"You're fond of me. We could have a nice, comfortable life together. Love might come later."

"Love is either there or it's not. Between us, it's not. No matter how much we want it, it's not there between us. Walter, you shouldn't settle for anything less than love. You're too nice a guy not to be happy."

"But I'm not nice enough for you." The hurt in his eyes had grown.

" 'Nice' doesn't have anything to do with this, either. You'll meet somebody. You'll see. You'll fall in love and be glad that you and I didn't go through with this."

Walter's mouth opened but no words came out.

"If you'll be honest, you'll admit your main concern is about what people might say, what they might think. You can tell them it's your idea, if it will make it better for you."

"Image is important. Mother says . . ." He didn't finish. "I guess you've heard enough about what Mother says. I reckon I may as well go." He walked to the edge of the porch. "I'd never say I jilted you. I wouldn't want people to think I don't want to marry you." He smiled, but it didn't reach his eyes. "I'd still marry you if you changed your mind again."

Missy went over and kissed him on the cheek. "Give yourself a chance to be happy, Walter. There's somebody out there waiting to give you her love."

She watched him go. He still had time to make the service without being too late.

As he left her yard, and drove out of her life, she felt as though a weight she had been hauling around since she had said yes to him had been shoved off her.

She went back to the swing and pushed back and forth. Now what?

EIGHT

"How'd it go?" Sally tilted her royal-blue hat to the left as she stepped onto the porch. Missy was still on the swing.

"Just about how I expected."

"He didn't take it too well." Sally smoothed the skirt of her powder-blue suit.

"I wouldn't either if I were in his place, Mama."

"Me neither, but you had to do it." She touched Missy's shoulder and gave it a quick squeeze.

"I know." She sighed. "Still, that didn't make it any easier." Missy stared at her finger that was bare after so many months. How long before the mark faded? Longer than it would take for her guilt to disappear?

A car pulled into the yard. Sally hugged Missy close.

"There's Deacon Johnson. He's running late this morning." She touched Missy's cheek. "It's not the end of the world, you know." She walked down the steps. "I'm gonna have to build a fire under Jimmy about my car."

Missy blinked at the name.

"See you after church. I'm staying for afternoon service, so I'll be late." She smiled at her. "The worst is over, baby."

Mama was right. It couldn't get any worse. Missy had made a mess of things, and Walter had gotten right in her mess. She went into the house and got the phone.

"I was wondering how long it would take you to find

your right mind," Nettie said after Missy told her about the phone calls and about breaking up with Walter. "What shook you awake?"

"I should have done it a long time ago. I never should have told him I'd marry him."

"I won't say I told you so, even though I did. I guess this is what they mean by better late than never."

"I guess so."

"I'm coming over. You make the tea and I'll provide the sympathy. You sound like you could use some."

Missy couldn't smile as she hung up. She had another call to make that could be as hard as talking to Walter had been.

"Connie, the wedding is off." Missy braced herself for the reaction from the woman who would have been her sister-in-law. "I don't want you to make the trip home for nothing. I'll pay for your dress, if you want me to."

"The wedding is off? Did my little brother do something stupid to tick you off?"

"It's not Walter's fault. It's mine."

"Is it Mother? Look, Missy, don't blame Walter for how Mother is. I love her dearly, but I swear I couldn't wait to leave home. I can't take her more often than once a month and not for too long a time then." Her words stopped.

Missy waited.

"Would you consider giving Walter another chance? He's really a nice person, he just has a blind spot where Mother is concerned." Her sigh was as heavy as Missy's had been. "I'm his sister, but I could strangle him when he starts quoting her like her mouth is the Bible."

"I know Walter is a nice man. He'll make some woman happy. I'm just not the right one for him. I don't love him. I wish I did. My life would be so much simpler if I did." It was Missy's turn to sigh. "I'm sorry, Connie. I really am."

"I'm sorry, too. I was looking forward to having you for my sister-in-law. I need somebody to talk to about Mother, and you would have been perfect."

"You can still talk to me any time you want about anything you want, if you can forgive me."

"There's nothing to forgive. I think I knew from the start that things didn't seem right between you and Walter. There weren't any sparks, no tension. Still, I was hoping . . ." Her words trailed off. "If the feelings aren't there, they aren't there, and you can't change that. You can't make yourself love somebody. Don't worry about the dress. Who knows? I might find someplace to wear it." She laughed. "Take care of yourself, Missy. I'll see you the next time I come to visit Mother and Walter."

Connie took things better than Missy had expected. Had everybody known she was making a mistake except her? Did everybody she knew realize she didn't love Walter? She shook her head. Deep inside she had known, too. Her mistake was in thinking she could marry him anyway.

She went back out to the porch swing. A hard push sent it into motion. *Walter, please find somebody in a hurry to take away the pain I caused you.*

"Okay, I'm here," Nettie announced before she even turned off the motor. "You look like you survived okay."

"Come on in. The tea is iced, but I think it will work as well with your sympathy as hot tea would." Nettie gave her a hug and followed her inside.

"Tomorrow I'm sending out notices," Missy said after they had gone back out to the porch, "but some people still have to be called. I hate to ask you, but will you call our friends and tell them? I don't want to go into a long explanation with each one. You can tell them I realized I made a mistake."

"It will be my pleasure to call anybody you want me to."

"I don't want to talk about this anymore." Missy twisted her hands in her lap. "I don't want to think about it." She stared at her finger as if she expected to find the ring back in place. "Tell me about you and Kyle."

"That will be my pleasure, too." Nettie turned toward Missy. "He's everything I ever dreamed of, and more. He's the finest, sexiest man I've ever seen, but he's also considerate, strong, intelligent, sensitive, and he has a sense of humor. Did I say he's fine and sexy?"

Her giggle made Missy smile.

Nettie's voice got low. "I didn't think it was possible to feel this intense about somebody. I love him so much I get the shakes thinking about him." A smile broke across her face. "I never felt this close to anybody before. I didn't think feelings this strong were possible. The man turns me on like nobody else ever has." Her face reddened. "Just thinking about him gets me all hot and bothered." She rolled her glass across her forehead before she drank the rest of the tea. Her gaze softened on Missy's face. "You'll find somebody who does the same for you."

Missy didn't tell her she already had, but she had let him get away. Now he had somebody else.

After Nettie left, Missy sat thinking of what could have been "if only."

First thing Monday morning she called Reverend Butler, the last step in undoing her mistake. He had already heard the news from several people, but he thanked her for making it official. He didn't sound surprised, either.

"It's best to find these things out before the wedding. Too many folks nowadays dwell on the wedding, and give no thought to what comes after. That's how they end up in divorce court. It was wise of you to change your mind before you became a bride to a man not right for you."

Missy agreed and hung up, but she didn't feel any better.

When the phone rang a few minutes later, Missy knew it couldn't have anything to do with a wedding that wouldn't take place. Everything had been canceled, including the groom.

"I'm calling to see if you still intend to take the teaching position I offered you." Mrs. Parsons didn't waste time getting to the point.

"Yes. I'll be there for the interview with you at one o'clock on Tuesday as we planned, if that's still all right with you."

"Of course. That's fine. I kept that time slot for you as we planned, just in case you're still coming. If you decide to take the position, we'll be pleased to have you join our faculty. Your references are impeccable, but with your wedding called off, I wasn't sure if you intend to remain in the area or if you'll go back to Philadelphia."

"I'm home for at least a year."

"That's all we ask of our new teachers. It takes a year for both sides to see if it's a good mix. We'll see you Tuesday, then. After we talk, if we're in agreement, I'll show you your classroom so you can get a feel for it. I'll have your class list, and go over it with you, if you'll have the time."

"I'll have as long as you think we need." She breathed deeply. "I don't have anything else planned."

Not for the rest of my life, she thought after she hung up.

She was having lunch when the phone rang again.

"I hear you need a ride over to the school tomorrow."

"Yes." She waited for Jimmy's "I told you so" about her wedding, but it didn't come.

"What time do you have to be there?"

"You mean the grapevine didn't give you that information? Somebody's gonna be charged with dereliction of duty. I don't know why folks bother with telephones. They could use the money they pay for phone bills for something they really need."

"Folks just care about each other, is all. That's how it is in a small community. Sometimes it works to an advantage."

"I know."

She thought of how neighbors had come together for her and her mama when Missy's father had been killed, and again when her grandmother died two years ago. If the support hadn't been there, Missy wouldn't have gone back to college.

"It's just that sometimes I wish they didn't care so much. Like now." She exhaled hard. "Forget all that. Is my car fixed?"

"Not yet. I fixed the timing belt and I'm still checking the alternator and other things. Under that hood I found what could be several accidents waiting to spring into action if I don't take care of them."

"How much is all this costing me?"

"I can't say yet, but it will be reasonable."

"That's what they always say." She wasn't as afraid of the cost as she would have been a week ago. Now she could afford to pay a lot more than she could have when he picked up her car.

"I'm not 'they.' Don't worry. Now, what time should I pick you up?"

"You don't have to do that. I can get a ride. Don't worry about me."

"I feel responsible since I have your car tied up and all. What time? Is it a secret?"

"Of course not." She told him the time.

"Why don't I come over early and we can grab some lunch on the way?"

"I'll eat before I go."

"Good. What time will you have it ready?"

"I'm just going to warm up some leftovers."

"I like Miss Sally's leftovers."

"You don't know what they are. You don't even know if Mama cooked it."

"It doesn't matter. All her cooking is good. So is yours, so don't tell me you fixed it and try to get out of it that way. See you at eleven-thirty tomorrow."

"Don't you have to work?"

"I'm the boss. Being able to work flexible time makes up for all the long hours I put in before anybody else gets in, and after everybody else calls it quits."

"I guess eleven-thirty is okay." Her wish that the school was within walking distance didn't help any more than it had when she was young.

"Welcome back, Missy." Jimmy's voice was a whisper before he hung up.

Back to what? She shook her head. She didn't want to think about it. Instead she picked up the phone, and called Patty about her offer to help get out the new announcements.

"I'll pay for doing it, if you want me to. I did call the wedding off."

"I can't let you do that. Regardless of what happened, the notices would have had to go out anyway because of our mistake in booking the hall. Tell me what you want them to say, and I'll get right on it. It won't take long."

Missy told her how to word it.

"I'll bring them over as soon as they're done. If I had your mailing list, I could have the computer address the envelopes and print them out."

"That's kind of you to offer, but I'll do them by hand. I'll just consider it part of my punishment."

"Don't beat yourself up. Better to find out before the wedding than after. It's a lot cheaper to call a wedding off than to get a divorce later. See you in about an hour."

While Missy waited, the back-to-what? question kept coming up and she kept pushing it back down. *What did Jimmy mean?*

By the time the announcements were finished and in the mailbox, it was time to start supper.

The smell of chicken baked with herbs from her mama's garden filled the kitchen. Missy heard the car pull up and popped the brown-and-serve rolls into the oven.

"My mouth started watering when my foot hit the bottom porch step. If you keep this up, you're gonna spoil me." Sally kissed Missy's cheek.

"You deserve it. Now go change. The bread will be out by the time you finish."

"Yes, ma'am. I don't know when we switched places, but if it means coming home to a ready meal, it's fine with me."

She came back into the kitchen a few minutes later. A whole lot faster than when Jimmy T brought her home, Missy thought.

"How was your day, baby?"

"I talked to Connie."

"How did she take it?"

"She was real understanding about it. She said she wasn't surprised. Seems like everybody expected this, except me and Walter." Missy took a deep breath. "I got the new announcements from Patty, and we addressed them. They're in the mailbox ready for pickup. How was your day?"

"Clarissa came over and got her dress for Saturday. She said be sure to tell you she expects you there. She's got the feeling you intend to skip her big day. I told her that wasn't the case; that you'll be there if I have to tie you to my arm."

"Mama, I don't think I'm up to it. The last thing I want to do right now is have anything to do with a wedding."

"Missy, you've got to go. Clarissa is a sweet child. She never did anything to make you skip her wedding."

"I know, but I don't think I can."

"Sure you can. This is the ideal time. Everybody will be giving attention to Clarissa and forget all about you."

"Mama, you know that's not true."

"You planning to stay in this house for the rest of your life? You're going to the wedding with me. You can't make me go by myself."

"I'll think about it. I'm not promising anything."

"I guess that will do for now." She smiled. "I didn't tell you the good news. I got a pleasant surprise this afternoon. Jimmy brought my car over. I have wheels again." She did a little turn before she sat at the table.

"That's great. After supper can I borrow your car to run over to the post office? I-I want the announcements on their way as soon as possible." She blinked. "I've got to try to put this all behind me. I don't need to know that the evidence of my mistake is sitting in the mailbox at the end of the yard."

"Sure, sugar, but don't be so hard on yourself. You did what you could to fix things as soon as you made up your mind. Things like that can't be rushed. Folks know that, even Walter. You got to let time take care of the rest."

"I guess you're right." Her eyes widened. "Hey, I can take you to the shop tomorrow and use your car to go out to the school to see Mrs. Parsons. I'll let Jimmy know not to come for me."

"Jimmy was gonna take you?"

"Yes, but he doesn't have to, now."

"I got some running around to do tomorrow. I need my car. Sorry."

"You don't sound very sorry."

"You know how I keep my feelings inside."

"Sure you do." Missy looked hard at her. "Mama, Jimmy and Julie are going together. You have to know that."

"Sugar, if weddings can be called off, I know 'going together' isn't written in cement anywhere. You and . . ."

"Please. Let's just eat. I really can't talk about any of this now."

Sally's look was just as hard as Missy's had been. Then it softened.

"You have outdone yourself today, Melissa," she said. "Every bit I put in my mouth is delicious."

"Thanks, Mama." Missy smiled as she reached for a roll.

She was finishing up in the kitchen, and she still hadn't managed to stop thinking about Jimmy. She'd pull out a memory, and Jimmy would shove it aside, and be right back in her mind. *He's Julie's now,* she kept telling herself, but that didn't keep him away. She hung up the dishcloth as her mama came in.

"It's for you." Missy dried her hands and took the phone. What now?

"Hi, Missy. This is Julie."

Why? Missy wondered.

"I just want to tell you how sorry Jimmy and I are about your wedding being called off. We were so looking forward to attending together. I thought I could get some ideas from your wedding for my own."

Julie's giggle felt like a slap.

"Your own?"

"Oh, yes. Any day now I expect Jimmy to ask the question I've been yearning for. He doesn't like to rush into things, you know. He always likes to be sure he's not making a mistake. I can understand that. After what happened with you and Walter, I know you can understand about not making a mistake, too. It must be so embarrassing for you."

Happiness and sadness were tumbling together inside Missy. If Julie was so sure Jimmy was going to propose, it was almost true. Missy frowned. Had Walter lied when he said Julie and Jimmy were engaged or had the grapevine been wrong? She sighed. It didn't matter anymore. Besides, Julie would probably call next week with her wedding date to ask Missy to be a bridesmaid. Missy was glad that Julie didn't know how Missy still felt about Jimmy.

"Thanks for your call. Good-bye."

Missy didn't know if Julie said anything else, and she didn't care. Julie had already said too much.

Julie and Jimmy. Even their names sounded good together. Would Julie have Mama make the wedding dress after Jimmy proposed? Why not? It wasn't supposed to matter to Missy what Jimmy did. She didn't want him anymore, did she? She kept telling everybody that she didn't.

She was thinking things over as she drove to the post office. Maybe there really was a lot wrong with her car. It had been so long since she had had it checked, and Jimmy had always been a good mechanic. Just because he wanted her to be safe didn't mean anything else. It certainly didn't mean she meant more to him than his other customers did. Jimmy cared about all of his customers. He was a caring person.

Caring wasn't the first word she would use describe how he had been with her, although it was one part of how he was. What he had shown her when she was in his arms went beyond plain caring.

He had taught her how to love him and she learned well. So well that, years after it was over between them, she was still having trouble getting past it.

Never mind that he wanted somebody else, her body still wanted him.

Just thinking about him tempted her. She shook her head. It was no use. If she started up with Jimmy T again, she would end up the way she did the last time: hurt. He still was content with staying here while she wanted more.

Besides, things were moving too fast. She had just broken off with Walter. It was her doing, but it still hurt. Not as much as when she and Jimmy broke up, but it did hurt. She couldn't survive a hurt like that again. Especially not now. Maybe not ever. She wasn't about to jump right into something new, even if Jimmy were available. Which Julie had plainly let her know he wasn't. No, Missy was going to take a lot of time to think things through before she got tangled up with anybody again. Even Jimmy. Especially Jimmy.

She made her mind leave Jimmy and move to a safe subject: her school things. She decided to make a list of the classroom charts and pictures she had brought with her. Fourth graders here wouldn't be much different from fourth graders in Philadelphia. Some of the units in the curriculum were sure to be the same.

She got out a pen and pad and began making her list of what she could remember was in her boxes and bags.

At least there was one thing she was looking forward to.

NINE

Missy was free again. Jimmy knew his grin was out of place while he was struggling to find the problem with Mr. Davis's pickup truck, but he didn't care. His grin widened. There wasn't any problem, with a car, truck, or anything else, that he couldn't solve now that the hard one was gone. Missy wasn't going to marry Walter Wilson in the middle of July or ever.

Jimmy could be the one waiting for her with Reverend Butler when she decided to get married. If he took things carefully, if he didn't rush her or blow it again, *he* would be the one standing in his tux watching his bride coming to him. Watching Missy. She'd have on that lace-and-pearl dress in the picture she had shown him, back when she was going to wear it for him. It was probably the same gown Miss Sally made for her when Missy was planning to be Walter's bride next month, but there wasn't any reason why she couldn't wear it for Jimmy. It was going to be her only wedding. She had said she wanted her wedding to be perfect because she only intended to get married once.

I'll make her so happy she'd never consider leaving me. If she wants to go somewhere to visit, I'll be right there smiling and carrying our bags. If she wants to move . . . he shrugged.

Mechanics were needed everywhere folks had cars and trucks. He had learned that where you lived didn't matter as much as who you lived with. He thought he had learned it too late. He was glad to be wrong. The idea of him and Missy together again made his smile wider.

Missy as Mrs. Jimmy Tanner Scott. Mrs. Melissa Scott. Perfect. He would take her anywhere she wanted to go on their honeymoon. On their wedding night he would show her how much he loved and cherished her. He would tell her how afraid he was that he had lost her. Then he would show how much he had missed her. He'd kiss her mouth that was waiting for him. Only him. Always him. He'd explore her body with his hands and his mouth until he knew it better than he knew his own. Together they would remember how to pleasure each other, and love each other. They would become one, and sail to undiscovered peaks wrapped in each other's arms, two parts, after so many years, finally joining to become one whole again.

Each morning she would be there with him in their bed, and they would travel their love journey all over again.

"Hey, Jimmy," Lester shouted. "You find a big sale on oil somewhere or did you buy out the company?"

Jimmy looked down. A puddle of oil had spilled over the toe of his shoe and was oozing away from the truck, down the drive, and toward the street.

"If oil could fix the problem with Mr. Davis's pickup, I reckon his truck is more than good to go." Benny's laughter mixed with Lester's.

"Boss, I ain't never seen you so moon-eyed before," Lester said shaking his head. "I wonder if it has anything to do with a certain called-off wedding?"

"If I'd a thought about it," Benny broke in, "I'd a hit you up for a raise while your mind wasn't paying attention. If I'd a been quick enough, I might even be the owner of this fine garage about now, and you'd be working for me." Benny's laugh was louder than Lester's.

"Never you mind." Jimmy's laughter joined with theirs.
"I got things under control here."

"Yeah, it sure looks like it." Lester let out another laugh
louder than before.

Then the men got back to work. Jimmy wiped the oil
from the motor and the exhaust manifold. He was going
to have to give Mr. Davis a free steam cleaning, but that
was okay. His laughter disappeared.

Cars and trucks were easy. Walter wasn't the only thing
between him and Missy. Walter had come after their
breakup, he hadn't been the cause. With him gone from
between them, their differences were still there. Jimmy
had to convince her that they could work through them;
that their love was greater than their problems.

Fixing things with Missy was going to take a lot more
work than fixing any car or truck, but when it finally happened, it would be worth the effort.

Missy spent all day Monday trying not to remember that
Jimmy was coming over the next day. Her mama had never
made her clean house the way she had cleaned today. You
could eat off the floor, the tops of every piece of furniture,
even the walls if you could figure out how to keep the
food from sliding to the floor.

Every closet in the house was neat enough to pass anybody's inspection. Yeast bread was rising in the pan, and
still Missy had too much time left over to think about
tomorrow. She tried to do a book of crossword puzzles,
but Jimmy's name came up whenever there were enough
spaces to fit it. She was glad when her mama came home
and talked about her day. Missy made her drag out her
story until it was time for bed.

She went to her bedroom because she didn't have anywhere else to go. It wouldn't have mattered even if she
did. Thoughts of Jimmy had traveled with her all day, and

she had no reason to think they wouldn't have gone out of the house with her.

She got into bed because it was late, not because she was sleepy. Sleep would have to fight with her thoughts, and she didn't expect sleep to win.

She crawled under the top sheet. The moonlight found the crack between the side of the window and the shade and threw patterns on the wall. She looked for pictures in the pattern the way she used to do when she was young and didn't want to go to sleep.

Tonight she did it to keep her mind busy with something else, anything else, besides Jimmy. It didn't work.

Missy dragged herself out of bed before her mama got up. The light coming in around the shade had turned to gray before sleep had come, but it hadn't stayed long. She was tired, but her mind was going too fast to let her body sleep.

She made a pot of tea stronger than usual. As she drank a cup, she thought of asking her mama one more time to lend her the car. If she thought she would succeed, she'd do it. She drained the last of the tea and poured more. Today she'd find out for herself if caffeine could really substitute for sleep.

She was on her third cup when a tap on the back door pulled her attention from her thoughts. She sighed and went to open the door.

"I came over early so I could bring more of your stuff."

Why did he have to look so good in the morning?

"Where do you want me to put this box? In your bedroom with your other things?"

"No." She did not want Jimmy in her bedroom again. Her jaw tightened. Maybe part of her did, but he wasn't going in there. For once the stronger part had more sense. "Put it out in the shed kitchen beside the washer.

It's going to end up at school. When I get my car back I can take it in."

"Why don't we take it today? We can do that while you have my muscle power to use. Why wait and carry it by yourself when you have me today?"

"Because I haven't even met Mrs. Parsons yet. You don't show up for a job interview with boxes of stuff like it's a given that you'll get the job." She glared at him. "But then again, you probably would. You'd probably walk into her office loaded down, set boxes on her desk and say, 'Show me my room.' If I do get the job, I haven't seen my classroom yet. I don't know what I'll need or where to put things." She crossed her arms. "I don't know if she still wants to hire me." *After the scandal I just caused,* she thought.

"You know the job is yours. How could it not be? Anybody smart enough to become a principal is smart enough not to let somebody like you get away." He stared at her. "Some of us are not so smart."

His stare grabbed her and tried to devour her. It could have lasted a few seconds or a few hours. He blinked and released her, then left her standing there, and went back for another box. When he went back outside, Missy followed him.

"Just leave those be," he told her when she reached to lift a box from the trunk.

"I'll do no such thing. It's my stuff. I loaded it all up in Philadelphia, I guess I can unload it just as easily here." She grabbed a small box. If Jimmy hadn't been watching, ready to say "I told you so," she would have put it back. Of all the boxes left, she had to pick the one with jars of paints. Full pint-size jars. And she had packed her art books on top of the jars. She took a deep breath and carried it into the shed trying not to struggle under the weight.

Two more trips for both of them, and Jimmy's car was empty.

"Come on into the kitchen."

"I'll follow you anywhere, honey, any time."

"Jimmy T, stop your fooling." Missy hoped he hadn't noticed the color creeping up her face before she turned her back to him. She didn't want to encourage him.

"I'm not fooling."

Missy felt her face get hot and she knew her color had deepened, but she didn't turn to let him see it.

"Pot roast. Do you know how long it's been since I had good pot roast? Of course you don't. I don't even know."

"When will my car be ready?"

"Where did that question come from? What does that have to do with pot roast?"

"It has nothing to do with pot roast. And it came from my mind, where it's been sitting since you towed my car in. It's still there because it hasn't been answered yet." This time she did look at him.

"Your car will be ready when it's ready. You don't want me to rush something as important as that. I might miss something."

"I don't want it to take as long as it's taking to fix the Tower of Pisa, either. What's wrong with it now?"

"I have to adjust the bands." He looked at her. "Don't tell me your music comes from the radio and tapes, and a band can't fit under the hood."

"Very funny. I know the bands have something to do with the transmission." She passed the breadbasket to him.

"You *were* paying attention some of the time."

"Of course." Missy blinked. *I was paying attention all of the time,* she thought. *It just wasn't cars and engines filling my mind.*

"After I adjust the bands and linkage, I have to see what else I find."

"I don't want to end up with zeros showing in my bank account. Maybe I should forget about Gertie, and think about a new car."

"No." Jimmy swallowed a big gulp of iced tea. He looked as if he were fighting to keep it from going down the wrong way. "Your car still has a lot of life left. I-I haven't been able to give it much attention, is all."

"Jimmy, is my car ready?"

"No, it is not. Don't you think I'd call you if it were? What kind of businessman would I be if I had ready cars sitting around taking up valuable space instead of back with the owners? Besides, I wouldn't make any money that way, would I?"

"Valuable space? You park on the street. And you'd make money if you'd fix the cars instead of letting them lay around your shop." She leaned forward. "I need my car."

"What's your hurry? I'll take you wherever you want to go whenever you want to go."

"I don't want to depend on you to carry me everywhere. What kind of a businessman would you be if you dropped everything whenever a customer wanted to go somewhere? No wonder it's taking forever to fix my car. You're never there to do any work. You're always here."

"Every customer doesn't need transportation." He stared at her. "And I'm not always here. I'm not here nearly enough."

Missy decided to ignore his last sentence.

"Your work is so slow I don't see how you get repeat customers. I'll bet you get complaints all the time."

"I do good work. That's why they come back. My customers don't complain. It's just taking me a little longer with your car than with most." He pinned her with a look. "You know I don't mind if you depend on me, Missy. Any time. All the time."

Missy's stare met his and was caught. Desire flared in

his eyes, and her body tightened in response. Somewhere a bird called out a warning. Missy blinked. The warning was too late and this was happening too soon. She wasn't ready for this. She cleared her throat.

"We'd best get going. I don't want to be late."

"I'm with you." Missy felt he still wasn't just talking about right now. What would Julie say if she were here? Would Jimmy have said all those things to Missy? Would he have looked at her the way he had, if Julie were here? What game was he playing? Was he trying to make Missy realize she had made a mistake years ago when she didn't try to make up with him?

Too many questions and not one answer. She was glad this wasn't a test to see if she deserved a job. If it were, she'd have to keep on looking.

Jimmy stopped outside the school twenty minutes early. Missy grabbed her purse and scurried out.

"Thank you for bringing me. I'll call Mama when I'm finished here. I can find something to do until she can come get me."

"I'll wait. Miss Sally is probably busy. She can't just close up shop in the middle of a workday. I'll take you back when you're ready."

"It's not necessary." Why did everything he said sound as if he were talking about something else?

"I know." His knowing didn't make him move.

"Jimmy, go on to your shop. Go finish my car."

"Don't worry. I can guarantee that the boss won't fire me." Missy glared at him, but he didn't leave. Finally she went into the building trying to ignore him, even though he was walking right beside her.

Missy met with Mrs. Parsons and reassured the woman that she still wanted the teaching position. Jimmy sat in the chair beside her as though he belonged with her. Mrs.

Parsons talked to both of them, and accepted that maybe he did.

She filled Missy in about general procedures, and gave her a packet with a handbook and a floor plan. Missy didn't need the floor plan. Everything was right where if had been when she was a student here. Only teachers' names had changed, and not all of them.

Their footsteps echoed off the concrete floors as they walked through the school. Missy felt strange as she always did when she was in a school empty of kids.

"I know there have been some changes since you went here. Probably not a whole lot, but nothing stays exactly the same."

Some things do, Missy thought. *No matter how you fight against it, some things don't change at all.*

They stopped outside a room near the end of a hall that had housed third and fourth graders when Missy was a student. Evidently other things stayed the same, too.

"This will be your classroom: Room 10. The classroom floors were refinished in this hallway yesterday, so all of the furniture isn't back in place yet. We like bright, cheery classrooms. I don't believe a stark classroom is a place where students are learning as much as they can. Don't you agree?"

"Yes, I do. I brought a lot of charts and posters with me."

"Good. I'm sure you can put them to use here. Also, each classroom has several computers. Next year we hope to add more to them. We have a variety of software available through the Instructional Materials Center. The students can also access the Internet. Some teachers match their classes with Netpals every year. Last term one of our sixth grades was matched with a class in Australia. At the end of the school year, we held an assembly and they shared their experiences with the other classes. If you need help with your computer program, the district has a specialist available. Most of the teachers can probably give you any help you need, though."

"I know a little about computers. My school in Philadelphia was a computer magnet school."

"Excellent. Maybe some of the others will be coming to you for help." Mrs. Parsons smiled and Missy relaxed a bit.

She stepped inside what was going to be her room, and took a deep breath. The smell of chalk dust, felt erasers and paper greeted her. The fresh wax odor would have told her about the floors if Mrs. Parsons hadn't. Classrooms smelled the same no matter where they were. She looked around. They all looked strange with empty walls and shelves, and no children.

Missy smiled. A shallow alcove by the last window was ideal for a reading corner. A bookcase would fit against the side wall, and the live oak right outside the classroom would give her students the feeling of sitting under the tree while reading. Maybe she could even get permission to paint a branch over the wall and ceiling in the corner.

"Would you like to stay or do you have to hurry back?"

"I'd like to stay awhile. I'm in no hurry." Missy smiled sweetly at Jimmy.

"Neither am I." His smile wiped Missy's away.

"I'll leave you, then. I have some paperwork I have to complete. If you have any more questions you can stop by on your way out, or you can give me a call." She held out her hand. "I'll see you the first day of school, but if you decide to come in before then, you won't have any problem. Mr. Henry, the custodian, is here mornings and most afternoons Monday through Friday. You might want to call ahead of time, though, and let him know when you're coming. Again, welcome to Jackson Elementary School." Her handshake was firm, like she was sure she knew what she was doing. Missy wished hers was, too.

After Mrs. Parsons left, Missy leaned against her desk, the

only furniture back in place, and looked around. There was lots of wall space for her charts and posters. The wall beside the closet was the perfect place for her American Inventor of the Month posters. She'd start with Elijah McCoy as she had last year. If she ever got her posters here.

"I need to know when my car will be ready. I need the rest of my things. I could put up my posters and charts. I could make sure I find the best spot for each one. I need to see how everything fits. I need my car, Jimmy T."

"I'll bring your school things over here. See how I'm saving you a trip? If you had your car you would have taken your school things into your house, and then you would have had to put them all back into your car and bring them over here. You should be thanking me instead of fussing."

"I'll thank you to give me back my car."

"It's not ready."

"If you'd spend your time working on it instead of playing chauffeur, it would be finished by now."

"I had to order a part and it isn't in yet."

"When they ordered a part in Philadelphia, they had it the next day."

"This isn't Philadelphia."

"The post office and other services work here just as well. The pony express has been replaced by something faster, you know."

Jimmy looked at her. The flash in her eyes was different from the look she had after he had kissed her, but it sent heat racing through him just the same. He hadn't shown a bit of sense when he left the argument in place between them years ago, but he had better sense now than to tell her how sexy she looked when she was angry, which she was. But then, she was sexy when she wasn't angry, too. She was just plain sexy, though it wasn't right to use the word *plain* with Missy. It would never be the right word for anything that had to do with her. "Be patient." He said it to her, but he could have been talking to himself. He understood her impatience. He knew how hard waiting was. Boy, did he know. "It won't take much longer." He hoped he wasn't just talking about Missy's car.

"You could have built a new car by now."

"Yours isn't the only job we have, you know."

"Jimmy Tanner Scott . . ."

"Next week. Your car will be ready next week." He had run out of time.

"You promise?"

"Don't you trust me?"

"Jimmy, I'm not fooling."

"Neither am I." He wouldn't have any trouble thinking of more pleasant ways to fool around with her, though. No trouble at all. In fact, just thinking about her with him . . .

"A week from Friday. No later. I expect to get my car back, and in perfect working order a week from Friday. You got that?"

"Got it."

"I'm ready to go."

"Sure thing. I'm with you." He tucked her arm under his. She tried to pull away, but gave up when he tightened his hold.

Jimmy let a small smile show itself. It felt almost like old times with Missy so close. He pulled her closer still to his side, but she didn't pull away this time. He slowed her down as they walked to the car, keeping her close for as long as he could.

He had less than two weeks to figure out his next move.

He didn't talk as he drove her home. He was too busy thinking.

Missy put her hands together over her head as she ran back toward the house, even though it wasn't doing any good. She might as well have put her hands to her side, taken her time and strolled back home. Water was running down her hair and shirt as if she were in the shower without a cap, and with her clothes on. She hunched her shoulders though she didn't know why.

The weather report hadn't mentioned rain. She wished somebody had told the rain. She stepped off the road as a car came closer.

"Get in." Jimmy stopped his car and reached across to open the passenger door.

"What are you doing out here?" She scrambled into the seat beside him.

"I'm not wearing armor, but I'm rescuing you. What are *you* doing out here?"

"I thought it was a nice morning for a walk."

"Sure it is. Perfect. If you were a duck or a fish, that is. You don't look like you sprouted wings or grew fins since I last saw you." In fact she looked as good as ever.

"It wasn't raining when I left the house." He watched her pull her shirt away from her body where it was plastered to her breasts, but the shirt clung back in place as soon as she let it go. He tried not to imagine his hands replacing the shirt.

He looked over at her again. *Thanks for hard, soaking rain,* he thought.

Twin hard pebbles pushed out Missy's deep pink T-shirt made darker by the rain. Jimmy's stare grabbed the pebbles as his body matched their hardness. He swallowed hard. Desire curled through him, and settled in his groin. He gripped the steering wheel to keep his hands to himself. *I wonder if her breasts feel as full and soft as I remember. Like smooth milk chocolate. They had tasted just as good.*

"What are you . . ." Missy's words stopped and Jimmy made his gaze creep up to her face. He watched her take in a sharp breath, and he watched it get lost. Her face was covered with the same desire that was swelling through him.

A boom filled the silence and Jimmy didn't know if it was thunder or his heart.

The rain poured down the windshield like a hose on top of the car trying to empty itself. It felt as if he and Missy had found a world of their own behind a waterfall. He eased her close, giving her time to pull away if she wanted to, but praying she wouldn't.

His lips brushed across hers. She opened her mouth and let him in. The tip of his tongue flicked along the inside of her lips. Sweeter than he remembered. She moaned and he swallowed her moan and explored deeper. His hand molded to her breast better than the shirt had. The hard tip tightened even more as she pressed harder against his hand. Soft and firm and perfect.

His thumb brushed across the swollen tip and another moan escaped from Missy. His hand found its way under her shirt and teased the other breast.

Her hands around his neck tightened when he gently tugged on the sensitive tip.

"Jimmy," she whispered.

He answered with a trail of kisses along her neck as he inhaled her sweet smell that had been missing from his life for too long.

"Missy, Missy. You don't know how I've missed you." His mouth moved back to hers.

"No, Jimmy. No." Missy sounded as if she had run all the way to town and back. She eased away. He let her go. "I'm not ready for this. I can't handle it."

"I'm not pushing you." He sounded as if he had been in the race with her. "I'll wait until you are ready." No matter how long. He wouldn't let her get away this time.

"Jimmy, don't. Don't talk like that." She looked in his direction, but she wouldn't look at him. "I don't want to talk about what just happened. Okay?"

He stared at her and struggled for control over himself. Definitely not okay. Nothing would be okay until she admitted they belonged together.

He ignored her question, and hoped she was asking herself and not him, but he also hoped the answer was still no.

He forced himself to look out the window, and away from her. If he kept looking at her, he wouldn't be able to keep from pulling her close to him again. If he pulled her close and felt her body against his again, he wouldn't be able to stop at a kiss.

"The rain has slowed down." How did that happen so fast? Or was it fast? How long had they been in the car? He always lost track of time when he was with Missy. There was never enough of it.

He looked at her. She had wrapped her arms around herself as if trying to put space between them. He caught her quick look.

That couldn't be fear, could it? She couldn't be afraid of him. Not after all there was between them.

He put the car into gear.

"I'd never hurt you. You know that, don't you?"

Missy looked away. She hunched her shoulders as if she were trying to hide inside herself. Trying to hide from him.

Jimmy let out a hard breath. How could she know he wouldn't hurt her? When they were going together, they had argued all the time. Once a week they had broken up, swearing never to go near each other again. She never cried during one of their arguments, but he wouldn't be surprised to know that she had released tears when he wasn't around. How could he expect her to believe he wouldn't hurt her again? What could he do to make her believe it?

"I came to bring you more of your things. The boxes and bags in my trunk are labeled school stuff, so I thought you might want to take them over to the school."

She was staring through the windshield as if she were outside, and not sitting in the car with him; not close enough for him to feel her body heat, heat that he had helped generate. His heat must be reaching her, too.

They were at the turn for her house before she answered.

"I-I have to change first." Her words whispered out. Where did that come from? She knew she should tell him to go. She should want him to go.

"I'll wait out here," he rasped. As if he had a choice.

He needed time and space to get himself together. In the house with her wasn't the place for it, and he wasn't sure there was enough time left in the day for the kind of control he needed. He watched her go into the house.

She still cared for him. He shook his head. The back windows were still steamed up from their little "caring" session.

All they had to do was touch and everything, including the time that had passed since they had been together, fell away and they were back to when they couldn't get close enough to each other. He just had to give Missy time to realize they belonged together again.

Missy scurried to her bedroom, grabbed a bra and panties from the dresser drawer and rushed into the bathroom as if she could outrun what had just happened with Jimmy.

"I can't go through this again," she said to herself as she peeled off her shirt and bra. The rest of her clothes followed. She draped them over the rod over the tub.

Julie's message, both the words and the meaning, came to her. Missy thought of the message Jimmy had just given her. *What are you trying to prove, Jimmy Tanner? We never did have problems when we were loving. It was all the other times that showed we couldn't make it together. If we could have spent all of our time making love . . .* She caught her breath.

She could think of lots worse ways to spend time, but none better. The things he could do with his mouth and hands should be against the law.

Warmth spread through her, and settled in her lower body. Jimmy didn't even have to touch her. One look from his green eyes darkened with desire, and, if she wasn't careful, she was halfway to where he wanted to take her and where she wanted to go.

No more. Not again. I should be smarter than this. I know how it will end. We'll have an argument, and neither of us will apologize, and that will be that. I'll walk around wondering why people can't see that my heart is missing and he'll be back with Julie. Let him stay with her and skip the hurting me part. I will not go through it again. It's too painful.

She rubbed herself dry harder than was necessary, trying to erase the effect Jimmy had had on her.

I'll be fine by myself. I was okay without him all those years in Philadelphia, and I can be all right here, too. I will be fine here. I'll only be here for a year. Then I'll take a job teaching overseas. That should be far enough away from them. I just have to get through one year. One year. She sighed. Why did a year have to have so many days?

Please don't let him and Julie get married before I leave here.

She pulled on the loosest sweater she owned and her baggiest jeans. She took a deep breath. *I have to remember the hurt that eventually comes from any relationship with Jimmy and forget the loving.*

TEN

The South Carolina sun was shining in Missy's bedroom window now as if it were trying to make her forget the rain it had let take over a little while earlier. She swallowed a lump. And what came after the rain? She shook her head. It wasn't the rain that she needed to forget.

Why did Jimmy have to go and touch her the way he did, when he loved Julie? While she was wondering, her body was remembering. She couldn't blame wet clothes for the way her breasts tightened now as if aching for his touch again. She pulled at the shoulder of her big shirt and was glad she at least had sense enough to put on something loose-fitting. No sense letting him know she was still as stupid as she was a few minutes ago.

As she went back to the car, she tried to find the strength to resist him. *Why did I agree to let him take me to the school? Why didn't I say no? Why can't I ever say no to Jimmy?* She squeezed her eyes tight. *Please don't let him bring up what just happened.*

She glanced at Jimmy as she got into the car. He stared at her. He didn't use words, but he didn't need any. His gaze said more than any words could. If his look were told in words, Missy would protest. How could she complain about a look?

She wished the school were two doors from her house instead of miles away. If the school were closer, she could

walk her things to her classroom even if she had to unpack
all the boxes and bags and carry two or three things at a
time. That would be better than sitting close to Jimmy
and trying not to remember.

She sighed. She'd been wasting a lot of wishes since she
got back home.

"Missy? Here we are."

She looked at Jimmy and wondered how long ago he
had stopped the car. His puzzled look told her it had been
a while.

She shook her head. She was glad he hadn't asked if
she was okay. If he did, she would have to say she was
losing it, but she was afraid the truth was that she had
already lost it.

She went to the trunk with Jimmy, and lifted out two
shopping bags. Rolled posters with rubber bands around
them stuck out the tops.

Jimmy grabbed a box and followed her into the building.

She stopped just inside the classroom. Her classroom.
She smiled. Bookcases stood against the walls and desks
were lined up in rows waiting for students. Her students.
Her smile widened.

"Where do you want this?"

"Put it on top of my desk, please." Her desk. That
sounded as if things were getting back to normal. Now if
she could get herself there . . .

Jimmy went back to the car for another load and Missy
followed, trying not to notice the way his muscles bunched
as he went down the hall, trying not to remember how
they felt under her hands when she had been allowed to
touch him, back before he gave Julie that right. Missy tried
harder not to remember.

She tucked a small bundle under each arm. The sooner

they got all of her stuff into the classroom, the sooner Jimmy would leave and the sooner she could gain control of herself. She slid the bundles up higher, tightened her arms and grabbed a bag in each hand.

Jimmy had barely put the last box down when Missy pulled herself up straight.

"Thank you very much, Jimmy. I know you have work to do back at your shop. I'm going to stay and put some things up around the room. Mama will pick me up when I'm finished. I appreciate you bringing me out here." Even to herself, she sounded as though she were talking to a casual acquaintance, and not to somebody who knew her body as well as she did. She held her breath. Maybe it would work.

"You didn't ask her. You couldn't have. You didn't know I was coming to your house, and I'll bet you didn't call her when you went in to change. She might have other plans."

"That's my problem, not yours."

Jimmy pushed a box back on the desk and leaned. *I knew I gave Miss Sally her car back too soon,* he thought.

"I'll stay and help you." Missy started shaking her head back and forth. He ignored it. "You're probably the only one in the building. You don't know how safe you'll be."

"Mr. Henry is here."

"I want to make sure you're safe with him."

"Jimmy, you know Mr. Henry is the deacon at our church. He's been there since before I was born. He was working here when I was a student. We've known him for years. Nobody ever says anything but nice things about him. We look on him as we would a grandfather."

Jimmy decided to try something else.

"I noticed you looking above the chalkboards and the windows. You need help putting things up high."

"Jimmy, go fix my car."

"It will be ready by a week from Friday. I promised."

Their stares held. "You know I always keep my promises."
He took a chance and lifted a poster from a bag and
carefully slipped the band off. "Where do you want this
one?"

"We can't put them up. We don't have a ladder."

The last word was barely out of her mouth before Jimmy
was gone. Before Missy could think of another excuse, he
was back carrying a long stepladder.

"Okay. Which one goes up first, and where do you want
it?"

Missy shook her head, but she started pulling out posters. She looked at each one and formed them into groups
on top of several desks. She rummaged in another bag,
pulled out a roll of tape and fastened a piece to the back
of each corner of the first one.

"I guess this one goes above the first chalkboard in
front."

Jimmy positioned the ladder and climbed it.

"It will make it more interesting if you tell me about
them as we hang them. That way I won't get bored." *And
I get to stay with you longer.*

"If you get bored you can go back to the garage and
work on my car."

"When did you develop that one-track mind? And
where did that salty bite come from? You've been away so
long that you've lost your southern hospitality." He
reached for the poster she held out. "Pretend I'm one of
your students. Tell me about this one."

There wasn't that much pretending in the world, Missy
thought. He was the teacher, at least when it came to lovemaking. He had taught her more that she had imagined
possible. His hands had performed magic on her body
every time he touched her. His mouth had . . .

"Is this the right spot?" Jimmy was pressing the last
piece of tape in place. "Tell me about this one."

Missy pulled her thoughts back to the safety of the posters.

"That's the first of the five steps in the writing process." As he hung the others in succession, she told him some of the stories and poems her students had written using the process.

Jimmy worked the ladder around the room, and Missy told him about her students' experiences with the posters and charts.

The last charts he put up were math posters on subtraction and regrouping.

"Last year Nina had a time learning that concept. We used bundles of ten craft sticks, different colors for ones, tens, hundreds and thousands. Each time she had a problem to do, Nina wanted to subtract the smaller number from the larger one, no matter whether it was on top or at the bottom. At first I had to have her actually work with the sticks. Then everybody else had gotten it, but she still struggled. After weeks of practice, she got so I just had to tell her to get the sticks, and she did the problem correctly. The day she got the process right the first time and without hesitation, the whole class gave her a standing ovation. Then I had her lead the class in marching around the room." Missy smiled at the memory. "It's times like that that make teaching worthwhile."

"I'll bet you're a dynamite teacher." He smiled at her the way he used to before so much had come between them. "Your kids are lucky to have you for their teacher. You really care about them."

Missy blushed and shrugged.

"I don't care any more about my students than other teachers do about theirs." She looked around the room. Posters and charts covered the walls above and even the space beside the chalkboards. "That's the last of them. I'll use the others during the year to replace the ones that are up." She rolled up the rest of the posters and put them into a bag. She set the bag on a shelf in her storage closet.

She was surprised at how smoothly things had gone. They hadn't had one disagreement. Jimmy had asked her questions, and her answers had given him a hint of her life as a teacher and a look at some of the students she had taught. She glanced at her watch. For the past three hours they had been like two regular people with each other. She hadn't once blown up and stomped away from him. He hadn't called her back to finish talking.

"What else is there for us to do?"

"Nothing. Anything else can wait until I get my car back."

Jimmy's sigh was loud enough to be heard down the hall if anybody had been there.

"There goes that one-track mind again."

They went to his car. This time Missy walked ahead, but she was thinking back.

Jimmy stopped the car and Missy looked around the small parking lot.

"Where are we?"

"Lunchtime." Jimmy opened her door. "The Owens' Family Restaurant is new, but word has spread about it already." He held out his hand. "Come on."

"We didn't discuss anything about lunch." She swung her legs out, but didn't stand.

"It's one o'clock. Almost past lunchtime. I'm not asking you for a commitment. I only want you to have lunch with me. What's wrong with that?"

She couldn't think of anything. As Jimmy said, it was only lunch.

She put her hand in his to help her stand, and wished she hadn't. The warmth flowed from his hand to hers and to her arm before she pulled away. That didn't help, though. It just kept on flowing until it reached her core. Then it spread out, filling her the way he had.

Jimmy was still staring at her even though their hands no longer touched. Did he feel the bond still there stronger than if they were chained together?

"Let's go inside." His voice sounded as though the last place he wanted to take her was to a public place.

She blinked loose. She knew the feeling.

She followed him into the restaurant. She slid across the red seat in the booth and Jimmy slid in across from her. For once she wished there hadn't been any empty booths. Jimmy was too close. His knees touched hers under the table. She sighed. If he were across town, he would still be too close. She had to find a way to break free of him for good. Only stupid people made the same mistake twice. If she tried hard enough, she'd discover how to turn off his attraction.

She looked around. It may have been after lunchtime, but there were plenty of people scattered around the room, and all of them were staring at her and Jimmy. To the left, Miss Henderson smiled and waved. Missy's smile wasn't nearly as strong as Miss Henderson's.

"Hey, Missy, Jimmy T." The waitress looked from one to the other. "I'm surprised to see you two together, but I'm glad you found us. This is Cousin Lou's dream and we're doing well, thank God." She stared at Missy. "You two back together?"

"No, we are not." Missy denied it before Jimmy could say anything. "Please tell that to anybody who says something to you about us." She didn't want Julie to get upset over nothing. "Jimmy took me to school because he still has my car. I think he must be building me a new one since he's taking so long to fix mine."

"I'm just being thorough, Willa. You know how I like to be sure when I do work. I have to test things out."

"Two days ago was way past the thorough point of testing."

"You know how impatient Missy can be." Jimmy turned a smile on Willa that could have melted butter still in the refrigerator. "Going North didn't help her manners any."

"My manners are fine, thank you. It's my car that isn't."

"You two *are* back together. I thought so. And you sound just like old times." Willa smiled as she looked from one to the other. "I recollect one of your arguments I overheard about which shop around here had the best barbecue. You two could sure stage a war of words back when we were in high school. I never did find out who won that argument. Do you remember?"

"No, I don't." She didn't remember an of their arguments except the last one. "I'll have the chicken salad."

"Bring her a cup of gumbo, too."

"I don't want gumbo. Just the chicken salad."

"You haven't tasted Lou's gumbo. Her daddy brought the recipe with him from New Orleans."

"It is good, Missy. You ought to at least taste it. Daddy's right proud of it."

"Go ahead and bring it." The longer this went on the longer she'd have to put up with Jimmy's company and the longer she'd have to fight her growing attraction to him.

She had to find a way to make it clear to Jimmy once and for all that she was tired of his playing games with her when he was going to marry Julie.

She was still searching for a way long after the meal was over, and all the way home.

"Jimmy, I am not going to get involved with you again. Okay?" *May as well get it out into the open.* They were outside her house but still in the car. "I'm just getting over that disastrous mistake that I made. Because of me, Walter got hurt. He hadn't done anything wrong. It was all my fault. I am not going to make another mistake. Back when we were going together, you and I broke up more times than either of us can count. I can't take that again. I need time to regroup; to get myself together." She shook her head.

Breaking up with Walter had hurt her, too, even though it was her doing, but it hadn't hurt more than when she realized Jimmy had moved on with his life, and was practically engaged to Julie. Now here he was again, stirring her up and making her remember old times with him. She couldn't take the heartache again. Maybe not going back to Philly wasn't such a good idea after all.

She would definitely leave Mayland at the end of the school year. She had to put some distance between them before she did something else stupid. She sighed. But first she had to get through the coming school year. She got out of the car.

She didn't want to, but she thought of the difference between the time Jimmy first came to Mayland and the way he was now.

Jimmy had turned into a ladies' man. Back when he first hit town, all the girls tried to get his attention, but he had ignored them. All except for her. At least she thought he had. Maybe he was seeing Julie on the side back then, and after their big breakup, Julie got to let the world know that Jimmy was hers.

Missy sighed. He must have decided to take advantage of her attraction to him. He was trying to start things up with her again even though he had Julie. Missy had to remember that. No matter how she felt with Jimmy, he had Julie. Julie had said so. Maybe Julie made him feel the same way he pretended that Missy did. She didn't know. There was a lot she didn't know anymore.

She swallowed hard and went into the house. She never looked back.

No, it was not okay that Missy didn't want to get involved with him again. It hadn't been okay when they had broken up years ago, but he hadn't had sense enough to realize it then. She wasn't getting away this time. If he had thought telling her so would have made a difference, he would have.

He pulled out of the yard.

If not loving somebody was as easy as saying you weren't going to, I would have been over her years ago, he thought.

A week from Friday, just as he promised, Jimmy pulled up into the yard. Missy ran to the door as he was getting out of her car.

"Thank you, thank you." She ran toward him and reached out, but stopped before she touched him.

"You're welcome." Desire flared in his eyes. "I wouldn't have objected to a warmer thank-you, you know." He put his hands in his side pockets.

"Yeah. Well." Missy blushed. "Come on in. What do I owe you?"

"A glass of iced tea is my delivery charge."

"Jimmy . . ."

"And you have to come to the Chargers softball game with me tomorrow afternoon."

"The Chargers game?"

"You have to remember them. You used to play first base."

"I'm not going to the game with you."

"Why not? They're on a hot winning streak. We expect them to take the championship this year."

"I'm not going to the game with you. I told you. I'm not getting involved with you."

"I invited you to a softball game. I didn't say anything about involvement. It's not like I suggested we go down by the creek out at my place. You remember that spot under that big willow where the ground is covered with star moss as thick as a mattress?"

He knew she remembered. He wasn't playing fair. That had been their spot. With the long willow branches brushing the ground around the edges, under the tree was like a woodland bedroom, and they had used it as such.

Missy looked away, hoping Jimmy hadn't seen the desire he had stirred inside her. By the creek was where he had taught her to make love. Sweet, hot love. Every chance they got. Until . . .

After Rhonda Patterson dropped out in the eleventh grade because she was pregnant, under that willow tree was where they had some heavy discussions, too. Nathan quit school and got a job after he and Rhonda got married. Some of the other girls quit speaking to Rhonda, but Missy didn't. She knew, no matter how careful she and Jimmy were, that could have been them.

It was a sunny October day when she and Jimmy decided to hold off on their lovemaking until she graduated and they got married.

The willow branches swayed in and out over them sitting under the tree that day. She told Jimmy how she wanted a long gown and him waiting for her at the altar. She had her wish book with her. She told him she wanted to know he was marrying her because he wanted to, not because he had to.

Together they had explored ways to please each other, but they hadn't had sex again. Sometimes it was Jimmy and sometimes she was the one to stop, but they managed. That was years ago, but she still remembered how it felt to be one with him.

She sighed. Julie didn't have to remember from a long time ago. Maybe her memory just had to reach back to last night.

"Missy." Jimmy touched her arm. She pulled away and he didn't pull her back. "I want you to come see a game with me." The look in his eyes said he wanted a lot more than that. It was easy to recognize a look when she was fighting to keep from letting the same one show in her own eyes.

"What's the bill for my car? What did you have to do to fix it?"

"I changed the timing belt."

"The timing belt? That's what you said was wrong at the beginning. What about the alternator? How about the 'accidents under the hood waiting to happen'? What about all the other things you talked about that were wrong?"

"You're the first person to complain because the bill was smaller than expected."

"Jimmy T, you said . . ."

"I never said those other things were wrong. I said I had to check them out to make sure they were okay." He shrugged. "I do a thorough job when I work on a car."

"Gertrude should have been ready in two days."

"Gertrude." He shook his head slowly.

"I like the name Gertrude."

"Anything you like is fine with me."

Missy looked out to the road. Nothing was there, but she had to look somewhere. Anywhere but at Jimmy.

"Who's coming to take you back to the garage?"

"Nobody. They're all busy fixing cars. You know I like to get cars back to the owners as soon as possible. You have to take me back to the garage." He smiled. "Or I can wait until your mama gets in. She'll be glad to run me into town. You and I can spend the rest of the day together, and you can tell me all about Philadelphia. Who knows? I might decide to visit there one day."

"You don't want to travel, remember? You're satisfied to stay here forever."

"That was a stupid, narrow-minded statement, and I've regretted making it ever since." He shook his head. "That's what started our last argument. The one that counted. I've changed my mind about a lot of things since then." He stared at her. Desire reared up in his eyes, and reached her. "But I haven't changed my mind about everything." His words came softly. "I'll always feel the same way about some things, some people; one person."

"Don't. There's no way I'm going back to those volatile times between us. I never knew when an argument was going to break out. I told you I don't want to hear it again."

"I'll wait for you until you do." He didn't move, but it seemed as though he had closed the space between them. No way was she going to let him wait here with her for her mother to come home.

"Let me get my purse." She glared at him all the while battling for control. "I don't believe nobody could follow you to take you back."

"I have a busy garage."

She wanted to remind him that if he spent more time at the garage and less time bothering her, he'd get a lot more work done.

Bothering her was right. He'd been bothering her since she had looked down the road in the direction of his house when she first got back home. When would he stop having this effect on her? If the answer wasn't 'in the next five seconds,' she didn't want to hear it.

She got in her car hoping Jimmy didn't plan to talk his trash all the way to town.

The ride to Jimmy's garage felt ten times as long as it actually was. Missy had thought the worst thing would be for Jimmy to spend the ride trying to talk her into letting him get close again. She was wrong. Jimmy didn't say anything. At least not with words. He didn't have to. His look was stronger than any words he could have used.

She spent the drive trying to remember the way to the place she could find without thinking, when she was alone. She fought to keep from turning the air conditioner up full blast to cool her off when Jimmy's thigh brushed against hers. She glared at Jimmy when she thought she could keep her real feelings from showing in her eyes. That didn't happen often.

"Thanks for bringing my car." She didn't bother to turn off the motor when she pulled up in front of the garage.

"What time should I pick you up tomorrow?" The man had more than his share of nerve.

"I'm not going with you. I told you. Take . . ." She swallowed hard. "Take somebody else." She almost said Julie. Wouldn't he enjoy hearing the catch in her voice if she had said that? Wouldn't he love knowing she would care if he did take Julie?

"I don't want anybody else." He stared hard. "I'll be by at one o'clock to pick you up. That will give us time to find a good seat."

"There's never a problem with finding a seat."

"So you think one-fifteen is time enough? Okay. See you then."

"I'm not going to the game with you. I'm not going anyplace with you. Not Saturday, not ever."

Randall pulled his head out from under the hood of the car he was working on.

"I mean it, Jimmy." Her words were suddenly too loud as a motor was shut off.

Benny peeped out of the garage door. Jimmy kept walking as if suddenly he had lost his hearing.

Missy watched as he turned the corner to go into his office. He never looked back. Blast Jimmy Tanner Scott.

She was still blessing him out when she pulled into her yard a half hour later.

No way was she going to that game tomorrow.

ELEVEN

Missy slowly drove her car into a space in the parking lot outside of the town ball field. She would go to the game. Where else could she go? Besides, it would be nice to see how her old team was doing. What she would not do, was go with Jimmy.

She turned off the motor, but she didn't get out. She leaned back against the headrest and stared at the field.

Starlings scratched for breakfast beside second base, and a flock of crows strutted and muttered in the outfield. Two squirrels scurried around under the tree near the fence. The bleachers, new since Missy had last seen the field, were empty.

The scrambling of two more squirrels playing tag up and down a tree on the other side of her car was the only sound that reached her. She felt as if she was the only person for miles around. She took a deep breath of the clean country air. Somebody had planted honeysuckle nearby. She looked around the vacant park. An empty swing swayed in the slight morning breeze. It was even too early for kids to be on the playground.

"What did you expect?" Her words to herself hung in the air outside the deserted field. "Folks don't even show up for a professional ball game five hours early." She felt like the third little pig in the fairy tale, only dumber. He had a good reason for arriving early. *Maybe I'm avoiding a wolf, too.* She glared at the field. Doggone Jimmy Tanner anyway.

If she had stayed at home, she knew he would have shown up early, but she didn't have a clue as to how early, so here she was waiting at the ball park as if it were ten minutes to game time instead of five hours.

She was glad she left the note for her mother on her bed instead of on the kitchen table. If she were lucky, her mama wouldn't know exactly how early she had left the house. The last thing she needed right now was her mama asking questions. She shook her head.

No, that was the next-to-the-last thing she needed. The last thing she needed was Jimmy bothering her. She took another deep breath. Or was that the first thing she needed?

She put the car in gear and headed into town. Maybe a cup of tea would soothe her. She shook her head. She doubted it.

Dottie Jones came over as soon as Missy slid into a booth in Stu's Place.

"I heard you were back in town. It's good to see you." She handed Missy a menu. "I expect you find things boring around here after all the years you spent in the big city."

"Boring isn't hardly the way I'd describe how things have been since I got home." She wouldn't mind a little boring. Boring would be nice about now, but the only way that stood a chance of happening was if Jimmy closed up shop and left town, and that was as likely to happen as today's game being called on account of snow.

"How have you been, Dottie?"

"Fine. Randall and me are still happily together. We got three kids now." She lifted her chin. "I know folks were counting backwards when Randall Jr. was born, but they got to nine before they got back to our wedding date." Her chin went up a bit more. "Our kids are stair steps, but however close they are, and how many kids we have is our own business as long as we don't ask nobody to help us take care of them."

"You're right about that, Dottie. Your business is your business." She smiled and was rewarded with a smile from Dottie. "You and Randall always did know what you wanted out of life. You were friends ever since grade school. Then it grew into something deeper when you got older." She shook her head. "It must be nice to be so sure."

There was a time when Missy had been sure, too. If she and Jimmy had been as sure as they thought they were, they'd be celebrating their anniversary about the same time as Dottie and Randall. Missy wouldn't have a teaching degree, but she and Jimmy would have had kids by now. Maybe a boy who looked just like Jimmy with that same slow smile, and that side-to-side walk of his and . . .

"We were just blessed that way." Dottie's voice cut into Missy's thoughts. She stared at her. "I'm sorry things didn't work out for you and Walter." She frowned. "To tell you the truth, I was surprised when I heard you were engaged to him. I always expected you and Jimmy T to follow me and Randall down the aisle."

Dottie wasn't the only one. Missy had expected that, too. She didn't answer. Instead, she let Dottie go on.

"The whole town was surprised the day Miss Elberta's announcement appeared on the society page of the *Mayland Times*." Dottie shrugged. "Still in all, your business is your business, same as mine belongs to me." She smiled. "I'm sure you know what you're doing, being a college graduate and all." Her smile widened as she pulled out a pad. She didn't notice that Missy didn't smile back. "Now, what can I get you this morning?"

Missy placed her order for tea and a breakfast that she knew she wasn't going to eat, and wondered what she would do for the next four hours and forty-five minutes. She should have all the answers, being a college graduate and all.

In spite of her predicament, Missy had to smile to herself. Why disillusion Dottie? Let her think a college degree came with instructions for the rest of your life.

Missy dragged her breakfast out as long as she could. After three cups of tea she felt she was going to float away. She looked at her still-full plate. She had rearranged the food, but it was still all there. What was she going to do with four hours?

She started walking toward the business district. So many years had passed since the last time she had been in town, it would be interesting to look at the displays in the shop windows. And it would use up some more time.

By the time she got back to her car after walking through town, she knew the details of every single item in every single shop window display. One thing was easy to remember. Every window had a poster of the Charger game schedule and a sticker declaring the shop owner a booster in good standing. A few had a WE CLOSE FOR CHARGER HOME GAMES sign on the door.

She sat in the car wishing the town were bigger.

Finally, with twenty minutes to game time, she drove to the field.

She walked toward the stands from the far corner of the parking lot, surprised at the turnout. A lot of shop owners must have forgotten to post a WE CLOSE FOR CHARGER HOME GAMES sign in their windows. They must have figured it was understood. The stands looked as if the whole town had come out to see the game. Jimmy had been telling the truth about the crowd, but there were still plenty of empty seats.

Missy climbed to the fourth tier and found a seat beside a family she didn't know. She had just settled in when Jimmy appeared at the gate. As if she had a tracking device and he were tuned to the frequency, he headed straight for her.

The fact that there wasn't any room beside her didn't stop him from coming over. Missy glared. Jimmy ignored it.

"Afternoon, Miss Harriet. Can I squeeze in here?" Jimmy flashed a smile at the woman sitting beside Missy, and she fumbled with the bags on her lap. She looked as if, if Jimmy had asked, she would have handed over the deed to her house and everything she owned to him.

"Of course, Jimmy." The woman smiled back and just sat in the same spot. Then she gave her head a little shake before she turned to the four children beside her. "You kids move on down so Mister Jimmy can have a seat."

"I appreciate it." There was his smile again, all lit up from the inside, and glowing like a large candle in a window. "Thanks, kids. I appreciate it."

Missy moved over too, but Jimmy sat right up against her as if the space were still too small. It was small, but not that small. His thigh brushed against hers a couple of times—three to be exact—before it settled as though it belonged there resting against hers. Missy had to battle not to look for smoke coming from where they touched. She would have moved farther away, but she knew Jimmy would only close the space.

It was going to be a long afternoon even if one pitcher threw a no-hitter, and the other only allowed one run.

The teams were still warming up when Julie came through the gate. She looked at Jimmy as if he had a homing device that she was set to.

"There's Julie."

"Well, Missy, I wasn't sure you knew I was here." Jimmy wrapped his fingers around hers.

"Stop." She tried to pull away. "Julie will see."

"So what if she does?" A frown creased Jimmy's forehead. He looked really puzzled. What was it with him?

"Don't you care?" She tried again to pull her hand away, but he tightened his hold. "Shouldn't you go sit with her?"

She wanted to say it wouldn't matter to her if he did, but she didn't think she could get the lie out.

"Why would I care about her seeing us?" He leaned closer and stared into Missy's eyes. He looked as if he was searching her face for answers to her questions and his. "Why should I want to sit with her?"

"Why?" She frowned at him. "Aren't you two going together?"

"We go out from time to time, but it's nothing serious."

"That's not true. That's not what she told me. She told me that you . . ."

Missy looked around. There were more people staring at them, now, than were looking at the field, where the players were in place, and "play ball" had just been ordered.

"What did Julie tell you?"

"You know." Missy looked around. Not a soul within ten feet around them was watching the game. A pop foul could have beaned any one of them if it came into this section of the stands. "I'm not going to go into it, now. Certainly not here."

On the other side of Jimmy, Harriet was watching them like they were a show on television, and something exciting was about to happen.

"When?"

"When what?"

"Let's get out of here. We have to talk."

"What about the game?"

"It's not important anymore. Come with me."

As Missy stood she caught Julie's glare. She looked

around. Folks were looking at her as if she were the one who just hit a long ball out to left field.

Jimmy reached for her hand, but she wouldn't let him hold it. Who knew what the crowd would do if they saw that?

She felt the stares follow her as she made her way behind Jimmy down the bleachers and out of the field. She wished she had sat on the corner just inside the gate.

By evening the whole town would be talking about what they had seen and heard at the softball game. The story would be passed on, and added to until it wasn't anything like what really had happened. Just like the kid's game Gossip, but this wasn't a game.

Jimmy grabbed her hand and led her to a picnic table under a maple on the other side of the park. This time she didn't try to pull away from him. The yells from the field behind them told her something exciting had happened, but it didn't matter.

"What were you talking about back there?" Jimmy sat on the table with his feet on the bench the way he used to when they were in school, and were going to spend the rest of their lives together.

"Julie told me that you two were practically engaged."

"She told you what?" His eyes widened.

"She said she's sorry about my wedding being called off because you and she had planned to come together. She said she was going to look for ideas for her own for when you proposed to her." Missy glanced at him. "She said she expected that to happen any day."

"She said what?" Jimmy's repeated the same question. His face looked as if it had never learned to smile.

"Jimmy, I don't know what kind of game you're playing. I don't want to be the cause of anybody getting hurt like I hurt Walter. I don't want to come between you and Julie."

"There is no me and Julie. As far as Walter is con-

cerned, he's a man, not some kid. You think he'd want
you to marry him just because you don't want to hurt his
feelings?"

Missy shook her head. It did sound silly put like that.

"Then I think it's best to drop the Walter stuff, get on
with your life and let him get on with his. Don't you
agree?"

Jimmy's voice wavered at the end as though he wasn't
as sure of himself as his words sounded.

Missy was glad she wasn't the only one feeling that way.

"There's never been anything serious between me and
Julie. Never."

"But back at the prom . . ."

"I only went with her to make you mad. I explained it
to Julie when she asked me to take her. She said she'd go
along with it." He looked at her hard. "I thought if you
saw me with her it might make you come to your senses.
Then you waltzed in on Walter's arm like that was where
you wanted to be. You . . ."

"Me come to my senses? What about you? You were the
one who said . . ."

"Missy, all of that happened a long time ago. Besides
being young, we were different people back then. Both
of us. I didn't have sense enough to know what was important, and what to let slide. And neither did you." He
stared off, but Missy knew he wasn't seeing the other side
of the street.

"You're not almost engaged to Julie?"

"Do you think I'd be knocking myself out trying to
spend time with you if I was in love with her?"

Missy shrugged.

"Do you think I'd have kept your car so long if she was
the one I want?"

I was right about my car. She blinked. It wasn't important
any more.

"Missy, why can't we get back to where we were?"

"I need some breathing time. Some time to myself. I'm not going to get involved with anybody. Not you. Not anybody else. I told you that. I can't make another mistake like I did with Walter. It hurts too much." She breathed deeply.

"You think it would be a mistake for us to get back together again?" He lifted her hand and traced around each knuckle as he used to do in the old days. Something stirred inside her, and settled below her waist, like in the old days.

She pulled away. She didn't want to think about the old days. The same differences between them then were still there beneath everything now, even under the feelings. What if she got called back to Philadelphia after this year? Or maybe she'd decide to go to some other place as she had been thinking. There were teacher shortages in a lot of places, even if not in Philadelphia. What would happen between her and Jimmy then if they got back together now? Her wanting to go places was what broke them up in the first place. She still wasn't through exploring the world, and he wasn't interested in even getting started.

"I don't know. I'm not sure about anything anymore. Things are still so . . ." She shook her head. "I just don't know."

Jimmy stared at her and let out a deep breath. He looked glad she hadn't said yes, it would be a mistake.

"We can take it as slow as you want to. Just don't cut me off without giving me another chance." He touched the side of her face. "Let's start over, Missy. Let's pretend we just met. Let's pretend there was never anything between us."

There isn't that much pretending in the world, Missy thought as Jimmy went on.

"I got the call about your car, and met you for the first time when I came out to tow it into the shop." His stare was full of hope. He squeezed her hand. "What did you think when you first saw me?"

Missy shook her head as she remembered how her heart felt squeezed, and her body ached for his touch when she saw him through the screen. She wasn't about to touch that one. She stared at their fingers laced together against his leg as though that's how they belonged again.

Jimmy squeezed her hand as if to show that they did.

"Standing at Miss Jenkins's door, you were the most beautiful woman in the world." His gaze caressed her face as surely as if he had touched her. He feathered a path from her hand, around her wrist and up her arm.

Missy watched as his fingers inched their way toward her elbow. His words were lost to her, blotted out as his fingers stroked the inside of her arm as they used to, leaving a trail of fire the way they used to when she and he belonged together.

"I still think so. Beautiful wide eyes, cute nose." He stroked a finger down her nose. "Cheeks the color and flavor of honey." His finger feathered down her cheek and stopped beside her mouth. Missy held her breath. "And your luscious, full mouth. Sweeter than anything I have ever tasted." He bent his head toward her. "There's nobody more beautiful or desirable in the whole world."

She watched him move close, closer. She licked her lips when his mouth got near hers. Peppermint tickled her nose. She closed her eyes, ready. Waiting. Tingling.

"But I don't want to rush things."

Missy's eyes popped open. She watched Jimmy move his head away from hers.

"After all, we just met. I don't want to start off wrong. I wouldn't want you to think I'm trying to rush you. I can look at you and tell you don't kiss on the first date, and this isn't even a date." He put her hand on her thigh, patted it and moved his away. Then he leaned farther back.

Missy blinked. Frustration and anger tumbled together inside her with a large dab of confusion thrown in. Her anger got stronger as the twinkle in Jimmy's eyes grew brighter. Jimmy Tanner Scott was a tease. Missy leaned back, too. There wasn't any reason to stay close anymore.

"What do you think, Missy?"

"About what?" Did she look as confused as she felt?

"You think you can be that good at pretending?"

"I can make believe as well as you can." *Make believe was what I'd been doing since I got back home, wasn't it?* She was so good at it she had herself convinced for a while. A short while, it's true, but she had managed to fool herself.

"Anything is possible if you believe, but first you've got to truly believe." Jimmy reached toward her, but pulled his hand back before he touched her.

Why did that disappoint her? She wasn't going to get involved with him again, she reminded herself. Why had he pulled back if he wanted to get close to her again? She tried to focus on his words.

"Remember when we decided things were moving too fast, and we pulled back on the intimacy? Rhonda and Nathan scared us when she got pregnant. We were kids then, and that made it harder to stop, but we held off." He changed position. "I had some hard times, no pun intended." He laughed. "But we both managed to get through it. If we could be together and pretend back then that we didn't want to be wrapped in each other's arms with me inside you, and you closed tight around me, we can pretend anything."

Images of them together under their willow tree flooded her mind. The striped blanket they had put over the moss was as bright in her memory as it had been years ago when it was their bed covering.

"I'm not even sure I'll stay here after the school year is over. I still want to go places, see new things. I'm not sure I want to go back to our times together. I've changed. I . . ."

"Think about it. Okay? I know we can work through our differences. Just think about it. I'll call you." He stared at her. "I would ask you to call me when you're ready to move our relationship on, but I'm afraid things would be stuck like this forever if I wait on you to make the first move."

He stood. He shoved his hands into his pockets as if he was unsure of what to do with them. "I'll call you, you hear?" Then, head down, he walked away.

Missy was still sitting at the table when the first people came out through the gates. She pulled herself from the bench and got into her car. She drove up and down a few roads before she decided to go on home. There weren't any answers out there.

She was barely in the door when the phone rang. *Let the machine answer,* she thought, until she heard Nettie's voice.

"What's going on?"

"What do you mean?"

"This is me, your old friend, remember. I'm on the first line of communication."

"Nothing's going on."

"That's not the way I heard it."

"If folks paid for each call they made, the phone company would clean up next month."

"I guess there's no truth to the current rumor that your wedding is back on, only this time Jimmy T will be the groom?"

"What?"

"That's what I heard not two minutes ago."

"I don't know why I'm surprised. Folks couldn't mind

their own business in Philly, either. I wonder if there's any place where they can."

"If so, there's either a nonstop pace and everybody is struggling to keep up, or everybody lives in total isolation. So give. What really happened?"

"Jimmy sat beside me at the game."

"That's it?"

"Not quite. We left the game and went out to one of the picnic tables to talk."

"No wonder you're stirring things up. You left a Charger game? That's practically against the law. They're gonna be state champions. I would have been there if I hadn't had to work. The few women who are not Charger fans come to my shop. You couldn't wait until the game was over? What was so pressing?"

"Jimmy wants us to start over. Why didn't you tell me he wasn't engaged to Julie?"

"Julie Gaskins? What gave you that idea?"

"Julie did."

"I didn't think even in her dreams that Jimmy would be serious about her. She has a better imagination than I thought. Now, what about it? Are you going to get back with him?"

"I don't know. I honestly don't know what I'll do."

"There's no time limit on making up your mind. Take your time, and do what you feel is best for you. At least 'don't know' is a step past 'no.' Now for the reason I called: let's go to that Chinese restaurant over in Florence that we love. I have a taste for their Grandfather Chicken. I don't know whose grandfather he is, but if he cooks like that, he can adopt me any time." Nettie's chuckle made Missy smile. She was still smiling after she hung up. Maybe Nettie could help her get her mind off her problems the way she used to be able to do.

* * *

It was bound to happen and two days later it did. Missy had been dreading her first meeting with Walter after the breakup. She knew it would be awkward and it was.

She was coming out of The Teachers' Store at the mall when she ran into Walter.

"How have you been?" Walter's gentle smile was the same. Missy was afraid to look into his eyes, afraid sadness would greet her.

"Fine, Walter." She made herself look at him. "How about yourself?"

"I heard you and Jimmy T are back together."

"We're not back together. He sat beside me at the game and we went out to talk. I don't need for you to tell me how you found out we were at the game together. Everybody seems to know that. Or why you think we're a couple again. They all seem to think that. Those few folks who weren't at the game were told by somebody who was." She didn't tell him about the rumor that Jimmy was taking Walter's place at her wedding. Maybe, by some miracle, he hadn't heard that one. "A national news agency would be proud to have an organization as efficient as the local grapevine." She sighed. "I don't think it's just in Mayland, either."

"I can't recall exactly who told me about what happened at the game." His look pinned her in place. "They weren't talking about the Chargers' win."

"Walter, I swear, when you and I broke up I was not seeing Jimmy T. I'm not seeing him now. After we left the game he asked me to go out with him again, but I haven't decided. I don't think I'm ready for that. Some differences are too big to overcome." She shrugged. "I'm not sure what will happen."

"I believe you, Missy. And I know you're right about differences." His smile was still gentle. "I reckon you don't have time for a cup of coffee? Or I guess it would be tea on your part."

"Sure, Walter. I got time."

"Hey, Missy."

Missy turned. Kate Turner's grin was wide, but it didn't reach her eyes. Missy wondered if she had a cell phone so she could spread this latest tidbit through the town as soon as she walked away. Most folks don't change after high school.

"Hi, Kate."

"How you been? I heard tell you were back in town. You and Walter getting back together? Or maybe you never broke up. And what about Jimmy? I heard you were with him at the game. Can't make up your mind, huh? Or maybe you decided you want both." She turned from Missy and faced Walter. "Hey, Walter. You charm Missy back? Wonder what Jimmy T will say about that when he finds out."

"Hi, Kate. How are you and Dexter getting along?" Walter's words were low, but they were powerful.

The smile disappeared from Kate's face and she stepped back.

"Same as usual. I got to go." She rushed past and never looked back.

"What was that about?"

"She and Dexter broke up three weeks ago. I heard he's seeing some woman over in Florence."

"There's a lot of that going around. Breaking up, I mean." Missy blinked. "You still want to get a cup of coffee?"

"If you still have time."

"Let's go."

They walked to the restaurant at the end of the strip. Missy didn't care who saw her. She wasn't doing anything wrong.

"Hey, Missy. I'm surprised to see you here."

Missy watch as Lois dropped first one menu and then the other onto the floor. She picked them up, wiped them

on her apron and handed them out. She stared from one
to the other.

"Hi, Lois. How have you been?"

"Busy minding my own business and wishing other folks
did the same." Her smile was wide. "What can I get you
folks?"

Lois was another one who hadn't changed since high
school. Missy smiled and gave her order. Walter did the
same.

Walter talked about a house he had just closed on.

"It was only on the market for a month before it sold."

"I'm not surprised. You always were a good salesman."

"Not always." He stared at her. Then he smiled again.
"I guess I knew from the start that you never got over
Jimmy. I just kept hoping that maybe over time . . ." He
shook his head. "That's over. No sense rehashing it. I
hope you all can settle your differences. I really do. You
deserve to be happy."

"Walter . . ." Missy swallowed hard and wiped at her
eyes.

"Missy, I've been thinking about what you said when
you broke things off."

Missy clinched her hands. She hoped he wasn't going
to heap guilt on her. She had just about gotten rid of the
old load.

"It's okay, really. You were right. My feelings were hurt,
not my heart. When I think of all the years wasted on an
illusion I had . . ." He shook his head. "I realize you did
me a favor."

He reached over and squeezed Missy's hand and she
squeezed back.

"Mother is trying to set me up with Marlene Claxton.
She works at the bank." He stared at Missy. "I told Mother
to mind her own business."

Missy blinked. She'd better have her hearing checked.

"She does interfere a bit," Walter went on. He shrugged. "More than a bit."

"I'm not going to touch that one, okay?"

"Okay." Walter laughed and Missy joined him.

"Remember Martha Duke? I took her to dinner last night. I had forgotten how much fun she is."

"I remember Martie." Walter and Martie? Martie had gone through green and purple before she settled for maroon for her hair color on senior day. "You mean Martie who saved her leftover chemicals for the last day of class, and mixed them over the Bunsen burner? That Martie?"

"Yes, that Martie. She came back about a month ago. She finished med school and plans to open a clinic." Walter's face couldn't hold a wider grin. "There's only one Martie."

"Martie's a doctor?"

"Just finished an accelerated program."

"Think that spot is still on the high school lab ceiling?"

"That was just a harmless prank."

"Harmless prank? She could have killed us all. At the time you fussed about her lack of respect for public property and how she had no sense of responsibility. Who are you and what have you done with my friend, Walter?"

"People change, Missy. Even me." He patted her hand. "You were right. 'Like' isn't enough. I'm glad you wouldn't settle for it." He squeezed her hand. "Thanks. And I'm glad you still consider me your friend. I like that."

When Lois set the little steel teapot on the table, Missy was still trying to digest the change in Walter.

"I reckon I'd best get back to the office." Walter placed his napkin on the table beside his empty dessert plate, and picked up the check. "It was great seeing you. I wish you luck with Jimmy."

"Make sure you invite me to your wedding."

Walter looked as though he had been sitting in the sun too long.

"I will if you promise to invite me to yours." He kissed her cheek and turned away.

Missy stared after him. Walter and Martie Duke. Miss Elberta would have a conniption big time.

Jimmy checked the diagnostic machine, left it and turned right back when he realized he couldn't remember what he had just read. He shook his head. He guessed things weren't moving as smoothly as he thought. Missy with Walter. Holding hands at the restaurant. Kissing.

After the third call giving him the news interrupted him, Jimmy knew it was true. He stared at the machine again and shook his head. Then he walked slowly into his office.

He had been pleased with how things went in the park during the game. Pleased? Shucks. If he had a couple of puddles and a rainstorm, he would have done a good imitation of Gene Kelly all the way home from the game. Missy had listened to him. True, she hadn't said she'd go out with him again, but she hadn't said she wouldn't, either. When he had leaned in close to her, she had leaned toward him. He swallowed hard. It had been all he could do not to kiss her. She had been ready. She had even parted her lips and closed her eyes. Jimmy squirmed.

If he had known that might be his last chance, he would have taken it. Right there in the park, in the middle of the day, regardless of who might see them, he would have held her close enough so he could feel if her heart was trying as hard to leap from her chest as his heart was from his. He didn't know how he did it this time, but it looked as though he had messed things up again.

He stared at the pile of papers on his desk, but he wasn't seeing them. He was seeing Missy and Walter together again.

TWELVE

The Fourth of July began with the early coolness that lulls you into believing the bright sunshine and searing heat won't come later in the day.

Missy woke up as excited as she always did on this annual cookout day. It was good to be home. Other towns celebrated on the weekend or the closest Monday. Not Mayland. The Fourth of July was the Fourth of July and, no matter what day it fell on, that was when the town celebrated.

When she was younger Missy had been glad because it meant she got to see a parade and fireworks when the Grand Strand celebrated and again when Mayland had its celebration.

Yesterday hadn't had any early fireworks. She had seen Walter, even had lunch with him. He had found somebody else and moved on. Everything with him had stayed calm and quiet, like always. She was still feeling mellow. In fact, she felt more at peace now than she had in a long time.

"You getting up or you plan to sleep the day away?"

Missy glanced at the clock. Eight o'clock. Couldn't her mother sleep in just once?

"I'm getting up. You won't give me any peace if I don't."

"Cranky as usual. Come on out to the kitchen when you're decent, and I don't just mean dressed, either."

Half an hour later, yawning, Missy went into the kitchen.

"The water's hot. Pour your tea and drink it so you can help me pack our lunch."

Missy looked at the table. Plastic bowls surrounded one platter heaped with fried chicken, and another with sliced ham.

"Mama, you got enough here to feed the whole town."

"If folks stop by, I have to be able to offer them a bite of something. It wouldn't be neighborly if I didn't." She looked at the table and grinned sheepishly. "I reckon I did overdo it a bit, didn't I?"

"Don't worry, Mama. We can eat leftovers for the next week." She looked at the table. "Probably the week after that, too."

"Don't get smart. Help me finish cutting the potatoes for the salad. I meant to fix it last night but I was just too tired. At least the weddings have slacked off. Several weekends I had to finish two gowns. The third weekend of June it was three." She flexed her hands. "I swear, if I have to sew on one more seed pearl I won't be responsible for my actions." She handed Missy a cutting board. "I never did see what's so magical about June for brides."

Missy winced.

"Oh, I'm sorry, baby. Me and my big mouth." Sally hugged Missy. Then she patted her cheek. "I'm so sorry."

"It's all right, Mama. I know how hard you've been working to make sure dreams come true." She managed a weak smile. "Maybe you can get some rest now that June is over. Of course, if you didn't insist on getting up at the crack of dawn every morning, you could get a lot more rest even during a busy workweek."

"I'm a morning person. I can't abide laying up in the bed."

"Tell me something I don't already know."

Missy cut one of the sweet potato pies, and slid the slice onto her hand.

"Melissa Miranda, you stop that. You know it's for later."

"Mama, I think three pies will be enough for the two of us."

"I meant to tell you something. I kind of . . . ," Sally mumbled. Not looking at Missy, she gave the table all of her attention.

She carefully moved the containers and platters around on the table as if looking for the perfect spot for each one. When she finally left them alone, they were where they had been before she had touched them.

"What did you mean to tell me, Mama?"

Sally acted as though she hadn't heard Missy, who was standing no more than two feet from her. She left her sentence hanging, and went out to the shed kitchen.

"What did you mean to tell me?" Missy licked her fingers. Then she cut another sliver of pie.

"It's not important." Sally set the large wicker basket on a chair. "Move the ham over and set the cooler on the table." She still didn't look at Missy.

"You wouldn't have brought it up if it wasn't important." Missy forgot the pie in her hand. She stared at her mama, who was looking like one of Missy's students caught pulling a prank. "Mama, what did you do?" Missy asked, but she had an idea of what her mother wasn't telling her. She hoped she was wrong.

"I invited somebody to share our lunch with us, that's all." Her mama still found somewhere to look beside at Missy.

"Does this somebody have a name?" Missy glared.

"It's just Diane."

"Uh-huh. And did you happen to include Miss Diane's son in the invitation?"

Sally took her time wrapping foil around the platter of chicken. She continued to mold it after she could have stopped.

"Mama, did you invite Jimmy to eat with us?"

"I reckon I did mention something to that effect."

"Mama, how could you?"

"I couldn't invite Diane and not everybody living in her house, especially her son. Besides, I don't see what's the problem with it. You're not engaged to Walter anymore. When I heard from a reliable source right there in my shop that you and Jimmy were back together, I thought this was a good idea."

"You know the most reliable source about me is me."

"Sometimes you keep things to yourself. Like when you decided to marry Walter. I had to hear it from Walter."

"I was going to call you and tell you."

"Yeah, and winter's going to come, too."

"I'm sorry, Mama."

"No problem. It's over and done with." She wrapped another bowl. "I hear Walter didn't waste any time grieving over you. He and Martie are so tight you couldn't fit a sheet of paper between them. You know you're still sweet on Jimmy. Why don't you quit fighting the attraction and admit it?"

"I never said I don't still have feelings for him."

"It's a good thing you didn't. I saw with my own eyes, right here in this very kitchen, how deep those feelings still run."

Missy blushed. It was her turn to fool with the containers that were already in place. "We still have differences we can't overcome."

"All differences can be pushed aside if you want to bad enough."

"I don't want to talk about it."

"Now see there, that's part of your problem. You leave differences sitting there, and never try to find a way around them. You've always been like that." She shook her head. "I kept hoping you'd outgrow it, but evidently you haven't. You're in what they call denial."

"Thank you, Dr. Sally, but I don't want to talk about this." She looked hard at her. "I'm not going to talk about it, okay?"

"Okay, baby." She sighed. "I'm just saying you can't keep on ignoring it, hoping it will go away, cause it won't." Sally hugged her. "Just take today as it comes. Don't fight it. Let later take care of itself later." She squeezed her shoulders before she let go. "Now, let's get this food packed and be on our way. There must be a hungry army waiting somewhere."

They laughed and finished packing the lunch.

Missy was glad her mother told her to expect Jimmy. Even when he knew she was going to see him, Jimmy was hard to resist. As for when she was surprised by him . . . She shook her head. . . . she remembered where that had led.

Missy and Sally got to the park at about ten o'clock. They found a spot as close to the tables scattered under the trees as they could. They weren't the only ones who believed in arriving early. A lot of cars were already in place.

They greeted other townspeople as they made their way to an empty table under a nearby tree. Missy was grateful they hadn't had to settle for one of the tables out in the open. The day was going to live up to July's reputation: hot and humid. Not a cloud blocked the already strong rays from throwing its full heat on the park. From time to time a weak breeze ruffled a few leaves as if it were practicing for a big gust later, but anybody who knew Mayland in July knew it was just a bluff. No breeze was going to give relief from the heat today. But nobody seemed to mind as they streamed into the park and claimed the last few tables waiting in the shade.

"I missed this last year. I don't know why I thought it

was more important to stay in Philadelphia for the celebration than to come home for the summer."

"Because you let your citified ways take over. I don't care if they do call themselves the Cradle of Liberty, there ain't nothing they can do on the Fourth of July that can hold a candle to the way we celebrate down here."

"You wouldn't be biased, would you?" Missy smiled at her. "Let's go look a the schedule," Missy said after they set the cooler and basket on the table. She grabbed her mama's hand. "I want to see what games we're going to play."

"You know it's the same old stuff as every year: relay races, three-legged races, potato sack races and every other kind of race they could think of. Last year, for the first time ever, they didn't hold the pie-eating contest, nor the hot-dog-eating contest. I'm glad. It's a waste of food, and what kind of message are we giving kids when, every other day of the year we tell them to eat slowly, and chew their food properly, and then we encourage them to eat like pigs on the Fourth of July? Of course they'll still have the watermelon-seed-spitting contest. I reckon that's all right so long as we make it clear to the kids that spitting is not acceptable at any other time."

"That's right, Mama. One day won't do any harm." Every year they had this discussion about that particular contest, but it wasn't as heated after Missy grew up as it had been when she was a kid, and had participated in it. Back then, each year Missy had to promise her mother that she knew spitting was not acceptable behavior, that she realized it was only okay this one time a year, and that she'd never spit at any other time.

"Let's go." She pulled her mother's hand as she used to when she was a kid.

It was a good thing they weren't in a hurry. They had to stop at each table and greet people as if it had been years since they saw them last, instead of a week at the most.

"Hey, Missy. Did your mama tell you I made that coconut cake you like so much?" A tiny woman smiled. "Even though you didn't peep into my shop, even though it's right next door to your mama's, I still want you to have a piece. Make sure you come on by and get a slice later."

"I'm sorry, Mrs. Williams, but I only came to the shop the first day I got here. I promise to come in and see what shoes you have. You know how I love shoes." Missy's smile widened. "But not as much as I love your coconut cake. I sure will be back for a piece later. Thank you."

They moved on, but only got as far as the next table.

"Good to have you back, Missy. I got my peach cobbler same as usual." Mrs. Wallace pointed to a covered glass dish. "Come sample it later."

"We're going to make ice cream later, too," Mr. Wallace added. "Make sure you get you some."

After Missy promised to come back, she and her mama continued to where the events schedule was posted.

"You better take part in every race they got, and think up some new ones," Sally said. "I lost count of the food offers, but you know you have to sample all of them, or somebody's feelings will be hurt."

"Yeah, I know. All of that food sampling will be a hard job, but somebody has to do it." Missy laughed and Sally joined in.

They finally got to the schedule and Missy gave it all of her attention.

"I have to do the potato sack race. I do it every year. I have to see if I can keep from breaking my record for the most falls." She pulled her finger down the list. "The hundred-yard dash. I have to do that, too. I used to be pretty good at it. I won the silver for my age when I was in high school. I'm counting on Jessica being out of the competition or at least being slower."

"I think you're in luck there. Jessica's due to have her second baby in two months. I don't expect she'll be doing any racing today."

"Good. Now if no ringer has moved to town since I left, I shouldn't have any trouble. I'm glad I did that jogging after school back in Philly and walking since I got back here." She chuckled. "I hope I haven't lost my edge." She laughed. "It won't matter if I have. It's all in fun, anyway." She read the rest of the list, commenting as she did.

Jimmy strolled behind Missy as she made her way to the schedule. Her white shorts and red-and-white striped blouse left no doubt that a woman was wearing them. Her hips swayed in that slow rolling way that drove him wild.

When he first mentioned her walk to her back in high school, she had no idea what he was talking about. He stopped trying to explain what he meant, but he took every opportunity that came his way to watch her move. And could she move. The writer who mentioned "poetry in motion" must have been talking about Missy.

She could cause a heat wave inside him in December. In July he didn't stand a chance. He moved in a direct line with her, but let the space between them stretch out. There wasn't any hurry. Walter had said as much and Jimmy believed him. Nobody ever said Walter wasn't honest.

Jimmy had called him hoping for the best, and not even thinking about preparing for the worst. Walter and Missy couldn't be back together. All those people who had called Jimmy and said so had to be wrong.

It took a while for Jimmy to decide to make the call.

He had to figure out a plan. In the end he attacked the problem head-on.

"You and Missy back together?" Nothing like subtlety to approach a sticky problem.

Walter had laughed.

Jimmy had never heard him laugh before. Walter had always been serious. Always. Maybe another time his laughter would be all right, but Jimmy didn't like it now.

"What's so funny? I asked you a serious question. Are you and Missy back together?"

Walter's laugh faded to a chuckle.

"What's funny is you and Missy. Still. I never realized just how funny you all are until now. Back when I had a major crush on her, I didn't find anything linking her to you the least bit amusing. Now . . ." He hesitated. "Now I can step back and observe. No, Jimmy, Missy and I are not back together. Martie wouldn't like it."

"Martie? Who's Martie?"

"You remember Martie. Purple hair, orange hair, green hair? I don't know which color hair you remember. It doesn't matter. That's in the past. Now it's a glorious, beautiful, rich, dark brown with auburn highlights. When the sun hits it just so, it's more beautiful than any color in a rainbow." His words drifted off and stopped. Then he started talking again. "No, Missy and I are not back together. We will not be back together ever again, and that's fine with me. We had a cup of coffee, that's all. Rather, I had coffee and she had tea like she always does. Folks have been calling and asking me if the wedding is back on, so I guess they've been calling you, too."

"You and Martie? Not you and Missy?"

"Jimmy T, you got it bad." Jimmy imagined Walter shaking his head. "I know the feeling. I got it bad, too, but for Martie, not Missy. The difference between you and me is, I'm doing something about it."

"You and Missy are not back together?"

"Good-bye, Jimmy. I got to go. Feel free to keep asking the same question. Be careful, though. Somebody might think you're looking for a different answer."

The soft click told Jimmy that he was the only one on the phone. He hung up and leaned back. A smile covered his face and smoothed out the crease that had been in his forehead. He hoped nobody came in and asked for a raise. He might give him a raise. He might even give away the whole dang shop.

He smiled now, as he remembered his conversation with Walter. It had been torture waiting until the picnic to approach Missy. He had made a headful of plans on the perfect way to do it, and scrapped every one. Why was love so difficult? "Because Missy won't cooperate" was the only logical answer. Logic. He couldn't count on logic when it came to her and him. Logic never entered into it. In the end he had decided to improvise as he went along. He was doing just that as he walked behind her, and imagined his hands caressing those hips that were causing his temperature to climb to dangerous levels.

He was grateful when she quit torturing him, and stopped at the schedule. He couldn't stand much more of just looking at her. Of course, it didn't help when she leaned closer and her shorts rounded to the contours of her cute, tight, tempting behind.

He closed the gap between them and bent over her shoulder. She still wore the same perfume that he had given her that last March that they dated. A "just because" gift he had told her.

Her face had lit up more than when she opened his gift at Christmas. She still wore the same scent. Did she think of him when she put it on? Did she imagine his hands on the places where she daubed it? Did she put a few drops . . . If he didn't stop he was going to be the first fireworks to go off.

"Don't forget the three-legged race," he said in her ear. Her hair smelled like spring rain. He closed his eyes and took a deep breath. "I still have my medal from when we won that six years ago. We have to see if we still have it after all these years." He tightened his hands in his pockets to keep from touching her. Too many years had passed. He knew he still had it for her, but did she still have it for him?

Jimmy's voice wrapped around Missy like a sizzling embrace. His aftershave shoved memories at her that almost made her lean back into him, and the heck with the folks all around them, and with whatever was making her keep her distance.

"Remember that day?" he asked.

She didn't want to remember. She didn't want to remember anything about her time with Jimmy, but wants never did control what happened where Jimmy was concerned.

"Hi, Jimmy. Where's your mama?" Sally smiled at him as if he weren't turning Missy's senses upside down.

"She's around here somewhere. She's got to make sure she speaks to everybody. Can't slight anybody, not even if she just saw them yesterday. We already put our basket on your table." He turned to Missy. "Let's go sign up for the races. We have to find a relay team to join, too."

"I'm not doing the three-legged race with you."

"Sure you are. It's tradition and you don't want to mess with tradition. Come on." He took her hand and tugged.

Her mother said take today as it came. His hand sent sparkles up hers that dragged her wants out of hiding. She'd have to try to do what her mother said. Jimmy wasn't giving her much choice, anyway.

After they signed up they scrambled with everybody else for a good place along the sides of the park to watch the parade. Let others march in streets. The Mayland parade marched down one side of the field, cut a line at the far end and turned and marched up the other.

The veterans marched at the front. Mr. Baldwin carried the flag as he had every year since Missy could remember the parade. He was older, but no less spry. Everybody watching stood a bit straighter, and some saluted as the flag went by.

The high school band was right behind with horns gleaming in the sunshine. When they reached the center of the field, they spread out like at a football game half-time show. The crowd hushed. "Yankee Doodle Dandy" was followed by "This is My Country." Missy joined her voice with the others. Jimmy's baritone came from beside her. She had forgotten how clear and exact it was. That was the only thing she had forgotten about him.

When the band started "You're a Grand Old Flag," Jackie Coleman, not even in grade school yet, led the majorettes. She stepped as high as the others. Her flawless baton routine brought cheers and encouragement.

"That's right, baby. You show them how it's done," came from further down in the crowd.

The gymnastics team came next, drawing gasps from the crowd at their high leaps and smooth tumbling. They finished with a pyramid that suspended all of them in time until they dismantled it as easily as they made it. Had they been inside, the cheers would have pushed against the ceiling. As it was, they soared into the cloudless sky.

The drill team followed, stepping smartly in their red pants and sparkling white shirts. They didn't seem to mind the heat as they performed a routine as complicated as one choreographed for a Broadway show.

"All right. This is what a parade should be."

Missy had forgotten how fantastic the parade was, and how much home-grown talent Mayland had.

She nodded and clapped her hands to the music with

the others as the team members cut corners as crisply as any military unit.

They left the field and the Cub Scouts came past, followed by the Boy Scouts. Last came the fire engine sparkling and shining in the sunlight. Smiles and more cheers followed as it slowly rolled off the field.

Folks gathered in small groups waiting for the kids who had performed to change and come back. They were greeted with hugs, kisses and pats on the back.

"Great job," and "I'm so proud of you" came from throughout the groups as families welcomed the parade members back. Then it was time for the games.

Missy questioned her good sense. Jimmy took so long tying the rope holding their legs together, Missy bet a kid learning to tie his shoelaces would have been faster. When did Jimmy become so clumsy? Why didn't she believe it really had to take him so long? Finally he finished. The look of satisfaction he threw at her told her her skepticism was correct. Why did he have to stand so close?

"Stop pulling away." Jimmy wrapped his arm around her shoulder and pulled her closer. "Put your arm around my waist. I won't bite you. At least not here in front of all these people. I'm not promising about later, though."

She pulled harder. This was definitely not the best idea she ever had.

"Don't pull away now." Jimmy put her hand around his waist and held it there. "The race is about to begin."

The cap pistol sounded and they took off.

At first Missy was only aware of the heat searing her where Jimmy's leg was tied to hers, but when Cliff and Dorothy passed them, her sense of competition kicked in.

"That's it. Just go with it. Pretend we're one person. We can do this," Jimmy assured her. "Our honor is at stake."

"Honor doesn't have anything to do with this. I just want to win." Missy concentrated on synchronizing her stride with Jimmy's. They passed the other couple, and ran across the finish line as smoothly as if they were one person.

"We can see that Missy and Jimmy T still have it," Judge Green said as he declared them the winners and placed gold medals around their necks.

Jimmy turned to Missy and smiled. As he stared at her mouth the smile faded leaving only want; leaving only need in its place.

Frozen in time, Missy watched as he inched his head down to hers. The flecks in his eyes darkened as desire flared in his eyes. She felt her face get warmer, and knew she was showing him the same feeling his face had showed her. She held her breath, waiting. Waiting. *I should move away. Now. Before it's too late.* Still she watched as Jimmy came closer. Closer still. She closed her eyes, ready. As he placed his lips firmly on hers, she knew it was too late to move. Way too late.

The crowd lined along both sides of the field roared its approval. Clapping and whistles grew louder as Jimmy wrapped his arms around her.

At first, when she heard the crowd, Missy tried to pull away from his kiss. She really tried. It should have been easy. Nothing was holding her. Jimmy's arms were still at his sides then. Nothing was holding her but his kiss. It may as well have been a chain and padlock.

"Jimmy," she sighed, but her word was swallowed by the kiss that was consuming her, taking her with him. His kiss was making promises and she was making him keep them.

Everything and everybody else faded, and only she and Jimmy existed in a timeless place all their own.

The whole length of her body molded to his hardness as if she were created with him in mind. This was where she belonged. With Jimmy. Like this.

Jimmy was the one who pulled away, slowly, as if to prepare her for the loss. When he did, Missy realized her hands had found their way around his neck as if this were a regular thing. She pulled back as if she had been burned, and blinked at him.

"Not in front of everybody," he said. "What will they think of me?"

Missy felt the blood rush to her face. The crowd was back around them. The twinkle in Jimmy's still-moldering eyes tried to tell her he had been in control the whole time. The huskiness in his voice said that wasn't true. Whistles and shouts grew louder.

"Way to go, Jimmy," somebody yelled. The crowd clapped in agreement. "Y'all go right on. Don't pay us no nevermind."

Missy jerked her arm away from him when he grabbed it. Then she strode off the field, redder than ever.

"Wait up." Jimmy caught up with her and matched her stride as easily as if they were still tied together.

"Go away."

"Is that any way to speak to your partner?"

"The race is over. You're not my partner anymore. I was a fool to partner with you, anyway. Go away."

"If you're a fool, you're a beautiful, sexy one."

She refused to look at him.

"I can't go away," he went on. "Winning teams are expected to hang out together. It's tradition."

"I never heard of such a tradition." She lengthened her strides.

"I just started it. Traditions have to start somewhere." His steps matched hers.

Finally she gave up and slowed her pace.

"Why don't you go find somebody else to bother?"

"There's nobody I'd rather . . ." He cleared his throat. ". . . bother. It's so . . ." He cleared his throat again. ". . . so stimulating bothering you." He put his hand on her arm and she let it stay. "Let's sit and watch the next races." He looked at the three gold medals swinging from her neck. "I assume you're through. You are giving somebody else a chance to win. Right?"

"I'm through. I didn't sign up for anything else."

"Good, let's find a shady spot." He held her hand.

She didn't pull away. *Just for today. This is just for today.*

"I don't know why I wore white shorts." Missy looked at the grassy spot beside Jimmy. "Maybe I'll just stand."

"You look great in them." That was the biggest understatement ever uttered in the history of the spoken word. "But then you look great in anything." His eyes darkened. "And nothing."

Missy took a step away, but he grabbed her hand.

"I can't help it if that's true. What I can do is promise to try not to mention it."

"That's a weak promise."

"It's the best I can do under the circumstances. Come on. Sit down. You can't stand through the rest of the contests. The water balloon toss, and the egg toss always take a long time, and we're tired from our race. Here." Jimmy pulled off his shirt and smoothed it out beside him. Close beside him. Too close. "Sir Walter Raleigh has nothing on me."

"I can't let you do that. Put your shirt back on. Grass stains are hard to get out." And the image of Jimmy without a shirt would be impossible to get rid of. Did working in the garage result in muscles like that, or did he lift weights?

She swallowed hard. If working at a garage could do that, every man in town should knock Jimmy's door down and offer to pay him for the privilege of working for him.

"Don't worry about the shirt. It will be worth a few grass stains to have you near. Come on. Sit down." He patted the shirt.

She reached to move it away from him.

"Oh no. The deal is, the shirt stays where it is, and I'll still keep my promise not to bite you."

Missy glared at him.

"Okay. I promise not to kiss you, either. At least not while you're sitting beside me. Okay? You know I always keep my promises."

Missy sat on the outer edge of the shirt. She wouldn't mind if one of the balloons burst on her. Maybe the cold water would cool her off.

After a while she managed to pay attention to the water balloon toss instead of Jimmy. She laughed with him as, one by one, the balloons burst and showered the unfortunate ones who missed catching them. The squeals of the losers only made the laughter stronger.

No matter how hard she tried, through the balloon toss, and then the egg toss, she couldn't ignore Jimmy. Not when he eased over so his thigh was against hers, and every few seconds it brushed against her leg, searing it; touching it in a stolen caress like a promise. His words about keeping his promises were as fresh in her memory as if only a second had passed since he said them.

Next time she'd wear dark shorts and the heck with grass stains. She only had to get through this one time.

Finally the winners of the egg toss, the last contest, were raising their hands in victory after the medals were placed around their necks. The last cheers sounded before the crowd broke up and folks wandered away.

Some kids raced to the playground equipment. Others tossed Frisbees around. Checkerboards and dominoes were brought out, and placed on tables. Folks gathered around the games, and were soon encouraging their favorites.

Missy went to her table.

"I'm starved."

"Me, too." Jimmy walked beside her. She didn't protest. Just today. She wouldn't let thoughts of faraway places and frequent arguments disturb her.

She sat at the table and didn't fuss when Jimmy sat beside her instead of on the other side. Just today.

"Mama, I'm stuffed." Missy pushed away her plate, and wiped her mouth on a pink flowered napkin. "I'll have a slice of sweet potato pie later."

"You had one at the house, but who's keeping track."

"I have room for a piece." Jimmy slid his plate to Sally.

"I'm with Missy on this. I'll get a piece later." Diane shook her head as Jimmy took a bite of pie. "I swear, I don't know where you're putting all that food."

"I'm a growing boy, Mama."

"If you're not careful, all your growing will be out." Jimmy laughed with them.

Missy doubted Jimmy would ever carry too much weight on his frame. If he did, it wouldn't take away from his appeal. Nothing would. She blinked. Where did that thought come from? More importantly, how could she get rid of it?

She was still wondering when they gathered with the others to watch the fireworks display sponsored by the Chamber of Commerce.

Jimmy's arm stole around her and felt as if it belonged. *Just take this day as it comes,* she thought as shooting stars and spider legs in the sky competed with Jimmy's caressing fingers on her arm for her attention. The heat from his body reached her, and lit a fire inside every bit as hot as any Roman candle.

His hands were causing shooting stars of their own to burst through her body. The fireworks would be jealous if they could feel. Sometimes not feeling was good.

THIRTEEN

Missy woke up Wednesday morning mulling over the cookout the day before. Yesterday she had taken her mama's advice. She had spent the day with Jimmy, keeping her mind in the present. For the most part. At times she had to battle with the past to keep it away, especially when he was so close that his touch seared her, and shot heat through her like water in the gully alongside the road during a sudden storm.

Yesterday she had walked with him, laughed with him and raced with him. She had sat on the grass beside him during the other contests, at the table when they ate and again during the fireworks that were mild compared to those that were going off inside her. At the end of the evening, although both her mama and Jimmy protested, she rode home with her mama. Through it all she had followed her mama's advice and not thought about to-morrow. Well, tomorrow was here.

She slipped out of bed and went to the kitchen. A note was propped up against the salt and pepper shakers on the table.

I've gone to the shop. I decided to let you sleep in this morning. I reckon that, after yesterday, you can stay in bed every now and again. Just don't let it get to be a habit. See you this evening.

                                                    You Know Who

Missy put on the kettle and fixed her cup of tea.

"I should mark this on the calendar. Mama let me sleep in."

She managed to keep thoughts of Jimmy away for a while, but they came pouring back as if the hot water released them as she filled her cup.

She shouldn't have listened to her mama. All yesterday did was let Jimmy find his way further into her heart. It would be that much harder to get him out. Nothing had changed. Not the way she felt about him, and not the different opinions they had about things.

Jimmy wants Mayland. I want the world. Jimmy is chicken and mashed potatoes and I'm whatever is different on the menu. Jimmy would live every day in T-shirts and jeans, while I want fancy dresses. I want live shows and he'll be satisfied with television every night.

She shook her head.

The arguments. The smallest thing could start one between us. Stuff like which shop has the best ribs. Neither one of us will ever back down, and, just like before, I'll walk away every time torn apart inside.

There was no reason to think it would be any different between them now than it had been years ago. She took a sip of tea.

She wasn't going to spend the rest of her life stuck in Mayland, wearing jeans and T-shirts every evening, watching television with Jimmy, and waiting for the next argument to show itself. That was not going to be her life.

What am I going to do? Anything else would have died in five years from neglect. Why hasn't my love for Jimmy?

She spent the whole day trying to figure it out, and

wasn't any closer to an answer when her mama came home.

"Clarissa picked up her gown this morning." Sally sat at the dinner table as Missy took her place across from her. "She has the funny notion that you plan on skipping her wedding come Saturday."

"I-I don't think I'm up to a wedding, Mama." Missy fidgeted in her seat. She stared at her empty plate. "Not so soon."

"You're being silly. So soon after what? Or before what? Nobody died." Sally leaned forward. "You were the one who called off the wedding. It's not like you were dumped. You got to move on with your life. Walter has. I hear he and Martie are gonna get married as soon as she finishes her residency."

"I can't do it. I just can't go to a wedding."

"Sure you can. You always could do anything you set your mind to. I know you've done harder things than this. It's just a wedding. In fact it's perfect. You can be seen by everybody, but they'll be giving their full attention to Clarissa. Nobody's gonna pay any mind to you." She threw a hard look at Missy.

Missy glanced at her, but quickly looked back at her plate. Sally went on.

"Clarissa's never been anything but kind to you. She's looked up to you since you were a junior and she was a sophomore over at the high school. You're the reason she went to college. You can't hurt her feelings like this. If she knew you were going to be in town, she most likely would have asked you to be in her wedding."

"Oh, Mama . . ."

"Besides, you can't let your poor old mama go by herself."

"Since when do you mind going anywhere by yourself?"

"Never mind that. Think about it. Think on all the

times I went somewhere with you when I didn't want to go."

"Mama, you don't fight fair."

"I'm not fighting at all, sugar, I'm trying to help you get through rough times." She walked around, kissed the top of Missy's head, then went back to her seat. "We won't talk about it anymore. Let's see if we can put a dent in these leftovers. We'll be eating them for a month. Please pass the ham."

Missy did, but she wasn't thinking about ham. She was thinking of the wedding. Everything her mama said made sense. Clarissa had never been anything but sweet to anybody, but especially to her. Clarissa wouldn't say anything the next time she saw Missy, but she'd be hurt. Missy sighed. She didn't need to cause any more hurt. She'd have to not only go, but look happy while she was there.

The early Thursday morning sun peeking through the lace curtains promised a sunny day. Friday and Saturday were supposed to bring more of the same. Missy groaned and turned over.

"Are you up, Missy? I'm on my way to the shop so I can't keep calling you. You said you have to meet Nettie, didn't you?"

"I'm up, Mama."

She heard her mama leave the house and drive off.

I must have been out of my mind when I agreed to go walking with Nettie before she opens her beauty shop this morning. She punched her pillow. *I must have been out of my mind, period, when I agreed to go walking this early. That's why cars were invented. So people wouldn't have to go everywhere on foot in the morning.* She turned over again.

Late afternoon and evenings were the time for walking and jogging, not the crack of dawn.

She was about to turn over yet again when the phone rang.

"Okay, Nettie, I'm on my way."

"No, you're not. You're still laying up in bed, aren't you?"

"I'm about to get up."

"You were about to turn over."

"Since when did you become psychic?"

"I don't need to be. I know you. I'll meet you at the high school track in exactly forty minutes. The later you are, the longer we walk. Got that?"

"Give some people a little power and they take over your life."

"You were the one who said walking together would give us a chance to talk while we exercise."

"I'm the one who must have been out of her mind when I agreed to go so early. Morning would be okay if it came later in the day."

"Quit complaining. You now have thirty-nine minutes to be at the track."

"Okay, I'll be there, but I'm not promising more than one lap, and I might have to crawl through that one."

"You get no sympathy from me. Thirty-eight minutes and still counting before W time."

" 'W time'?"

"Walk time. Wake up. Get with it. Get a strong cup of tea. See you in thirty-seven minutes."

Missy dragged herself out of bed and stumbled to the bathroom.

Twenty minutes later she had finished her tea and toast, pulled on jeans and a T-shirt and, still yawning, walked out the door.

Nettie was stepping from side to side as Missy pulled up beside the fence. When she got out Nettie stretched and twisted and stretched again as though she was going for a serious run.

"There's something wrong about driving to a place to walk. If you intend for this to be as serious a walk as you're preparing for, I'm gonna get back in my car and go home."

"Good morning, Miss Sunshine. Let's see if a little sweat can chase away the grouch and let Missy come out to play."

"Only a masochist would call anything this early play, but lead on."

Nettie laughed and led the way to the track. Two women and a man were jogging, but not together.

Missy and Nettie started out. They walked the first lap in silence.

"What are you wearing Saturday?"

"I was thinking about wearing what you see here." Missy pointed to herself.

"You're really gonna stir things up if you wear that sweat suit to the wedding."

"I'm thinking hard about maybe skipping the wedding."

"You can't do that. The whole town will be there."

"That's why I'm going to skip it. Besides, with everybody else there, nobody will miss me."

"You know better than that, girlfriend."

"Yeah." Missy sighed and shook her head. "I guess I know I have to go, but it's going to be so hard. Since I called off the wedding I've had to face folks staring at me like I came from Mars or something, but I've never had a lot of stares at one time. It was bad enough at the softball game when Jimmy came up and sat beside me, and I left the game with him. This is going to be much worse. I'm not sure I can do this without running away."

"Sure you can. Nobody will pay you any mind. Clarissa

will have the spotlight as she should. She's such a nice person."

"Mama said nobody will pay me any mind, too." She stared at Nettie. "I didn't believe her either."

"It will be all right." Nettie smiled. "I remember how Clarissa took to following us around when she first came to high school. Actually, she was following you. I just happened to be with you."

"Yeah. She was so timid. That's how I felt when I first got there, but I knew a lot of the kids from grade school and junior high. I also had you to hang out with. She was new in town and didn't know any of the kids. She looked so sad all the time. I had heard she was a good kid. I guess she picked me because her mama was working for mine when they first got here."

"Then you introduced her to a couple of girls from the church choir. She fit right in with them. You have a knack for knowing who will be right together. At least you used to."

Missy let out a hard breath that didn't have anything to do with her walking.

"Don't go there or I might decide one lap is enough."

"My lips are sealed, although I know you wouldn't leave me to finish this torture by myself."

They finished the lap in silence.

Missy was glad Nettie didn't elaborate. Jimmy was on Missy's mind enough without hearing his name. An ache started inside her and spread out as it always did when she thought about Jimmy. If only they saw things more alike; things that didn't have a thing to do with bodies wrapped together and loving each other.

They passed the bleachers and started into the second lap before words broke into her thoughts.

"You have to go to the wedding on Saturday," Nettie continued. "It will get you in practice for mine."

"Yours?" Missy stopped short and pulled on Nettie's arm.

"Kyle proposed last night." Nettie's smile could have replaced the sun.

"Why didn't you tell me?"

"I just did. I got in too late last night to call you."

"Then why are you here with me and not with him?"

"He had to leave town this morning on business and he won't be back until Sunday. Besides, I promised to go walking with you this morning, and I would never break a promise to a friend."

"Right. You expect me to believe that if Kyle were in town you'd be out here walking with me? I don't think so."

They both laughed.

"Missy, you should have been there last night. Kyle got down on one knee right there in Harold's Restaurant. The place was crowded. You know how it is even on Wednesday nights. Anyway, there he was on one knee beside the table in the middle of the room. He took my hand, kissed the palm, and slipped this on my finger." She held out her hand. Sunlight glinted off a large center stone and smaller diamonds forming a half circle around it. "Makes me glad I'm left-handed." She waved her hand around.

"Oh, Nettie, it's beautiful." Missy leaned her head away and squinted. "I would have brought my shades if I had known this rock was gonna blind me." She hugged her close. "I'm so happy for you. You deserve it after all the frogs you've kissed."

"Those frogs have all gone back into the swamp and are forgotten." Nettie sighed. "It was so romantic. That's what folks will be talking about tomorrow, and maybe into next week, right along with Clarissa's wedding." She grabbed Missy's arm. "You have to go with me. Kyle won't be back until Sunday and I don't want to go alone. The bottom line is you need to go. For you."

"You sound like Mama. You been talking to her?"

"No, but great minds and all that."

"I don't know what to wear."

"That's a cop-out. You've got a lot of outfits that would be great for a wedding. Of course, if you want attention, you *can* wear what you have on."

"Attention is just what I want. I haven't had enough of it lately. Speaking of attention, did you know Walter and Martie discovered each other?"

Nettie stopped suddenly in the middle of the path. A jogger shook her head and slipped around them.

"What? Not Martie Duke with the green and purple hair? Who told you that?"

"Walter himself. I had a cup of tea with him. I assume her hair is a normal color, now that she's a doctor."

"A doctor? Has it been that long?"

"She just finished an accelerated program in med school, and is home for a little while. She plans to come back here and open a clinic after she finishes her residency."

Missy started walking and Nettie followed.

"Walter and Martie." Nettie grabbed Missy's arm and stopped again. "Wait a minute. You were seen in public with Walter, and I didn't find out about it? Nobody called tell me? Don't ever talk about the grapevine around here anymore. Somebody fell down on the job big time and will have to be replaced." She started moving again. "Come on. Tell me all about what happened when you were with Walter."

Missy took the next lap to fill Nettie in, and they took the one after that to talk about Martie's antics in high school.

When they left the track after an hour, Missy admitted she was glad she had come.

"I'll come pick you up Saturday unless you want to do this again tomorrow."

"Sure. Let's meet at four tomorrow morning. That way we can finish before the sun is up."

"I take it that's a no to the walking."

"You are so intelligent."

"Thank you. I'll pick you up Saturday morning."

"Don't bother. I'll catch a ride to the church with Mama. She gave me her 'You can't let your poor old mama go all by herself to the wedding' speech."

"Mamas are good at stuff like that. I think they take lessons in how to create guilt in their children." She laughed. "If she wants to leave the reception early, though, I'll run you home." She looked at her watch. "Miss Emily is probably waiting at my beauty shop door. See you tomorrow."

Missy caught one last flash of Nettie's ring as she waved before she got into her car.

Clarissa's wedding Saturday, Nettie's soon after and Walter's probably next. Maybe Walter and Martie would marry before Nettie and Kyle.

She sighed as she put the car into gear. *Am I the only one still confused about what I want that I can have?*

Missy went home and looked through her closet. May as well get it over with. Her mama and Nettie were right. She had to go to the wedding.

She took out every dress, put them back one at a time and took them out again. Why was she going through so much trouble?

Her answer was to pull out two more outfits, try them on and look at them critically.

Finally, she narrowed her choices to the deep peach and the royal blue. Blue was Clarissa's wedding color. Missy put the blue dress back in the closet. It shouldn't matter, though. If she was lucky, nobody would notice her at all tomorrow. If she was lucky. She took the peach dress to the ironing board. She didn't expect to be lucky.

She made it through the rest of the day by thinking about Clarissa and how happy she'd be. She was glad for her.

Now she had to get through tomorrow. She hung the ironed dress on the hook in the shed kitchen. Today was easy. Saturday was the day that had her worried.

Saturday morning the sunlight slipped in when the breeze disturbed the curtain in Missy's bedroom window. Songbirds were already singing. It was going to be a perfect day for a wedding, and Clarissa deserved it.

"Missy, stop dawdling and get on up. The morning is too beautiful to waste it laying up in the bed. Throw on your robe, and come on out and share a cup of tea with me."

Missy groaned, but got up and pulled on the pique robe her mama had given her for her last birthday.

A short while later she was sitting at the table across from her mama.

"I reckon we can leave here about ten-thirty. I have to swing by and pick up Dorothy."

"What?" Missy put down her cup. "What happened to my 'poor old mama going all alone'?"

"I just said that to get you to go."

"Mama, you lied to me."

"Mothers are allowed to lie when there are extenuating circumstances; when it's for the good of their children."

"Says who? Did somebody give you a *For Mothers' Eyes Only* rule book?"

"There's that smart mouth again. I don't know who you got that from. I'm sure it wasn't me." She took a sip and held her cup between her hands. "Now, if I had said

Dorothy just called this morning and asked to catch a ride with me, that would be a lie. A bold-faced one."

"I'd like to see what else you have in your secret book."

"I hope you get a copy of your own one day." She took another sip. "Do you know all of my friends are grandmothers? Some of them several times over. Dorothy's daughter is expecting for the second time, and here you are waffling over . . ." She stared at Missy. "Tell me. Exactly what are you waffling over? Do you know if you don't get a move on, by the time you do get married and have a baby I'll be too old to play with the child?"

"Mama, I am not getting married and having a baby just so you can have grandchildren. Besides, when I was engaged to Walter, you kept complaining about me planning to marry him."

"I was trying to save you from a mistake. He wasn't right for you. Deep down both of you knew it. It just took a while for you to admit it." She stared hard at Missy. "We both know who is right for you. Has been for years. I never saw two people so made for each other." She smiled. "It's just taking you so long to see it. I declare, I know you didn't get your thickheadedness and your procrastination from me."

"Mama, I'm not going to talk about Jimmy T."

"See? I told you we both knew. Actually, all three of us know. You're the only one who's too mule-headed to admit it."

Missy glared as her mama's smile widened.

"Now what dress did you decide to wear?"

At 10:30, Missy stood at the door waiting for her mama to come out of her bedroom. She took a quick look in the mirror over the mantel and patted her hair one last time. Should she have left it down? She was still getting used to the shorter cut. She opened the gold clip holding her hair in place on top of her head, and refastened it.

"As soon as you're done primping, we can go."

"I'm ready." Missy took a deep breath.

"Do you like this?" Sally twirled around and her pale green chiffon skirt swirled against her legs. "I saw a picture of a dress like this in a fashion magazine. Perfect for a wedding, I thought, so I made it."

"It's beautiful, Mama." Missy blinked. She took a deep breath. "You hadn't planned to wear it to my wedding, had you?"

"Course not. I put that one aside. I'm not blowing it on somebody else's wedding. I haven't given up on you yet."

"I hope it will still be in style when my day comes. *If* it comes."

"It will, baby. It will." She took Missy's arm and walked out to the car.

The church was filling up fast when Missy slipped into a pew with her mother. Flowers of every shade of blue mixed with a variety of white blossoms tumbled from displays at the front of the church. Blue and white sprays were tied to each pew with wide blue satin ribbon. Jason Stanley played soft organ music as Mount Olive Church quickly filled.

Walter walked in with Martie and sat two pews in front. He didn't see anybody or anything but Martie. Missy smiled.

"Slide over a bit unless you want to sit by the aisle. If so, let me get past you to the other side."

Missy stopped smiling. She refused to look at the person talking to her.

"There's no room. Go sit somewhere else."

"Come on, Missy. Slide on over. You can make room."

Missy tried to ignore him. Jimmy stood by her pew. He wasn't going away.

"Baby, for somebody who doesn't want to attract attention you're doing a poor job of showing it."

At her mother's whisper, Missy looked around. The people in the pews around her were all focused on her. She moved over and her mama and everyone else in the pew shifted away.

"Why did you have to squeeze in here?" she whispered, but folks didn't look away. "Look at all the room in the pew right in front of us."

"You know why. Now quit fussing and go back to smiling in case anybody's looking at us."

"You know everybody's looking at us." She glared at him. "And I don't feel like smiling. I don't feel like putting up with any . . ."

Suddenly the music changed. Jason played a string of chords meant to attract attention. There was a hush and then murmuring filled the air as the little Thompson boys unrolled a white carpet down the center aisle and took a seat with their mother at the front. Missy smiled. She remembered when the twins were born. Their mother, Sonya, was only two years ahead of Missy in high school.

"No. I don't wanna." Carl Littleton's voice joined the music. Missy and everybody else looked at the back of the church. Carl stood with the white laced-trimmed pillow clutched in one hand. His other hand was wrapped around his mother's leg. "No, no. I don't wanna. Everybody's looking at me." His last word dragged out and hit a high note that completely drowned out the music. He dropped the pillow and grabbed his mother with that hand. Chuckles drifted from a pew here and there.

I can understand not wanting everybody looking at you, Missy thought.

She watched Carl's father hand the pillow to the usher while Carl's mother led him out. Chuckles stopped and were replaced by *ah*s as little Janie Adams wandered down the aisle scattering rose petals from a lace-covered basket as she made her way to the front. Every now and then she stopped to wave to somebody. When she finally reached the front the chuckles started again, followed by clapping as she turned to the congregation, put down the basket, held both sides of her pink dress and bowed low.

The music changed again as the rest of the wedding party glided to the altar. When the wedding march sounded, Missy stood with the others. She swallowed hard and tried not to remember that next week was supposed to be her turn.

A radiant Clarissa slowly made her way to her husband-to-be. She was more beautiful than ever. Tears shone in her eyes and Missy felt her own fill. She was glad she was here to share Clarissa's day, although she doubted if Clarissa knew anybody but Franklin was there. Their gazes met and held each other as if they were alone in the church.

Missy knew that look. She had exchanged it with Jimmy so many times. She knew how looking at a special somebody could make the rest of the world fade away until nothing and nobody existed except the two of you, and that was okay. She knew that love could take over and really conquer all, as somebody once said.

She swallowed hard. She also knew it didn't always work out like that. Sometimes, no matter how badly you wanted it, love wasn't enough.

She slipped a tissue from her purse and quickly dabbed her eyes. Then she forced herself to concentrate on the two people who had found a way to make it work out for them.

Vows were exchanged and Missy tried to ignore Jimmy sitting close. She looked down and noticed his fingers wrapped with hers and clutching them tightly. When had that happened? She didn't pull away. Instead she stole a glance at him. His look was as intense as Franklin's was. What was Jimmy thinking?

Reverend Butler presented the new couple to the congregation, the music changed and a beaming Clarissa and Franklin marched out of the church.

Soon Missy was outside with everybody else throwing birdseed and watching the kids blow bubbles at the newlyweds as they made their way to the waiting limousine.

"Come on. I'll give you a ride to the hall." Jimmy's voice sounded huskier than usual. He was standing close enough for Missy to feel his body heat almost as much as she had when she was sitting beside him. It seemed like, lately, he was always that close.

"I'm riding with Mama." She took a step away, but she still felt like he was touching her.

"You go on with, Jimmy, Missy. I just remembered something I have to do before I . . ."

"Mama, if I'm going to the reception, I'm riding with you. That's all there is to it."

"Okay, baby." Sally's voice was soft. "Let's go. Dorothy's riding with Thelma."

Neither said anything during the ride. Missy was grateful for her mama's silence. She needed time to build up her courage to face the rest of the day.

Sally parked in the last empty space in the lot. They got out of the car.

"Thanks, Mama." They both knew it wasn't the ride Missy was thanking her for.

Missy took a deep breath and let it out slowly. She managed a slight smile. The worst was over. The rest of the day would be easier. No pews. No Jimmy sitting close enough to fire up old memories.

FOURTEEN

Missy walked into a picture from a book of fairy tales turned to the page after the wedding. Blue and white was everywhere: in the flowers, in the wide satin ribbons and crepe paper streamers. Vases of blue and white flowers had been brought from the church and placed on stands around the walls. More flanked the stage. Pale blue and royal blue cloths with white lace-skirt overlays covered the tables scattered throughout the room. Wide white ribbons trimmed the bottoms and pulled up every so often so they looked like scallops. Large blue bows and sprigs of baby's breath held the loops in place. Different varieties of blue and white flowers filled cut-glass bowls in the center of each table. A crystal candle holder with a tall golden candle stood on either side of each bowl. Paper wedding bells hanging from blue crepe paper streamers were fastened around the walls. The hall was no longer just a hall. It was a perfect setting for a beautiful bride. Clarissa did it up right.

Missy went to the table with the chart showing where each guest was sitting. Then she went to her table. Jimmy was sitting to the left of the seat that had her place card in front of it.

"You don't belong here."

"Sure I do. I have an invitation. Franklin and I go way back. We used to hang out together. Remember? I was almost in his wedding, but another buddy wanted it more than I did, so I bowed out."

"I'm not talking about you being here at the reception and you know it. That's not supposed to be your seat. Your name wasn't on the chart for this table." She knew that. His name would have jumped out at her if it had been there, and she would have switched her seat to a table at the other side of the room.

"Sure it is. See?" He held up his place card. "There's my name." He set it back on the table and patted the chair beside him. "Come on, sit down."

"That's supposed to be Mama's seat."

"She wanted to sit with a friend. I don't remember who."

Missy looked around. At the far side of the room her mother was sitting with people Missy had never seen before. She doubted her mother had met them before she went to the table.

"Come on, Missy, sit down." Jimmy patted the chair again and turned up the volume on his smile. "Relax and get comfortable. Pretend I'm not here."

Fat chance she could do either of those things. She was supposed to get comfortable with Jimmy sitting right next to her all dressed up in his tan suit, and looking better than any model from any men's fashion magazine? How had she forgotten how good he looked in fancy clothes?

She sat, but shifted away from him. Jimmy T looked good in anything. Or nothing. She shook her head. *Don't go there. That's a closed book. Don't open it again.* Forget he was here, he said. She had as much chance of doing that as she had of forgetting all that had happened between them.

Jimmy's smile was warming her insides and spreading heat through her whole body, in spite of the air-conditioning working perfectly. It was going to be a longer day than she had imagined.

Missy was relieved when Clarissa and Franklin's arrival was announced. She had something else to set her mind on.

The newlyweds paused in the doorway and Jimmy handed Missy the disposable camera from the table.

"You do the honors. What with keeping your wish book all these years, I know you have more of an idea of what shots a bride would like. Just pretend that's you and me standing there getting ready to greet the guests at our reception. The wedding is over and we're both looking forward to tonight."

Missy dropped the camera. She tightened her hands to stop the shaking. She didn't look at Jimmy. She picked the camera back up and tried to forget Jimmy's words. She almost managed to make the picture his words formed disappear. Her and Jimmy on their wedding night. She blinked.

They'd probably be arguing because she wanted to go to the islands and he wanted to go to the motel on the highway ten miles away.

"Go on. Clarissa wants pictures from every table and you're not ready."

Jimmy's voice broke in and Missy raised the camera.

She snapped right along with everyone else as the new couple made their way to the front of the hall, pausing every few feet so more pictures could be taken.

The receiving line formed and somehow Jimmy was right behind Missy. When his hand found the middle of her back, it felt too right for her to protest.

"I'm so glad you could come." Clarissa hugged Missy.

"Maybe you two will decide to join us." Franklin pumped Jimmy's hand.

"I'm just waiting for Missy to say the word. You know how women get cold feet about these things." Jimmy tightened his grip on Missy's waist when she tried to move away. She was the only one not laughing.

Jimmy took her hand and led her back to the table.

"How could you?" She threw him a glare.

"I'm telling the truth. You know all you have to do is say yes. I'll know what the question is."

"Cut it out. I don't want to hear anymore about it today. Is that clear?"

"Yes, ma'am." His crooked grin was at home with the twinkle in his eyes. "How about tomorrow?"

"Jimmy, behave yourself." Missy slowly shook her head.

"Okay, but I warn you. I'm not as much fun when I behave."

Missy was glad she was sitting. If not her legs would have collapsed.

Jimmy's arm found its way to the back of her chair. That seemed right. His fingers stroked across her shoulders, plotting a trail of heat. That seemed right, too. Disturbing, but right. That part of their relationship had never been a problem.

She and Jimmy were always in sync when they stopped telling and discussing and got to showing and doing. Lovemaking was harmonious from the first and got better with each practice. And, for a while, they practiced every chance they got. How could it have been perfect and then gotten better?

Missy wasn't aware of anything else but her memories until she felt a gentle tug on her hand.

"Let's dance."

When had the musicians gone on stage? When had the music started? Had the bride and groom had their first dance together? What about the other traditional dances with parents and mother and son and father and daughter before everybody else got on the dance floor?

She must have missed those, too, because folks from

other tables were swaying to the music as they made their way to the hardwood floor.

Missy wished the musicians had picked a fast number instead of this slow song that reminded her too much of what had been between her and Jimmy, but would never be again. She thought of the Top Ten numbers. There were fast songs on the chart. Why couldn't they be playing one of those?

Jimmy eased her close, fit his body to hers, rested his chin on her head, and then Missy didn't let herself think at all.

The singer sang of love ever after and kisses and happiness, and Missy almost believed such things were possible with her and Jimmy. Almost. She heard murmurings and looked around.

She and Jimmy were the only ones left on the floor. How long ago had the music stopped?

As she led the way back to the table, Jimmy's hand against her back seemed to belong there, but she eased away from it. A year from now she'd definitely be somewhere else, and Jimmy would still be here in Mayland, happily stuck in place.

They danced again several times, but Missy didn't forget that her time here was temporary. She had sent for a booklet from the government describing teaching opportunities overseas on military bases. She expected it to come any day. Then she'd decide where she wanted to go and what part of the world she wanted to see next. Maybe if she put distance between her and Jimmy, the pain of what couldn't be would dull until she could cope with it.

Each time Jimmy held her close during the rest of the reception, she had to remind herself not to get too comfortable in his arms, even though they made her feel as though she were home. *Temporary,* she thought, *it's only temporary.* But it sure felt permanent.

Nettie came over to the table and told Jimmy about Kyle.

"I'm here to tell you dreams do come true." She smiled.

"I hope so." Jimmy was talking to her, but he was looking at Missy. "When do I get to meet him?"

"Funny you should ask. That's what I came over for. I want you and Missy to come to dinner Tuesday evening. You all can get acquainted and I can practice my cooking skills."

"I-I'm not sure I can make it." The first chance she had Missy was going to strangle Nettie. Slowly and with great pleasure.

"Of course you can. You're on vacation. You don't have a schedule. Besides, I picked Tuesday because that's the day you and I were supposed to go shopping for shoes, so I know you don't have anything else planned. Now, instead of walking around the mall complaining about how long I take, you get to sit and talk. You should be glad for the change."

"Nettie . . ."

"I got to go see Miss Barbara. I promised her. Bye."

"I didn't put her up to that," Jimmy said when Missy stared at him. "You know how she is."

"Yeah, I know exactly how Nettie is."

"So, what time should I pick you up on Tuesday?"

"I'll drive over there myself."

"No problem picking you up. It won't take me any time to swing by your house. And if it did, I wouldn't complain. I'd never complain about spending time with you."

"Don't push it, Jimmy." She turned her back to him. If she tried hard enough maybe she could ignore him.

"Attention, everybody. The bride is ready to pass on the pleasure. Let's see who's next. May we have all single women out here, please?"

Missy watched women scurrying from all of the tables,

but she didn't move, not even when Jimmy nudged her shoulder. He nudged again, and she leaned away from his hand. She refused to look over at the table where her mother was sitting.

Clapping filled the hall when Clarissa walked up onto the stage. A few women in the group standing in front jockeyed for position. Finally, Clarissa took one last look at the group, stared at Missy and turned her back.

Oh no. She wouldn't, Missy thought when she saw the look Clarissa gave her. Clarissa wouldn't dare. . . .

Missy blinked as the bouquet landed in her lap as if it had been placed there. She owed Clarissa payback. Big time.

Cheers and hoots and clapping sounded. Missy stared at the flowers as if willing them to sprout legs and get off her.

"May as well pick them up, smile and take your bow," Jimmy whispered in her ear. "Those flowers aren't going anywhere, and you're holding things up. The men are waiting for the garter toss, so I better go. Wonder what it means if I catch it after you got the bouquet? What do you think, huh?"

Missy didn't have to look at him to know there was a gleam in his eyes. She sighed and stood. She sat back down so quickly that if anybody had blinked they would have missed it.

There was a roar as Franklin moved to the stage. He and Clarissa kissed before he led her to the chair with blue and white bows tied to each corner. Cheers sounded when Franklin slowly eased up her skirt, reached further up her leg and pulled off her garter. Right now Clarissa didn't need blusher. The cheers grew when he waved the garter into the air.

"Wish me luck," Jimmy brushed his lips across Missy's cheek and joined the other single men on the floor before she could react.

She didn't watch. She wished she was as sure about picking lottery numbers as she was that Jimmy was going to catch the garter.

It didn't make her feel any better when Jimmy came back and took his seat beside her, still twirling the white lace-trimmed garter on his finger.

Somehow she made it through the rest of the reception. She got a slice of cake and ate it.

"You know you're not supposed to do that. You're supposed to sleep on it." Jimmy wrapped a hand around her shoulder. "I reckon it doesn't matter, though. We both know you'd dream of me, so why waste a perfectly good piece of cake?"

Missy didn't know what came after that. Too much was going on in her head to pay attention to what was happening around her.

She was glad when her mother told her she was leaving. Being in Jimmy's arms and pretending to dance was worse each time. She knew what "sweet torture" meant.

Jimmy offered to take her home, but, despite her mother's urging, Missy refused. She couldn't stand the torment. The more she let herself care for him again, the harder it would be when she left Mayland for good.

"Sleep well tonight, though I doubt I will." Jimmy's words were soft. "Be talking to you real soon."

Missy's hand shook as she picked up her bag. She knew he was making a promise and Jimmy always kept his promises.

Missy was sitting on the floor of her room surrounded by boxes, piles of papers and stacks of books when the phone rang Monday morning. She knew who it was before she picked it up.

"Hello, Jimmy."

"Morning, darling. I see we're still on the same wavelength. There's hope for us yet. I know this little restaurant in Andrews. What do you say we go there for dinner tonight?"

"I can't."

"Why? And don't give me some excuse like you have to wash your hair or polish your nails."

"I don't need an excuse. Things are moving too fast."

"How can dinner be too fast? We haven't had a date since our new agreement."

"Jimmy, I'm seriously thinking about applying for a teaching assignment on a military base overseas. I'm just waiting for the information to come."

Silence stretched between them.

"You're really doing your best to put space between us, aren't you? You're serious. Are you going to look at a globe and try to find a spot exactly halfway around the world from here before you make your decision?"

"I keep telling you we still have the same differences as we always did. I don't intend to spend the rest of my life arguing every day about dumb stuff. I keep telling you it won't work out between us. You know I do. You're just too pigheaded to listen to me. You always were. You always will be." If she didn't know better she'd think he had hung up on her. Finally he spoke.

"I guess I hear you now. Real clear. I thought we could talk out our differences. Work them out. They don't seem that big to me. I didn't think they were too hard for us to work through. I thought, if we both set our minds to it, we could make it work. I thought . . ."

Missy could imagine him shrugging.

"Never mind. You know what I thought. I showed you enough times every chance I got." He sighed. "I reckon I've pushed you hard enough long enough." Again heavy silence hung between them. "I'll be seeing you around, Missy. Stay sweet even if it's not for me."

He hung up, but instead of feeling relief, Missy felt an

emptiness fill her. She sat holding the phone as though waiting for somebody to come on the line. As if she were waiting for Jimmy to come back on and make her change her mind.

By the time she finally hung up and stood, Jimmy had probably fixed a couple of cars and was working on a third.

Jimmy did his best to concentrate on finding the trouble with Deacon Albertson's car, but after looking at the diagnostic sheet three times, he gave up and went back into his office.

The door clicked shut behind him. He was just wasting his time trying to get any work done after his conversation with Missy over an hour ago. He let out a sigh as heavy as his heart was feeling. That was the last conversation he'd have with her except maybe a hi whenever he was lucky enough to run into her. He'd see her in church, but he'd sit way on the other side. He was through bothering her. She didn't want anything more to do with him. It finally got through his thick skull that she meant what she had been telling him all along.

He let out a hard breath. Once he had suggested they could just be friends. That could never happen. He didn't have any friend he wanted to hold close and kiss senseless as he wanted to do to Missy. As he'd always want to do with her. As he still, right this very minute, wanted to do with her.

Maybe he had been wrong all along. Oh, Missy still had feelings for him. She didn't try to deny that. She couldn't. Not after the way she still responded to him whenever he kissed her.

Whenever he was near her, desire heated up in her eyes to match the desire that raced through him. She couldn't hide it from him. He had seen so much of it before he let her get away from him, but maybe her feelings weren't as strong as he thought. Maybe it was only wishful thinking on his part to believe they could overcome their differences.

He didn't want to continue to make her unhappy. He didn't want to push in if she really wanted him out of her life as she kept telling him. What made him think he knew more about what she wanted than she did?

He once knew a fellow who didn't know when to quit a relationship and break away. That guy had made his ex-fiancée miserable. Jimmy loved Missy too much to torment her like that.

If he had given Missy the ring he had bought the day before their last argument when she was in high school, what would have happened? Would she have kept it or would she have been angry enough to give it back after they argued? There was a time he would have bet she would have kept it. Now he wasn't sure anymore. He shook his head.

He wasn't sure of anything anymore where Missy was concerned. He wasn't sure of anything except that he loved her and always would, but she didn't love him back enough to take a chance on a future with him.

Halfway around the world. She'd go halfway around the world to get away from him, and as soon as she could. She must be sorry she signed that contract with the school system. He knew she was sorry she came back. What kind of man was he? He had made her sorry she had come home and he was chasing her away.

He scribbled nothings on the pad in front of him as if he expected the markings to develop into suggestions of what he could do next to get her to change her mind. Then he dropped the pen and leaned his head back against the chair. He closed his eyes. He was too old to believe in magic anymore. The most he could hope for was for the next year to race past.

Some folks would say he was wishing his life away. They didn't know that, sometimes, having time zip away was less painful than taking each day as it came.

"What did you do to Jimmy?" Nettie greeted Missy at the door Tuesday evening.

"Hello, Nettie. What do you mean what did I do to Jimmy? I didn't do anything. I haven't heard from him since he called me yesterday."

"Come on in." She led the way into the living room. "This is Kyle." Nettie's voice got all soft when she said the name, and her face softened, too. "Sugar, this is my best friend."

"Nettie's told me so much about you, I feel I already know you." A strong dark hand gripped hers and a friendly smile in a dark chocolate face greeted her. Nettie had chosen well.

"She told me about you, too." Missy smiled back. "I'm glad she found you."

"Not as glad as I am." Kyle put his arm around Nettie's shoulder and eased her against his side.

Missy would swear Nettie glowed as she looked into his eyes.

"Maybe I should go and come back another time?"

Nettie looked at her and laughed.

"It wouldn't do any good. We'd be like this then, too. If fate is kind, we'll be like this for the rest of our lives." She crossed her arms and stood straight. Her soft look disappeared. "Now, what happened between you and Jimmy?"

"I told you, nothing."

"Maybe that's the problem."

"What are you talking about? What's going on?"

"That's what I'd like to know. Jimmy called me an hour ago and told me he wasn't coming. He didn't give me a reason, just said he hoped he wasn't causing any problem by canceling so late, but he thought you'd be more comfortable without him here." She kept staring. "Since when does comfortable and you and Jimmy belong in the same conversation? Did you have an argument? I mean a new one. You all been carrying on a running fuss for years. I thought it was finally playing itself out. What happened?"

"I told Jimmy I'm thinking about teaching overseas."

"Wow. You sure know which button to push to turn him away, don't you? You should. It's the same one you found years ago. I guess it still works." She shook her head. "Are you sure this is what you want?"

"It wouldn't work out between us. No sense in letting it go on, when I know how it will end up. We'd both be miserable and sorry. By then it would be too late."

"Must be nice to be able to see into the future. Remind me to get the set of tomorrow's lottery numbers from you before you leave tonight. Missy, how can you do this? How can you . . ."

"Baby," Kyle squeezed Nettie's shoulder. "Maybe you should back off a bit, huh?"

Nettie took a deep breath.

"Sorry, Missy." She hugged her and held her close. "I guess I did come on too strong. I only want you to be happy. You know that, don't you?"

"Yeah, I know. But this is something you have to leave alone. Jimmy and I just weren't meant to be together."

Nettie stared at her for a minute. Then her look softened.

"You all may as well sit on down. I'll have supper on the table as soon as the bread is ready."

Jimmy wasn't mentioned again, but all through dinner Missy's glance kept going to the empty chair across from her. Nettie and Kyle kept the conversation going. Missy may as well have not been there.

They moved to the living room, but that didn't help

Missy. When enough time had passed so she could leave without hurting Nettie's feelings, Missy stood.

"Thanks again for a great meal."

"You're welcome." Missy was grateful Nettie didn't mention that Missy hadn't eaten more than a forkful of anything.

"Nice meeting you, Kyle. I know I'll see a lot more of you."

"I'm sure you will. You take care, you hear?"

"I'll try my best."

"Talk to you tomorrow." Nettie hugged her. "For sure."

Missy managed a nod. Then she left.

Jimmy was so strong in her thoughts as she drove home that he may as well have been sitting beside her. They weren't even dating and they had had an argument. Not a long, drawn-out one like in the past. This one had been short but there was nothing sweet about it.

What was he trying to pull now? Had he really decided to leave her alone? If so, why wasn't she happy about it?

FIFTEEN

Two days later Missy wasn't any closer to the answers to her questions. Nobody mentioned Jimmy to her. Not Nettie when they went on their walks and not her mother. For the first time since she got back, her mother acted as if Jimmy never drew breath. In the past she had always found some excuse to talk about Jimmy, mentioned seeing him; heard something about him; anything. But now, not a word parted her lips about him.

It was as if he had dropped out of existence and a hole gaped in Missy's life where Jimmy used to live. Each time the phone rang, she expected to hear his voice at the other end, trying to sweet-talk her into going somewhere, anywhere, with him. How could she miss him more, when he was this close, than she had all those years when she was away?

She went into town both days on errands, but she didn't run into Jimmy. Not even at lunchtime when she was only a block from his shop. It seemed as if she saw everybody else in Mayland, but not him. Folks who had sat within hearing distance at the game or the reception looked at her funny, but they talked about the weather or asked about her teaching position. Not one person she saw had any comment to make about Jimmy. It was as though a secret pact had been made.

On Wednesday she didn't take her usual route home

from town. She drove passed Jimmy's garage. Three mechanics were busy, but Jimmy wasn't one of them.

The rest of Wednesday and into Thursday she stayed at home with her thoughts until they crowded her out of the house.

She took a ride that went nowhere near town. She didn't ask herself why. She already had too many unanswered questions to handle.

She turned off the main road onto the piece of land that Jimmy's grandfather had left him. Jimmy had added a gravel road that wound around stands of trees.

She and Jimmy had walked all over his twenty acres deciding what would go where when he built his place. A heated discussion about where a gazebo should go had gone on for days. Jimmy had finally given in, and decided Missy's spot just beyond the side yard was the best place after all. They had planned to put a swing set and sliding board near the side yard, too, for the kids she and Jimmy planned to have. They talked about maybe building a play fort together when the kids got bigger. From the gazebo they could sit close while they kept an eye on their kids at play.

Missy blinked and shook her head. Their kids. They had argued over whether to have three or four. They had never agreed on that. Now there'd be none.

She wiped her eyes as if she had lost the kids, even though she never had them. "Could have been" was tougher than what once was.

Missy let the road take her past what would later have been irises and daylilies in little clearings, if Jimmy had followed their plan. She had to see how close Jimmy had come to their dreams so far.

The fresh coating of oil covering the wide road kept her car from stirring up dust despite the dry surface. It led her through a few more turns before it ended at a garage wide enough for two cars with plenty of space left over for storage. Missy stopped her car.

A wide patch of grass was interrupted by a brick walkway leading up to the porch. Twine was still strung along the sticks marking the path. The bricks hadn't been walked on yet. Missy stayed in the car. She didn't have the right to be the first to use it. She didn't have any rights at all where Jimmy was concerned. Not anymore. She had walked away from them. She stared at Jimmy's dream.

He was building his new house exactly the way they had planned it when they were in high school. A wide porch wrapped around one side—the side where the gazebo would go. All that was missing from the porch were wicker furniture and a corner swing. They would come next. Missy sighed. Somebody else would pick out the pattern for the cushions she was going to make.

Jimmy had left the floor and railings in their natural wood finish, though they had a high shine on them. Natural like him. There never had been anything phony about Jimmy.

She looked at the bare bay window facing the porch. Who would pick the curtains now? That was supposed to be her department. She was going to pick the fabric and make them herself. Not now. Not ever. What color would Jimmy paint the walls when he was finished inside? Would he still use pale blue as they had talked about?

She swallowed hard and closed her eyes. Would there still be an herb garden under the kitchen window? Would the gazebo go where they had decided? What about the swing set? Would he still need it? A bitter taste rose up in her mouth, but she swallowed it.

Of course he would. Just because she had turned him down didn't mean Jimmy would spend the rest of his life alone.

He loved kids. Back when they were in school, whenever Jimmy popped the hood of a car, kids came around to see what he was doing. He was so patient with them. He'd make a great father. Missy closed her eyes for a minute. She didn't want to guess about who would be the mother of his children. She shouldn't care. She didn't want him, did she? She had told him that more times than she could remember. Wasn't she glad she had finally gotten through to him?

The gurgling of the creek reached her, but she resisted the urge to go look at their willow tree. She knew she couldn't handle the memories waiting there for her. The tree would be bigger. Things grew, if you let them; if you didn't stop the natural growing process.

She started up the car and drove home. Saturday would have been her wedding day. It would have been the happiest day of her life if she had made sure she knew what she wanted, and who she wanted it with, before she had agreed to anything. She had broken her engagement with Walter. She had dumped Jimmy. And she still wasn't any closer to knowing what she did want. Instead, here she was moping around and wondering how she had let her life get into such a mess and, more importantly, wondering how was she going to fix it.

As she opened the door to the house, the phone rang. She rushed to pick it up. She wouldn't think about why she hurried, nor would she try to analyze the reason she was disappointed when it was only a telemarketer trying to get her to change her long-distance carrier.

She thought about calling Jimmy, but what would she say? *I was wondering why you decided to leave me alone like I've been telling you to do since I got back?*

She went to the shed kitchen and sorted through the boxes of things that she hadn't taken to school.

Two hours later she looked at the three piles she had made: things to keep, things to throw away and things she hadn't decided about. Her future should be in the last pile.

She stood. She'd have to go through it all again. She had no idea what she put where or why. She did know her future wasn't there. She had to decide about that later.

Late afternoon, the mail carrier brought the brochure about overseas teaching, but Missy put it on the dining room table with the rest of the mail. It wasn't important.

The next day she made herself look through the booklet. None of the places offered were interesting anymore, and all of them wanted at least a two-year commitment. She wasn't willing to commit two years to a place she didn't care about any longer. A vacation would serve her purpose just as well. *When did I change my mind and why did it take me so long?* She didn't ask herself why she had changed it. She knew the answer to that question.

She had promised herself it wasn't going to happen. She had told herself, Jimmy and everybody else who mentioned his name to her, that she wasn't going to get caught up with him again; yet here she was, back in love with Jimmy. Or maybe it was still in love and finally admitting it.

She went out to weed the flower bed and vegetable garden. She picked the ripe tomatoes and cucumbers and looked around. If neatness counted, her mother's gardens would win a prize without Missy touching them. Not a weed was in sight for her to pull. That was okay. Yard work wouldn't help her this time. She had some serious planning to do.

She plodded into the house carrying the old wicker basket full of ripe vegetables as if it weighed ten times heavier than it did.

She had to call Jimmy. Maybe she should go over to the shop; that way he couldn't refuse to talk to her. She had to tell him how she felt; had to let him know her sense was finally back where it should have been years ago.

How should she do it? How could she say it to make

him believe her? What could she say to make him forgive her?

She turned on the small television on the kitchen counter to catch the rest of the noon news. Anything was better than listening to her thoughts. The announcer stopped in the middle of a sentence and recited from a sheet of paper thrust at her by a hand barely seen on camera.

"Less than fifteen minutes ago, local garage owner, Jimmy Tanner Scott, was struck by a hit-and-run driver while hooking up a car to his tow truck out on the highway. We take you now for a live report from the scene."

Missy dropped the basket of vegetables. Cucumbers thudded and tomatoes and bell peppers spread out over the floor. A tomato split open, but went unnoticed as seeds spattered the floor. It could have tap-danced across the vinyl for all Missy knew. No longer able to stand, her hands shook as she pulled a chair close to the counter and flopped into it.

"Please, no. Please, God, let him be all right. Please . . ."

"The driver swerved, hit Mr. Scott, swerved again and hit a tree before speeding away. The owner of the disabled car, Charles Hatch, had this to say:

"That man came barreling down the road like he was on a raceway or something. He was talking on one of them car phones. Them things should be against the law." The man brushed his hand over his head. "I never seen anything like it. Knocked poor Jimmy T over like he was a target or something, and took off like a bat out of . . ." He blinked at the camera. "You know what I mean. Jimmy, he just laid there. I-I never seen anything like it before. That man must a been drunk or something. I saw him weaving toward us and warned Jimmy. Jimmy, he got up right fast, but before he could get out of the way of that crazy man, it was too late. I-I hope poor Jimmy's not too bad hurt, but he was laying there so still. Didn't move at all. It was terrible. Just terrible. I hope he's not . . ." The man wiped his forehead. "I hope he's gonna be okay. It was my car he was hooking up. That hunk of junk broke down on me. It wasn't the first time. My wife, Bessie, she told me it was time to get a new car, but I didn't pay her no nevermind." He shook his head. "I didn't see that fool in time. If I had just seen him a mite earlier . . ." He shook his head again. "Jimmy got to be okay."

The man faded away and the reporter came back on.

"Mr. Tanner was rushed to County General. The extent of his injuries are unknown. Now to this . . ."

The reporter went on to the next item as if she were going down a shopping list, and in a hurry to get to the end.

Through the rest of the news Missy waited for somebody to say it was all a mistake, or at least to say that it wasn't as bad as they thought and Jimmy was all right. She was still waiting after the news went off.

She started to call County General, but hung up before the first ring. Hospitals only give information to immediate family, like wives. That left her out, but not for lack of Jimmy's trying.

The phone rang as she grabbed her purse, but she didn't take the time to answer it.

She got into her car and rushed to the hospital praying the whole half hour it took her to get there. She had to have another chance to tell him she loved him. It couldn't end like this. Even if Jimmy wanted nothing else to do with her, he deserved to live. He deserved a chance to find somebody who would make him happy. Even if it was Julie, Missy would dance at his wedding. *Please, God. Please.*

Missy pulled into a spot. Her parking would have made her flunk the driving test, but she didn't care. She ran into the hospital.

One of her friends from school, Carrie, was the nurse

on duty, but that didn't matter. All she gave Missy was sympathy, when what she needed was information.

"Missy, I'm sorry. I can't tell you anything about Jimmy's condition. You're not a relative. Hospital policy." She looked hard at Missy and shook her head. "Fact is, I don't know a whole lot." She leaned toward her. "They got him in surgery. If you go up to the fourth floor, maybe you can find somebody willing to give you some information."

Missy's gasp escaped. She grabbed the edge of the counter. She had almost convinced herself that Jimmy had suffered only cuts and bruises, and he'd come walking into the waiting room any minute.

Carrie patted her shoulder. "He's still in surgery. That means he's still with us. Hang on. I'm praying for him."

"Thank you. I am, too." Tears poured down Missy's face as she ran down the hall to find the elevators.

"The other way," Carrie called when Missy turned left instead of right at the end of the hall.

The elevator took forever to come down. When the doors opened, a doctor and a man in a business suit strolled off and stood for a while as if there was no need to hurry. Missy moved around them, not hearing their apology for blocking her way.

After a stop at the second floor for the woman who was still on the elevator, Missy was finally on her way to Jimmy. She'd worry about how she was going to get information about his condition when she got there.

When she turned the corner on the fourth floor the first person she saw was Jimmy's mother.

"Miss Diane, how is he?"

"Oh, Missy. I'm so glad you're here." She grabbed Missy and held her close.

Missy rocked her back and forth and patted her shoulder as her tears for her only child fell onto Missy's shoulder.

Missy swallowed a lump and let Diane cry. Finally the tears let up and Missy led her to a row of chairs. She handed her a tissue.

"My baby's been in there forever. When they took him in they said something about internal injuries, but since then nobody's told me anything. I-I reckon they're all too busy working on him. He's got to be all right. He's just got to be. The Lord wouldn't take him from me at his young age, would he? It's not fitting for a child to go before a parent. He's still real young. And he lives right. He's kind and he's caring. He's a good person." She wiped her eyes. "That doesn't mean anything, though, does it?" She wiped new tears away. "Last year the Baxters lost their four-month-old baby. Jimmy's a lot past being a baby." She twisted her tissue one way and then the other. "You don't think he's . . ."

"If they haven't come out it means they're still working on him. He'll be all right. He has to be. We need him too much for him to leave us." Missy did need him. Why had it taken her so long to realize it? Please don't let it be too late.

They were headed toward the chapel when the operating room doors swished open.

"Miss Diane? They're finishing up in surgery. The doctor will be out to talk to you directly, but I wanted to let you know Jimmy's out of danger and will be coming out soon."

"Thank you, Freda. Oh, thank you." Diane grabbed the hand of the young woman who was the same age as Jimmy. Her family lived down the street from where Diane and Jimmy lived when they first moved to town.

"The doctor is the only one who's supposed to give medical updates, but Jimmy will be all right. The doctor said so." She squeezed Diane's shoulder. "When he tells you that, you try to act relieved, you hear?" She smiled.

Diane managed a smile of her own through the tears.

"Thank you, Freda." Missy squeezed her hand and Freda squeezed back.

"You got to thank somebody higher up than me, and I don't mean the doctors. The way Jimmy was hit, he should have been hurt a lot worse. He's lucky to be here. We here at the hospital can't claim credit for him still being with us." She smiled at both of them. "I got to go. You all hang in there a bit longer. The worst is over."

Ten long minutes later the doctor came out.

"Mrs. Scott? I'm Dr. Stephen Garfield, chief of surgery. They'll be bringing Jimmy out soon. Aside from minor scrapes and cuts, he had multiple internal injuries. Among other things, he had a lacerated liver, and we had to remove his spleen. A broken rib punctured a lung, but we were able to take care of that after we repaired the other damage. We're not sure of the extent of his head injuries, but we do know, at the very least, he's got a concussion. He may be in a coma for a while; we don't know that yet. His leg was broken in three places. We had to go in and make repairs. We inserted three pins to aid the correct mending. He might walk with a slight limp, but at least we saved his leg. For a while I wasn't sure that was possible."

Missy thought of the three-legged races they ran. She thought of how Jimmy loved to play ball with the kids.

"It will take a good while for him to mend," the doctor went on, "though we don't expect any complications."

Diane gasped and grabbed Missy's hand. They clung to each other as the doctor continued.

"I know this is all a shock to you, but I believe in fully informing the family so they know what to expect." He gave them a slight smile and his voice softened. "The bottom line is that we expect full recovery. It will take some time and he'll experience discomfort for a while, but I expect him to leave here in a few weeks or so barring any complications. Keep in mind it might take as long as a month. He was pretty banged up."

"Complications? You mentioned complications before. Wh-what kind of complications are you talking about?"

"The chances of any complications are remote so I won't go into them at this time. I'm just following my policy of having the family know everything about the patient's condition. There's no sense dwelling on possibilities. Mr. Scott was a mighty lucky man. His guardian angel must have been on duty today." This time his smile was wider.

Missy closed her eyes and sent up a prayer of thanks.

"Can we see him?" Diane asked.

"He'll be heavily sedated for a while, and remember there's also the strong possibility that he'll be in a coma. We won't know until later. For now, we'll take it one step at a time."

"But can we see him?"

"He won't know you're there."

"I know, but we still want to see him."

"Of course. I understand." He looked at Missy. "You do realize only family members will be allowed in the intensive care unit?"

"She's practically family." Diane took Missy's arm and held it. "They're almost engaged. You have to let her in to see Jimmy."

Dr. Garfield stared and shrugged slightly. "They'll be taking him to the East Wing. You can wait for him over there. If they give you any trouble tell them I said it's all right."

"Thank you, doctor. I-I . . ." Diane swallowed hard. Tears gathered in her eyes. "I can't thank you enough."

"I had some help from upstairs on this one." His face softened. "Now if you'll excuse me, I have to go change."

Diane held tightly to Missy's arm as they went to wait for Jimmy to be brought over to the East Wing. This time the wait wasn't quite as hard as it had been outside the operating room, although they were both anxious to see Jimmy and see for themselves that he was still with them.

Twenty minutes that seemed like months later, Missy heard the gurney coming down the hall before she saw it. She rushed over, but stopped short when she reached it. She gasped and Diane grabbed Missy's hand. If she hadn't been told it was Jimmy, she wouldn't have recognized him. Diane probably wouldn't have, either.

Banged up didn't begin to describe how Jimmy looked. His face was badly swollen and bruises covered almost every inch of skin. Stitches crossed his forehead where that wayward curl had once rested. A wide bandage wrapped around his head above that. A smaller bandage crossed his nose. Had the doctor mentioned a broken nose? The skin that wasn't bruised, and there wasn't much, had lost all color. Blood was being pumped into one arm and a bag of clear liquid was hooked up to the other.

How could they lie to her and Diane and say Jimmy would be all right? He looked as if they had only a few minutes to say their last good-byes.

New tears poured down Missy's face. She started into the room closely behind the gurney. She didn't know how much time Jimmy really had left, and she wasn't going to waste any of it.

"I'm sorry," one of the nurses pushing the gurney said, turning to them, "but you have to wait here until we get him settled into bed."

"But we don't want to miss one minute with . . ."

"It won't take long, and we can work faster without anyone else in the room. It'll just be a little while longer; then you can come in. I promise. There's a lounge at the end of the hall. You can go have a seat. You'll also find some vending machines in there in case you want coffee or something. We'll let you know when we're finished."

She smiled and pushed the gurney into the room. Another nurse followed her and closed the door.

Missy wasn't going any farther away from Jimmy than she had to. Definitely not way down to the end of the hall. How could the nurse think they could think about food at a time like this?

She squeezed Diane's hand and held it for a while. Together they paced in a small circle in the hallway outside the room. Why was time passing so slowly today?

Finally the nurses came out of his room.

"You can go in now, but you do realize he won't know you're there. He's still sedated. He won't be awake until tomorrow evening at the earliest. Probably not even then."

Tomorrow or later? Why not until tomorrow? Missy swallowed and, although she didn't like what she heard, she nodded.

"We know he won't know we're there, but we'll know it." They rushed in. Missy pulled a chair close to the bed for Diane and stood beside her. Tears filled her eyes again and spilled over. They came slowly at first, then they picked up speed. As fast as Missy wiped them away, more formed.

Jimmy's leg was raised up and held in the air by a pulley attached to a bar fastened over the bed. A machine attached to Jimmy's chest by long lines sent pinging noises from behind the bed. Another gave low beeps from a stand at the side. The only thing not moving was Jimmy. His hands lay still and pale at his sides.

Gently Missy brushed her fingers across his hand, carefully avoiding the tube coming from the plastic bag hanging on the pole beside the bed.

"He's so still." Diane's words were weak and low. She sobbed. "I-I don't know why I'm whispering. He can't hear me. He can't hear anything at all. Oh, Missy, what if he never . . ."

Missy squeezed her shoulder.

"Ssh, don't think like that." She rubbed Diane's back, then hugged her close. "He'll be all right. The worst is over. The doctor said so. You heard Freda say so, too."

Diane wiped her eyes. Missy wiped her own.

"We can do this. You and I can get through this. Jimmy has the hardest job. He has to get well for us. We just have to be here for him."

Diane sniffled and wiped her face again.

"I'm glad you're here with me. I couldn't do this by myself. Everybody thinks I'm so strong, but I'm not."

"You're stronger than you think. We'll take this a step at a time. Jimmy will get through this." Missy swallowed the tears trying to start again. "We know he's strong. He'll get through this. He will."

She looked down at Jimmy. He hadn't moved an inch since they came into the room. She struggled to believe her own words.

Please don't let my words be a lie, she prayed.

The streetlights outside the hospital came on and made shadows on the walls of Jimmy's room. He still hadn't stirred. A nurse came in, turned on the ceiling lights and checked Jimmy.

Missy wished the nurse hadn't bothered with the lights. In the dark room it was easier to pretend that Missy had exaggerated how bad Jimmy looked. With the light glaring overhead and shining on him, there was no way to escape the truth.

From time to time the nurse came back. A couple of doctors came in. They all assured Missy and Diane that there was no cause for concern. Missy's eyes were telling her differently.

Finally, at eight o'clock the nurse came in and convinced them to leave.

"He'll be the same for the rest of the night and at least

through tomorrow. One of the reasons is the medication we're giving him. You all need to go on home and get some sleep. You won't be helping him any if you come down sick." She smiled. "Just try to get some rest. We'll take good care of him. I promise." Her smile widened. "I always keep my promises."

New tears streamed down Missy's face. That's what Jimmy had said to her. She squeezed her eyes tight. She wished he had promised to get well. She took a deep breath. *Please let him be all right.*

It took a while, but she finally talked Diane into leaving the hospital by convincing her she would need her strength later to help Jimmy recover when he came home. And he had to come home.

Missy concentrated hard on her driving through the narrow dark country roads as she took Diane home. Although she drove slowly, it still took all of her effort to pay attention to the road when her mind wanted to stay on Jimmy.

She glanced over at Diane. She was staring straight ahead as if she was interested in what was out there. Missy knew she wasn't seeing anything. She was having trouble herself seeing just what was on the road ahead.

They would pick up Diane's car from the hospital tomorrow if she was in any state to drive by then. She certainly wasn't in any frame of mind to drive tonight. Missy was barely making it herself.

She was still struggling to keep her mind off what happened. If Jimmy hadn't gotten the call to tow the car he wouldn't be in the hospital. She would have begged his forgiveness by now and he would have given it. She would have confessed her love for him. They'd be back together.

She took in a deep breath. If he had been hit differently, if the doctors weren't as skilled, if his guardian angels hadn't been with him . . . She had come so close to losing him for good.

How could she have thought she would be satisfied without Jimmy? For once she was honest with herself. She had missed him while she was away. She had denied it. She had dated others, but nothing ever came of it. They weren't Jimmy.

She dropped Diane off and headed home. Why had it taken her so long to admit the truth? And was it too late?

SIXTEEN

SIXTEEN

Missy parked the car in front of her house and turned off the motor. She leaned her head on her arms against the steering wheel, waiting for her legs to get strong enough to carry her into the house. Finally, after deciding waiting any longer wasn't going to make it any easier, she got out of the car. As she climbed the steps to the porch, the door swung opened.

"I've been waiting for you, baby." Sally stepped onto the porch, rushed over to Missy and wrapped her in a hug. "I tried to call you when I saw the noon news, but the phone rang and rang. I was hoping you were in the yard puttering around or anywhere but in front of the television. I didn't want you to hear about Jimmy's accident that way." She squeezed Missy's shoulder. "I reckon I was too late calling. Carrie called me from the hospital to tell me that you were there with Diane."

She pulled Missy closer and led her into the house, trying to give her some of her own strength.

Missy didn't speak. It was taking all of her energy just to put one foot in front of the other.

"Nettie called," Sally went on. "She was all concerned. She said she was going to close up her shop, and come on over to the hospital, but I told her it wouldn't help. I said she can help most by being there for you as Jimmy gets well. I told her I can take care of you right now."

Missy was still in a fog as Sally led her to her room. She still hadn't said a word.

Sally gently pried the purse from Missy's fingers, and rubbed her cold hands between her own.

"Carrie called me back when Jimmy came out of surgery. She said she's not supposed to give out information about the patients, but she did anyway. She told me he's holding up real good and that the doctors say he's going to be all right." She stared at Missy's pale face before she touched it. "He's probably doing a whole lot better than you are right now."

Missy released a heavy breath and shook her head.

"You don't know how bad he looked, Mama." Tears filled her eyes and spilled over. "You don't know. You just don't know. I-I could barely recognize him. He didn't look like Jimmy; like my Jimmy. His face was all swollen and bruised. He looked like . . ." She shook her head and swallowed hard. Still she whispered. "He looked like the doctors and nurses are lying to us about him ever getting well." Her last words came out with a sob. "I can't talk about it."

"Yes, you can. Come on, talk to Mama. Don't keep this bottled up inside. It will help you if you let it all out."

She sat on the bed beside Missy and tried to rub the tension from her shoulders.

Missy started, slowly at first, to tell her mother what had happened at the hospital and what the doctor had said. Her words stumbled when she described what Jimmy had looked like when the nurses brought him to his room. She shook her head in a futile effort to get rid of that image.

"They're talking about a coma and maybe complications and all sorts of things."

Sally squeezed her shoulders.

"They said maybe those things will happen. You got to latch on to the 'maybe.' They aren't sure. They said the same kind of things when Mrs. Greenfield had her accident. To look at her now you'd never know that accident had ever happened. Jimmy's a lot younger than Mrs. Greenfield was at the time. About thirty years younger. He'll be all right. He's strong and he's healthy. You know how I always tell you don't borrow tomorrow's trouble? This is one of those times. You just think about how he's gonna get well. It doesn't matter how long it takes. He's gonna get well."

"What if he doesn't? I love him so much, and I never told him. I kept pushing him away. Now it might be too late." Fresh tears started to run down her face. "What if I never get another chance to tell him how I feel?"

Sally brushed her hand along Missy's cheek and gently lifted her chin. She smiled at her.

"You'll get the chance. Maybe you need to start thinking of how that crow is going to taste when you have to eat it as you confess your love to Jimmy."

Although tears glistened in her eyes, Missy smiled back.

"That's better." Sally patted Missy's hand. "Now you try to get some sleep. You got to look your best in case Jimmy decides to wake up tomorrow. How will you feel if the way he remembers you confessing your love is with bags under your eyes, and a tired old look on your face?" She squeezed Missy's shoulder once more before she walked to the door. "I'm coming back here in fifteen minutes and I don't want to see you still sitting there in that same spot. You hear me?"

"Yes, ma'am."

"Good. Jimmy's going to be okay. He's tough. It might take a little time, but everything will turn out all right. Now go on and try to get some sleep. Morning will be here soon enough and you'll insist on going over to the hospital as soon as they'll let you in."

Missy didn't deny that that was exactly what she planned to do.

After her mother left the room, Missy dragged her shirt over her head and stripped off her jeans, but that's as far as she could manage. She crawled between the sheets and pulled up the covers, knowing that sleep wouldn't come.

Whenever she closed her eyes, she pictured a car barreling toward Jimmy and her eyes popped open. Finally, tiredness got the better of her and she drifted off to sleep for a short while. When she did, she dreamed of him getting hit and she woke up crying.

When daylight slanted into the room, she woke again and gave up any chance of going back to sleep. She dragged herself out of bed as tired as she had been when she lay down the night before.

She wished yesterday had been a bad dream and Jimmy was in his shop working on somebody's car as he did every day, but she knew the accident had been real. It would be a long time before Jimmy worked on cars again. If ever. She shook her head. *No. Don't think that way. You'll fall apart and never get it together again.*

She took a shower and decided to wait until a decent hour to call Diane. Maybe Jimmy's mother had had more luck with her sleep the night before than Missy had.

As she dressed, she glanced at the calendar hanging on the closet door. Today was July 15. Her wedding day. By the end of the day, if things had gone according to her old plans, she and Walter would have been man and wife. She sighed.

That was in another lifetime, back when she was still denying her love for Jimmy. Now she wasn't sure she'd ever get the chance to tell him how wrong she had been.

When she was growing up her mother used to tell her how stubborn she was. Back then she denied it. Now she couldn't. Hardheaded. That's what she was. She hoped she had come to her senses in time to fix things.

The phone rang and she picked it up.

"Hello, Missy." Walter's pleasant voice reached her. "I hope I'm not calling too early, but I wanted to catch you before you left for the hospital. I'm sorry about Jimmy. I don't want to bother her, but you tell Miss Diane that if there's anything I can do, she's not to hesitate to call on me."

"Thanks, Walter. I'll tell her."

"How are you holding up?"

"I guess I'm okay. Jimmy's the one we have to worry about."

"I hear he's on the mend. He's going to be all right. I know firsthand how stubborn he can be. You know it, too. He can let that work for him now. You hang in there. You be strong. You're no slouch yourself when it comes to being . . . shall I be kind and say headstrong?" He chuckled. His next words were soft. "You let me know if there's anything I can do for you. You need a ride to the hospital this morning? Maybe you don't feel like driving. Martie and I can play chauffeur for you and Miss Diane."

"I'm okay with driving. I got us both home last night, and I'm a little steadier this morning than I was then. Thanks for the offer, though. I'm going to call Miss Diane in a little bit. I'm hoping she was able to get more sleep than I did."

"I hope so, too." Walter hesitated. "You know what today is?"

"Our wedding day."

"It seems so long ago that we made those plans. We were different people back then, weren't we?"

"Yeah. It even seems a long time ago that I canceled those plans. At least the ones that didn't cancel themselves."

"Yeah. Talk about not meant to be." He laughed. Missy couldn't remember ever hearing him laugh before. It was a pleasant, relaxed sound. She managed a laugh of her own. Walter continued.

"I've got somebody here who wants to talk to you."

"Hi, Missy. Happy Unwedding Day. I hope you won't think this inappropriate in light of Jimmy's accident and all, but I didn't see any harm in calling to thank you for Walter. If you hadn't had the sense to dump him I never would have found him. If we were planning a big wedding, I'd ask you to do me the honor of being one of my attendants, but I learned from your experience."

"My experience? How's that?"

"Walter told me how everything fell apart and then you called the wedding off. Just in case Walter's the jinx, I'm going for a small wedding with hardly any notice. The fewer things we have planned, the fewer chances of things falling apart, and of Walter changing his mind and backing out. I never would."

Walter laughed in the background. Then his soft voice sounded as though he was right beside Martie.

"I'd never back out on Martie and I don't intend to let her change her mind about me, either."

"I'd never want to." There was a pause long enough for a kiss. "We're not waiting until I finish my residency." She hesitated. "Things can happen that you can't plan for. Walter and I are going to have a small service in Reverend Butler's study next Wednesday afternoon. Only a few close friends will be invited. Afterward, we'll go back to Miss Elberta's for cake and punch. I know you'll be at the hospital most of the time, but if you can get away for a few minutes we'd love to have you come."

"I'll try. Congratulations. Or should I say best wishes? You're not supposed to congratulate the bride-to-be. It sounds too much like she was in a hunt or something."

"If that's true, then congratulations are definitely in order. I have been hunting Walter for years. I've had my eye on him since high school, but he was blind to every female except a certain somebody we all know. I tried all kinds of ways to get his attention, but nothing worked. The man never even knew I existed." She laughed. Then her voice was serious. "I guess if you have patience and wait things out, you get what you want. That's what you have to do, Missy. You have to have patience and wait things out. Jimmy will be all right. You've got to believe that."

"I-I'm trying real hard to believe. And you're right about needing patience. I never was known for having much of it." Missy managed a small laugh. "As the saying goes, I need patience and I need it right now."

When she hung up they were both laughing. She didn't know about Martie, but her own laughter quickly disappeared.

She was drinking a cup of tea when her mother came into the kitchen.

"Morning, baby." She gave her a hard look. "I'm fixing you some breakfast."

"I can't eat anything."

"You have to eat something. Starving yourself won't help Jimmy get any better any faster." She pulled eggs and cheese from the refrigerator and grabbed the small green basket of mushrooms. "I'm going to make you one of my famous mushroom and cheese omelettes. You always loved that."

"Mama, I don't want an omelette. I don't want anything to eat. I can't think about food."

"When's the last time you ate?"

Missy frowned. Then she shrugged.

"How can you expect me to keep track of something like that?"

"See that? You don't even know." Sally beat the eggs and chopped mushrooms and slivers of cheese. "Next thing I know, you'll be in a bed in a room at the hospital and Diane and I will both have to go visit our babies. I'm too busy to take time off from work to visit you in the hospital and sit all day because you did something dumb like not eat." She poured the mixture into the hot skillet. "You don't want to do that to your poor mama, do you? I'd end up sick with worry and they'd probably put me in a bed next to yours so I could still keep an eye on you." She tilted the pan and moved the eggs around. "And I know you don't want to add to Diane's worry."

"Mama, you're carrying things to the extreme."

"I just know how one thing can lead to another." She eased the omelette onto a plate. "You know how I worry about you."

"I know." She stared at the table. "You know I don't want to worry you or Miss Diane." She shook her head slowly. "But I know I won't be able to eat."

"You try. You give it a good try." She set the full plate in front of Missy and adjusted the toast on the side.

Missy stared at the plate for a long time. Then she looked up.

"Mama, do you know what today was supposed to be?"

"A lot has happened since you made those plans for today."

Missy nodded.

"Walter and Martie called this morning. He offered his help, and she thanked me for him. I was so concerned about hurting his feelings I never considered that somebody might be waiting for him to be free." She stared at her breakfast again, but didn't pick up the fork. "I read somewhere that life is what happens to you while you make plans. I know that's true in my case. I had everything set for a dream wedding right down to the clips for my hair when I went on my honeymoon. Everything was going to be perfect." She brushed a hand across her eyes. Everything except for one thing: The groom was the wrong man. How could I have been so wrong for so long?"

"Missy, don't think about any of that. It's all in the past and you shouldn't let it trouble you. You can't change it. You realized your mistake before it went too far."

"Did I? Jimmy's in the hospital. He still doesn't know I love him. I don't know if he ever will."

"Don't talk like that. Of course he will." She put the fork in Missy's hand. "Try to eat. You need your nourishment."

Missy took one forkful of eggs and forced it down. Then, because her mama was looking, she took another. Then she gave up. "Sorry, Mama."

"At least eat your toast. I spread some elderberry jam on it. I know how much you like it. You were always after me to buy some. When you were younger, I couldn't keep enough in the house. Go ahead and try it, baby."

Missy forced down two bites of toast. Then she set it back on the plate.

Her mother sighed.

"I guess I can't complain," she said. "You gave it the two-bite try."

Missy smiled, but it was weak.

When she was little and didn't want to eat something, her mother always told her to give it two bites before she made up her mind about whether or not she liked it. Sometimes back then, two bites seemed like a lot. This morning it did, too.

"What time are you leaving?"

"I don't know. I'm fixing to call Miss Diane now."

She dialed Diane's number. Although it was still early, Diane answered as if she had been sitting by the phone waiting for Missy's call.

"This is one of those take-things-one-day-at-a-time situations," Sally said after Missy hung up. "Remember that. You know Jimmy won't be dancing around his room this morning. But you know he came through the operation and is on his way to mending. It takes time. Sometimes it seems to take so much time for something you can't hardly stand it." A faraway look came into her eyes. "You have to, though. You have to go on no matter what." She looked at Missy. "In this case you got something to pin your hopes to. He's still here and the doctor says he'll be all right. It will be hard, but you have to wait until he's back to normal. You're both young. You have time to wait." She wiped her eyes. "Go on, now. Diane is waiting." She put a couple of sandwiches and some fruit into a bag. "In case you get hungry later. I know how folks don't want to leave the hospital room. This is better than the junk food in those machines, anyway."

Missy thanked her mother, took the bag and left.

When they reached the hospital Missy drew in a deep breath and clutched Diane's hand. They walked into Jimmy's room as if they were afraid of what they would see, but anxious to make sure Jimmy was still among the living and breathing.

He looked as though he was lying in the same position as when they had left the night before. The machines were still hooked up, but today only one bag hung from the pole. It dripped clear liquid into his arm. The bruises on his face had turned purple. Green tinged the outer edges. Missy knew that was normal for bruises, but her knowing it didn't stop her from feeling as though something were wrapped around her heart and squeezing hard.

His chest went up and down just deep enough to assure her that he was still breathing.

She brushed her hand against his face and tried not to look at the bandage wrapped around his head.

On the other side Diane stroked a finger down his hand as if she was afraid of breaking something.

"H-he's s-so still."

"Part of that is because of the medication." A nurse

came in and walked over to the bed. She took Jimmy's pulse. Then she nodded, checked the machines and wrote her findings on the chart before she faced them.

"How is it? How's he doing?"

"His pulse is where it should be, considering what he's been through. Dr. Garfield is making rounds so he'll be here before too long. He'll fill you in on Mr. Scott's condition." She smiled as she left the room.

As if he had been waiting in the hall for the nurse to leave, Dr. Garfield swept into the room, nodded, spoke to them and strode over to Jimmy.

Missy and Diane watched as he checked Jimmy's condition, adjusted the machines and consulted the chart. He lifted Jimmy's eyelids and shone a light into his eyes before he scribbled on the chart.

They waited, though not patiently, until he finished and turned toward them.

"He's progressing nicely. His vital signs are good."

"But h-he looks like he hasn't moved."

"That's not unusual in cases like this. We have him on medication that's partially responsible for that. We . . ."

"Partially?" Missy had trouble getting the word out. "What else is making him this way?"

"Remember, he does have a head injury. We had to go in to relieve the pressure." The doctor's voice was soft. "Coma isn't unlikely in cases like this. We'll keep a close watch on him."

Missy wished she had some of the patience the doctor was showing them.

He thrust his hands into his pockets and continued.

"The body has a way of adapting itself to situations so it can heal. I'm not overly concerned. He's reacting normally to his injuries. I'm going to decrease his medication a bit and we'll see how he reacts to that. If we get a positive reaction, we'll cut back some more." He looked at them hard. "You do realize that even if I do, he still won't wake up right away. I expect it to take at least several more days. Maybe longer." He touched Diane's hand. "He's doing well, Mrs. Scott. This is an excellent hospital for head-trauma cases. His other injuries are healing nicely. I don't have to tell you about how cuts and bruises heal in spite of how bad they look. We've all had experience with those, haven't we?" He smiled. "I'll be back this evening to check on him again." He patted Diane's shoulder and nodded to Missy on his way out. "You two take care of yourselves. Neglecting your own well-being won't help Mr. Scott. When he comes to, he'll need your strength to help him. He'll still have a way to go to full recovery. We can't rush things. If he's like most of my patients, though, he won't be very patient about his recovery. He'll need you to help him give his healing the time it needs."

Missy nodded, but she wasn't sure if Jimmy wanted even that from her. After the way things were between them before he ended up here, he was probably through wasting time on her. He had sounded as if he was tired of chasing her, and had decided to move on without her.

One thing at a time. One thing at a time. Let Jimmy wake up. Let him get well enough so he could tell her he didn't want to see her again. That would cut her to the core, but she'd manage to stand those words if he'd just wake up. Until then she'd be right here every day with Miss Diane, praying for him to open his eyes, waiting for his crooked smile to shine on her again. She blinked. Waiting for him to tell her to stay in his life.

SEVENTEEN

It was hard, but on Wednesday afternoon Missy made herself leave Jimmy long enough to go to Walter and Martie's wedding. They had changed the place from the pastor's study to Miss Elberta's house.

Missy walked up the wide porch and, although the door was open, she knocked on the screen door.

"Come on in."

Was that Miss Elberta's voice sounding so friendly?

Missy went in and stopped just inside the door.

Baskets of flowers of every color lined the wide hall. Huge bows tied smaller baskets to the bannister.

"Come on in, Missy." Miss Elberta smiled and took her arm. She led her inside with the other guests.

"I'm coming by to see Jimmy tomorrow. It's been hectic getting things together on such short notice but we managed. I should say they managed. They had their own plans in mind. I did talk them into having the ceremony here, though. An office is such a cold place to hold a wedding."

"You've done a beautiful job."

"I can't take the credit. Martie and Walter made all the plans. I just helped them with the phone calls needed to put things in place." She looked around. "It does look festive, doesn't it? I wanted to have it in the yard, but I got voted down." She shrugged. "That's not important, is it."

"No, it's not."

Miss Elberta brushed her hand down her pink chiffon dress. "I know I'm a bit overdressed, but I wasn't going to let this go to waste hanging in my closet." She smiled at her. "Maybe I'll wear it when you and Jimmy get married, too. After all, I had it made for your wedding. I just thought it'd be you and Walter." She glanced over at her son tugging on his suit jacket. His hand moved to his bow tie and fiddled with it even though it was straight before he touched it. "He's so nervous even though he's so much in love."

"It's a big step he's taking."

"That's true. You know everybody. I'd better go check on the hors d'oeuvres. Walter and Martie were going to just have cake and punch, but I talked them into a little more than that. After all, it's not every day my only son gets married. I want things to be perfect." She smiled before she hurried to the kitchen.

Missy walked over to Walter.

"Congratulations. I know you and Martie will be so happy."

Walter's face had a glow she had never see before.

"I know we will." He kissed her cheek. "Thank you."

Missy smile at him.

The opening notes of the wedding march silenced the talking. Everybody turned toward the stairs and watched as Martie walked slowly toward them. A wide white lace shawl framed her shoulders and her white silk dress swirled around her legs as she made her way to her husband-to-be. Her face was lit from within by a twin to the light inside Walter. They looked at each other as if they were the only two people in the room.

Missy sighed. They belonged together.

Missy stayed long enough for them to cut the cake after

the short service. Then she went back to Jimmy where she belonged.

Walter and Martie returned from their honeymoon in Bermuda, but Jimmy still hadn't come back from where he was. Missy was full of hope each day when she went to see him. By the end of the day the hope had disappeared and she had to find some more the next day.

More than a few days had passed. Didn't Jimmy know that? Didn't he know he was supposed to be back from wherever he had gone? Why didn't he realize it was past time for him to come back to them?

July was on its last day. Missy forced down the last bite of toast and gulped the last of her breakfast tea. It tasted like cardboard washed down with water, but her body would know the difference.

"You want me to fix you something?"

"No thanks, Mama. I had some toast and tea." They had this same conversation every morning.

"What kind of breakfast is toast and tea? Your body's going to protest big time if you don't start sending down some real food in the morning. Breakfast stands for breaking the fast of the night before. It means you're supposed to eat."

"I do eat. Honest. I told you, somebody brings us platters for supper every day. I haven't felt like it, but I have been eating. I have to. It's the only way I can get Miss Diane to eat. This thing is really taking a heavy toll on her."

"Yes. I can understand how it would. I know how I'd feel if it were you in there. Tell Diane I'll be stopping by later. I'm bringing you all lunch again today. And this time I'm going to sit there and watch to make sure you eat it. If I don't, you'd throw it all in the trash as soon as I left."

Her mother had been bringing lunch every day for the

past two weeks. At first Missy tried to talk her out of it. She knew how much work her mother had waiting at the shop, but she insisted and Missy knew it wouldn't do any good to argue about it. When her mother set her mind to something, there wasn't any way to make her change it. And she was right. If she didn't stay while they ate, the trash can would get a lot more nutrition than they would.

On her way to pick up Diane, Missy said her morning prayer for Jimmy to wake up. It was the same prayer she had been saying every day since the accident. She'd be glad when the Lord decided it was time.

They went into the hospital and the smell of rubbing alcohol, antiseptic, medicine and sickness greeted them as it had every day for the past few weeks. When would Jimmy be home where he belonged?

When she and Diane got to his room he was as still as he had been since the day he was first put in this bed. It was no longer in the intensive ward, but it was still in the hospital.

The bruises had disappeared. The stitches in his forehead were taken out long ago, and the wide bandage around his head had been replaced by a smaller patch. Only a faint thin pink line showed at the sides. His leg had been lowered to the bed and the thick cast lay against the sheet. Except for the needle still hooked up to his arm, Jimmy looked as though he was on the way to recovery. But that was all looks. It was all on the outside. Jimmy still hadn't awakened. He hadn't even blinked.

"Good morning." Dr. Garfield strode into the room as he had every day since Jimmy had been there. He examined him and checked the one machine still connected as he usually did. This morning when he checked Jimmy's eyes concern flitted across the doctor's face. It was gone almost as soon as it appeared, but Missy saw it and her heart tightened. Something wasn't going the way it should be. The doctor's words confirmed her fears.

"I expected Mr. Scott to be more responsive by now."

Although Missy wasn't surprised at his words after the look on his face, she still gasped.

"I can't find any reason for his condition to still be as it is. His wounds are healing nicely." The doctor shook his head. "Perhaps the head injury was more extensive than we thought. That is the case sometimes. Perhaps we were a bit too optimistic; expecting too much too soon. We won't dwell on that. The body knows when it's ready for the next phase. I want you to talk to him while you're here. Talk about anything and everything." He looked at Diane. "Remind him of things from his childhood. Talk about what he got for Christmas when he was a kid. Remind him of his favorite toys. Pull out every incident you can remember, the more dramatic the better." He turned to Missy. "I understand you've known Mr. Scott since you were in high school?"

Missy couldn't speak so she nodded.

"Talk about those times. Anything you can remember. Play his favorite songs. Read passages from his favorite books. The important thing is to keep bombarding him with words and memories. Tell him how his favorite teams are doing. Have friends come over and share their memories, too. We can't do too much of this. Quite often those are the things that help pull a patient back." He smiled. "Don't give up hope. I haven't. I still expect a full recovery for Mr. Scott. It's just taking him a little longer than I expected." He looked from one to the other. "I hope you both like to talk. You'll be doing a lot of it. I'll look in on him again this evening."

Missy and Diane stood in place as if somebody had poured a bottle of glue around their feet. Then they moved to opposite sides of the bed.

Diane held Jimmy's hand but no words came from her.

Missy took a deep breath. Where should she start? Sud-

denly she couldn't think of anything. Then she took another deep breath and started talking.

She reminded Jimmy about when her mother let him
look under the hood of her car the very first time. Jimmy
had the schematics he had borrowed from the automotive
shop teacher in one hand and a flashlight in the other.
She reminded him about how she had teased him for
using a flashlight in broad daylight, but he had said he
had to see into dark places.

Missy's words stumbled. She hoped somebody found a
way to drag Jimmy from the dark place where he was.

She talked until she was hoarse. Diane thrust a cup of
water into her hand. Then Diane took over.

Missy heard stories about Jimmy when he was little. She
heard about the time he was sure he was getting a pony
for Christmas even though they lived in the city. It was
almost suppertime before Diane talked him into coming
downstairs to see his toys.

The Christmas he was eleven, money was tight and
Jimmy knew it. He swore he didn't want anything and
refused to give her a list. Diane scraped together enough
to get him kits for two model airplanes.

"You still have them. You put them on the mantel in
your new house. They're waiting for you." Diane's voice
broke. New tears slid down her face.

Wake up, Jimmy, Missy urged silently. *Forget about me. See
what this is doing to your mama?*

But Jimmy slept on.

Each story Diane told gave Missy a deeper understanding of Jimmy, and with the understanding her love grew
stronger than she thought possible.

Her mother came with their lunch. When they told her
what the doctor had said about talking to Jimmy, she
talked while Missy and Diane picked at their food.

Missy heard about how Jimmy stopped by her mother's shop every day to see how she was doing.

" 'Just checking up to make sure you stay out of trouble,' you always said." Sally wiped her eyes. "You need to wake up so you can check up on me again." Her voice lowered. "I miss you, Jimmy Tanner Scott. Come on back to us."

Missy stared at the bed. Her mama's words were so strong she expected Jimmy to open his eyes and say, "Yes, ma'am."

When he didn't Missy went back to staring at her plate.

A while later Sally stood.

"I reckon I'd best be getting back to the shop." She touched Diane's shoulder. "If it's all right with you, I'll tell Nettie to come on by later." Diane nodded and Sally continued. "I reckon I'll call Walter, too." She looked at Missy. "I know how you love to run your mouth, but even you can't talk all the time."

She hugged Diane and kissed and hugged Missy.

"I'll most likely stop by later after I close up. You all hang on."

Over the next few days it seemed that everybody in town came by and talked to Jimmy. Most of the stories were funny. All of them gave Missy further insight into this man she had been foolishly pushing away for too long.

Julie was one of the first to come. She stood in the doorway and looked at Missy as if waiting for permission to come in.

"Evening, Missy."

"Hi, Julie."

Diane glanced up and nodded. Then she turned back to Jimmy.

"Is it all right for me to be here?" Julie asked. "I mean, if it's not I'll go. I just thought I . . ."

Missy looked at Diane, who wasn't aware that Julie was still there.

"Sure, it's okay," Missy said. "We need all the help we can get. Come on in."

Julie hesitated a few seconds longer. She looked at Missy.

"About all those things I said to you. I'm sorry if I gave the wrong impression about me and Jimmy. I just . . ." She shrugged. "It was wishful thinking."

"I understand." Missy's voice was soft. She meant her words. "I might have done the same thing if I were in your place." She swallowed hard. "There's nothing between me and Jimmy, either."

"Yeah, but everybody knows there will be."

Missy didn't say it, but everybody must know something she didn't. She wasn't sure of anything anymore where Jimmy was concerned.

"Go ahead and talk to him. The doctor said to talk about anything."

Julie nodded. Then she went over and stood by the bed.

"I won't stay long."

"Stay as long as you want." Missy pointed to a chair. "You'll be more comfortable if you sit." Then she went over to Diane.

"Let's take a little break. Julie will talk to Jimmy for a while. Okay? Let's take a little walk. Come on."

Diane nodded but she held on to Jimmy's hand. Missy eased her away and into the hall.

Maybe Julie could get through where she couldn't. Maybe it was Julie's voice he wanted to hear. Maybe Julie hadn't been as far off the mark as she thought when she talked about her and Jimmy thinking about getting married.

Missy swallowed the lump clogging her throat. If Julie was who Jimmy wanted, then Missy would bow out. She'd had her chances with him and had wasted every last one.

She'd survive if he chose Julie, just so long as he woke up.

Missy walked Diane down one corridor after another. She couldn't have told what they passed along the way, but the walk had to be good for Diane. While she sat beside Jimmy she barely moved. Missy managed to keep her away for about twenty minutes.

"I-I think we should go back now," Diane said when they reached the end of another hall. "Jimmy might wake up and I want to be there."

Missy led her back, but she didn't expect Jimmy to be any different than he had been when they left.

When they got back to the room Missy was sorry to see that she had been right.

Julie stood. "I-I talked to him about the prom." Her eyes widened and her body got stiff. "I hope that was all right."

"It's fine. Anything you want to talk about is okay." Maybe that's what Jimmy wanted to hear. Maybe it was Julie talking about their times together that would give him a reason to come back.

Julie smiled and her body relaxed. "I'd like to come again, if it's all right."

"Come back any time you can." Missy glanced over at Diane, who was back to holding Jimmy's hand as if she had never left. "We appreciate your help. She stared at her. "You might be the one to wake him up."

A sadness showed in Julie's eyes and she shook her head slowly.

"I doubt it."

The next day Walter came by.

"Hi, Miss Diane." He touched her shoulder. "Missy." He hesitated, then went over and kissed Missy on the cheek.

"Sit here." Missy stood, walked over to the window and stared out as if there was something she wanted to see.

"Jimmy T, it's time to wake up, now." Walter said. "You took Missy back and she needs you here. It's not fair, now that I can pass you on the street without you glaring at me, that you stay stuck here in the hospital. You know Martie and I are married. She wants to come by and see you, but her feelings will be hurt if you don't see her back." Walter smiled.

Then he started telling Jimmy about a time they were in school that Missy didn't know anything about. Jimmy didn't answer.

August came, bringing its usual South Carolina heat, but the only time Missy spent outside was getting in and out of the car at home and at the hospital.

None of the rooms they passed on the way to Jimmy's room had the same patients that were in them that first day. Everybody had gone home, more patients had taken their places, and most of them were gone, too. Only Jimmy stayed as though he had no plans to leave any time soon.

Jimmy used to say these days of August were called the dog days because dogs were too hot to do anything but laze around. Missy smiled, but it didn't reach her eyes.

She'd remind Jimmy of that when she and Miss Diane got to the hospital.

"You remember that, don't you?"

"I remember." Jimmy's words were weak and soft, but Missy heard them.

Tears streamed down her face, but this time they weren't pushed out by sadness. She yelled for the nurse, who ran into the room.

Missy and Diane hugged each other as the nurse

checked Jimmy. When she shined the light in his eyes, he turned his head away.

"Welcome back, Jimmy." She smiled at Missy and Diane. "I'll call Dr. Garfield."

"Do you know how worried you had us?" Diane held one of Jimmy's hands while Missy held the other.

Jimmy took a deep breath and shifted in the bed. Then he opened his eyes and looked at them.

Missy had never seen such a wonderful sight.

"Hi, Mama, Missy."

After Jimmy awoke his recovery was fast, as if he were trying to make up for lost time. Missy went to see him every day. When a week later he still hadn't smiled at her the way he used to, she reminded herself that he didn't know how she felt. She'd tell him today.

"Hi, Missy."

"I have to talk to you." Missy glanced at Diane, who nodded at her.

"No, I have to talk to you."

Missy held her breath at the harsh look on his face.

"You don't have to come anymore. Mama is driving again."

"Jimmy, don't." Diane looked at Missy. "Missy has been so supportive, so helpful."

"I appreciate all you did for Mama, but I don't want you to keep coming out of some sense of obligation."

"I'm not. Jimmy, I . . ."

"Fact is," he interrupted her, "I've been doing a lot of thinking. I've had a lot of time for it." He stared at her. "I don't want to see you any more. It's time we both get on with our lives."

"Jimmy, you don't know . . ."

"I don't want to hear it, Mama. I don't want to discuss

it. I've made up my mind. Now if you'll both excuse me, I'm feeling very tired." He closed his eyes.

Missy stumbled from the room and hurried to the elevator. What happened to accepting it if he didn't want her anymore? How did she think she could do that?

"Missy, I'm so sorry." Diane caught up with her in the hall. "I'll talk to him. I don't know what's going through his mind."

"Please don't. We don't want to upset him. He made himself clear. We have to respect his wishes and let him get on with his life." She felt her eyes fill. How was she going to get on with hers?

"You're sure?"

"I'm sure. Let him concentrate on his recovery." She smiled although it was hard with her heart broken in so many pieces. "Why don't you go back to him? He'll be okay now that I'm gone."

Jimmy opened his eyes as soon as he heard them leave. *It's better this way. In another year she'll be leaving town for good. I'm not letting her get close enough to break my heart again. Not that she really wants to. Even the doctors aren't sure what shape I'll be in. My leg might not ever get back to normal. I won't let anybody, not even Missy—especially Missy—be with me because she feels it's her duty.*

Jimmy's therapy went as well as the doctors expected. At first they were concerned about his memory, but it was fine. It was too good. He remembered every second he had ever spent with Missy. In a way, that was good. It was all he had of her now.

She did what he had told her. She never came back to see him in the hospital, nor after he got home.

EIGHTEEN

"Jimmy's coming with me to church this morning." Diane's words caused fear and hope to battle inside Missy.

Every evening Diane had called with a report on Jimmy's progress. Missy knew when Jimmy began getting around on crutches. She knew when he started using only one. When he went to town for the first time in more than a month, Missy knew it was going to happen before he even got in the car. She knew all about what was going on in Jimmy's life. She knew he hadn't mentioned her at all. This was worse than all the times they had broken up. This time they hadn't even had an argument.

Diane told her each day that, even though Jimmy didn't mention her, she knew he was thinking about her. In spite of his progress, he wasn't happy.

"He mopes around like he lost something. He has. He's just too thickheaded to admit it. You have to be patient a little longer."

Missy was patient. She didn't have a choice. She hoped Diane was right. She took a deep breath. She hoped it didn't take him five years to see things as they were. She sighed. If it did, though, she'd wait. Five years was better than never.

Jimmy was coming to church today.

Missy went back to her room and pulled out two dresses. She went to her mother's room.

"Which one?" She held up a solid blue two-piece and a rose flowered one. "I think the blue, but the flowered one might be better."

"It doesn't matter, does it?"

Missy sighed.

"No, I guess not." She swallowed hard. "I'm so nervous."

"I can understand, but try to relax." She stared at her. "I reckon this means a nice full breakfast is out for this morning."

"I can't eat." She took a deep breath. "This is the first time I'll see him since that last day at the hospital."

"I know it's his first time back at church, but he's still Jimmy."

"I know, but . . ." She sighed. "Maybe what I'm planning to do is a mistake."

"You got to go with your heart, baby."

Missy nodded.

"I guess we both should drive."

"I reckon."

"Let me get dressed. I want to get this over with."

"No matter what time you get there, the choir won't march in until eleven."

"I know." Missy smiled at her. "I'll see you later."

Missy arrived before 10:30 as if she didn't believe the service wouldn't begin until eleven no matter how early she got there.

Others drifted in and took their places in their favorite pews. A ripple started among the pews just as the choir lined up to march in.

Missy looked with the others to the aisle on the far side and held her breath.

Jimmy, leaning on one crutch, made his way to a pew.

Diane let him sit on the corner. He settled in and never looked Missy's way.

The choir marched in and she was glad to have somewhere else to look.

She made herself sit still and tried her best to concentrate on the service. Finally it was time for Reverend Butler's comments. When he asked, as he always did, if there were any more announcements, Missy stood.

Her legs tried to collapse, but she stiffened them and stayed on her feet.

"Yes, Missy? Do you have something to say?"

She cleared her throat twice before she spoke.

"Yes, sir. May I come up there to the front?"

"Of course. Come right on." His smile gave her the strength she needed to move forward.

As Missy walked to the front of the church, she clutched her hands together to stop their shaking. It sounded as if the whole congregation were holding their breath.

She turned to face them. For once she didn't mind the attention.

"I have . . ." She swallowed. "I want to ask . . ." Again she stopped.

"Go right on, Missy. We're all friends here."

That was true. She stood straighter. Her voice trembled, but she didn't care. She looked at Jimmy.

"I have to ask Jimmy something."

She looked at him and a feeling of calm spread through her as she let her love show. She took a deep breath.

"Jimmy Tanner Scott, I love you. Will you marry me?"

Everybody was staring at her and she didn't care. Nothing mattered except Jimmy.

He stood and stared back at her. She saw as much love as she felt reflected in his eyes. He smiled at her and everything was finally as it should be.

"Right now," he answered right away, "if we had a license."

Everybody clapped.

"The waiting period is only three days." Lil Perkins, a notary, stood. "Come in tomorrow and fill out the papers."

"Our hall is free Thursday evening." Patti stood in her pew.

"I can do up some mixed flowers to make you right proud," Lureen said from the back.

Before Missy could respond, Mrs. Butler stepped out from her place in the front pew.

"I don't think I'm stepping out of line when I say the Women's Auxiliary will be pleased to fix the food. I hope you don't mind chicken."

Missy laughed. "I don't care what food we have, or even if we have food. It's not important. I appreciate your offer. I appreciate everybody's offers."

Jason turned on the piano bench.

"I think I can coax a song or two from my keyboard as my gift to you."

Missy was laughing and crying at the same time.

"I'd be happy to walk you down the aisle to Jimmy."

Everybody turned to look at Walter. For several seconds there was silence. Then the church filled with clapping and cheers.

"This is better than any soap opera," somebody said from a pew to the left.

"Amen," Mrs. Carter said from the right.

"Something told me to hang on to that wedding present I bought," Mrs. Dale yelled from the choir loft.

"It's about time," somebody shouted from the back. Everybody laughed and clapped again. "Amens," came from all over the church.

"I reckon choir practice is canceled for Thursday," Reverend Butler announced. "We're having a wedding here, praise the Lord. One long awaited by everybody in the whole town, I have to add."

"Amen," Jimmy said as he made his way to Missy as fast as his crutch would let him. She met him halfway. There, in the middle of the aisle, with the whole congregation watching, he lifted her hand and kissed it. Then he gently lifted her face to his. Their eyes met and they got lost.

Everybody faded away and Missy and Jimmy were alone standing in the middle of nowhere. He lowered his mouth to taste hers and she raised her lips to meet his. Cheers, louder than ever, filled the air followed by a standing ovation.

Missy looked at all the faces smiling at her. Love and caring shone from them.

"In light of all that just happened," Reverend Butler continued, "I reckon it won't do any good to deliver the message 'What Do You Do?' since we already witnessed one answer to that question. Instead I'm going to talk about 'And the greatest of these is love.' "

Thursday evening Missy, in the gown her mama had made her and holding a bouquet of mixed colored carnations and baby's breath, stood in front of the packed church and exchanged the traditional vows with Jimmy. Jimmy sealed their vows with a kiss and wrapped her in his arms.

Later they'd eat chicken and peas, and dance to Jason's music in the sparsely decorated hall with not an orchid or a rose in sight.

It was August, not June or even July. It was Thursday evening, not a Saturday afternoon. It wasn't her dream wedding. It was better. It was perfect.

COMING IN MAY 2001 FROM
ARABESQUE ROMANCES

Do You Have the Entire
SHIRLEY HAILSTOCK
Collection?

__Legacy

                0-7860-0415-0 $4.99US/$6.50CAN

__Mirror Image

                1-58314-178-2 $5.99US/$7.50CAN

__More Than Gold

                1-58314-120-0 $5.99US/$7.50CAN

__Whispers of Love

                0-7860-0055-4 $4.99US/$6.50CAN

Call toll free **1-888-345-BOOK** to order by phone or use this coupon to order by mail.

Name_____

Address_____

City_____ State _____ Zip _____

Please send me the books I have checked above.

I am enclosing $_____

Plus postage and handling* $_____

Sales tax (in NY, TN, and DC) $_____

Total amount enclosed $_____

*Add $2.50 for the first book and $.50 for each additional book.

Send check or money order (no cash or CODs) to: **Arabesque Romances, Dept. C.O., 850 Third Avenue, 16th Floor, New York, NY 10022**

Prices and numbers subject to change without notice. Valid only in the U.S. All orders subject to availability. **NO ADVANCE ORDERS.**

Visit our website at **www.arabesquebooks.com**.